SCENT OF DANGER

SINCLAIR & RAVEN SERIES

WENDY VELLA

OTHER BOOKS BY WENDY VELLA

The Lady Seals Her Fate

The Lady's Dangerous Love

The Lady's Forbidden Love

Regency Rakes Series

Duchess By Chance

Rescued By A Viscount

Tempting Miss Allender

The Lords Of Night Street Series

Lord Gallant

Lord Valiant

Lord Valorous

Lord Noble

Stand-Alone Titles

The Reluctant Countess

Christmas Wishes

Mistletoe And The Marquess

Rescued By A Rake

For Blake
"If you live to be a hundred, I want to live to be a hundred minus
one day
so I never have to live without you."
- Winnie The Pooh

PROLOGUE

$\mathcal{I}$t is said that when lowly Baron Sinclair saved the powerful Duke of Raven from certain death in 1335 by single-handedly killing the three men who attacked his carriage, King Edward III was grateful. Raven was a wise and sage counsel he had no wish to lose, therefore, he rewarded Sinclair with the land that sat at the base of Raven Mountain. Having shown himself capable of the duty, Baron Sinclair was now, in the eyes of the King, to be the official protector of the Ravens.

Over the years the tale has changed and grown as many do. There were rumors of strange occurrences when a Sinclair saved a Raven in the years that followed. Unexplained occurrences that caused many to wonder what it was that the Sinclairs were hiding, but one thing that never changed was their unwavering duty in the task King Edward III had bestowed upon them.

To honor and protect the Raven family was the Sinclair family creed.

CHAPTER 1

*B*eing a Sinclair was both a blessing and a curse, Cambridge Sinclair decided as he burrowed into the collar of his thick coat. A blessing because he had six wonderful, if at times slightly annoying, siblings. Two brothers and a sister-in-law, one perfect niece, and one equally perfect nephew.

"What appears to be the problem?"

Cam turned to look at the owner of the voice. Mr. Quixly stood behind him, also waiting in line to enter the lecture. His thick gray brows were drawn in a frown. Like Cam he was dressed for the brisk weather that had descended on London early in November. He knew the man by sight, but they were on nothing more than nodding terms, for which Cam had always been grateful. Quixly was one of those men who would find fault in a visit from a celestial being. Short, squat, with an unappealing visage, he was not someone who could afford to scowl, and yet it seemed to be a permanent fixture.

"Pardon?"

3

"Why are we standing about waiting, Mr. Sinclair, in this dastardly foul weather?"

And I should know this why?

"The doors have yet to open, Mr. Quixly, and there appears to be a disturbance up ahead."

"Ridiculous that we have to queue simply because these fair-weather types wish to listen to the great man, when normally the place has any number of empty seats."

"Indeed," Cam said, as the man actually had a point. Normally they were not forced to wait for admittance when attending lectures, but because tonight's speaker had a handsome face and smooth way with words and was a benefactor of the Prince Regent, he had become something of a phenomenon in the astronomy world. Many had come to hear him, and most of them were women who would no doubt sigh and giggle when the man walked on stage.

Looking to the front of the queue again, he noticed a woman appeared to be debating with Mr. Lotus, who was the curator of the institution they were about to enter. He was waving his hands about, as was the lady, which suggested she was displeased about something. Likely she wanted to ensure a seat at the front so she could bask in Fossett's magnificence.

Being taller than most he could see over the heads in front of him, but could hear nothing. Cam wished his sister Eden was with him; she had exceptional hearing.

"Can you hear what the disturbance is about, Mr. Sinclair?"

"As I am only one space ahead of you, Mr. Quixly, I fail to see how I could. A woman appears to be in conversation with Mr. Lotus, is all I can tell you."

"A woman!"

Mr. Quixly's tone indicated women were not his favored gender, unlike Cam. Lowering his eyes to the large bonnet

4

before him once more, he again contemplated his lot in life. He'd been doing that a lot lately.

The curse of being a Sinclair was that he and his siblings were born with heightened senses. Cam could smell foul breath or rotten food from two hundred paces. Even now someone nearby was emanating vile odors that made his nostrils twitch. His siblings had often teased him about needing to wear a nose peg. Cam had actually been tempted a time or two. He tended to breathe shallowly when in public and usually through his mouth rather than his nose.

"I merely wish for you to show him my paper!"

He heard those words because they were shrieked. The woman who was talking to Mr. Lotus was displeased about something. She leaned in closer now, and he could only surmise the gesture was meant to intimidate—not a terribly sound notion when the top of her head reached Mr. Lotus's chin.

"I will not be sent away, and will hand my paper to Mr. Fossett myself!"

Why did he know that voice? Cam went through the list of women he was acquainted with. It was considerable.

"Mr. Fossett does not like to be approached or bothered with such things; he is an important man. Please go to the back of the line like everyone else, madam, or I shall be forced to stop you from entering these premises." Mr. Lotus sounded harried.

Looking skyward, Cam wondered if they were in for snow. It was certainly cold enough. He hoped the woman did as she was told so they could enter soon, or his face would be numb, and then his nose would turn red.

"Cold enough for you, Mr. Sinclair?"

"Indeed it is, Mrs. Vex." He nodded to the woman barking at him as she passed to join the line. Large, with a square jaw that had a mole that drew the eye like a beacon, the woman had attended every lecture Cam had, and was considered something of a bluestocking.

"Stuff and nonsense going on up there if you want my opinion."

"Indeed," Cam said, not sure what was going on, but not wishing to get offside with the woman.

"Wouldn't hurt that windbag Lotus to hand the woman's work to Fossett. He'll read it or he won't!"

"Just so," Cam said with a nod. This seemed to appease her, as she moved on.

"I shall take my place, but I think your behavior exceedingly shabby!"

The woman who was debating with Mr. Lotus began to turn toward Cam, and he felt a strange surge of anticipation grip him. He inhaled to see if he recognized her scent, and shock ran through him. He knew only one woman who wore orange blossom.

"Emily?" Cam shook his head to clear it, sure he was not seeing who he thought he was. Reaching his side, she stopped, the horror on her face telling him she was about as happy to see him as he her.

"What are you doing here?"

Emily was the half-sister to James, the Duke of Raven, Eden's husband. Cam and she had disliked each other excessively from their first glance. The feeling had not alleviated but grown over the years. Emily often made Cam feel as if he had a pebble in his shoe—not painful, but bloody annoying.

"I-I am to attend Mr. Fossett's lecture." She raised her chin, defying him to say a word against her.

"You do realize it is on Galileo and heliocentrism?"

Her soft gray eyes narrowed as she glared at him. "Oh dear, I had thought it was flower arrangement."

This time it was Cam who narrowed his eyes. The woman had a smart mouth, which she rarely used unless he was nearby. Beneath that black velvet bonnet was hair the color of the honey he drizzled on his morning toast. She was slender, and he'd often thought her willowy, but to her face he called her skinny. He personally liked women curvaceous and less caustic.

"As it is likely that I am standing between you and this lecture, one would think you could find your way to being nicer," Cam said.

"Why are you standing in my way?"

"Where is your maid?" Cam asked instead of answering her question.

The gloved fingers at her side clenched briefly, then released.

"Not here."

"You are surely not attending alone?" Cam looked around but saw no one that would be keeping her company. He knew most of the staff in her household. "In these conditions?"

"I am, and usually do so."

"I don't believe James or Max would like the idea of that."

Her lips formed a straight line.

"My brothers trust me. Besides, I have always walked about London alone, I see no reason to change that."

"It's cold enough to snow, and the streets are lined with ice. That alone, without the other ten reasons, should have been enough to make you use common sense."

"Only ten? I am surprised."

"You," he pointed a finger in her face with a total disregard for manners, "are a mouthy woman."

"Thank you." Her chin rose.

"It was not a compliment, as you are only mouthy in my company. You have your family fooled into believing you are a sweet natured, timid individual."

"I'm sweet natured!"

7

Cam scoffed. "How is it I have yet to see you at any lectures?" He raised a hand as she opened her mouth to speak. "Wait, I have it, you slip in at the rear, then leave before everyone else."

"I have no wish to discuss this with you."

She attempted to walk by, but he grabbed her arm, effectively stopping her.

"You sneaked out of the house, didn't you, and your family see no reason to question your actions as usually you are the epitome of well behaved, or squirreled away in your bedchamber?"

Emily looked uncomfortable and Cam realized he was on to something.

"How long has this been happening? Hiding in your room, where your family rarely venture, and then slipping out when they are not looking?"

She kept her eyes forward.

"I have no idea what you are talking about. I would never lie to my family."

"Lie, no; evade, yes."

"I don't have time for this."

"And what of your reputation should anyone chance upon you gadding about London alone... on foot?"

She scoffed. "I hardly think I can do any more to ruin my reputation, Cambridge."

She attempted to leave once more, but Cam simply tugged her with him as he stepped to the side and out of the line so those behind him could enter, as the doors had finally opened.

"What does that mean?"

She had a way of looking at him that made him want to gnash his teeth. When Emily was near he had the urge to behave very badly... and often did. She brought out the worst in him and Cam had no idea why.

"I'm the bastard daughter of a duke." The words were cold and clipped. "I would have thought it obvious."

"What does that have to do with anything?"

"Don't be ignorant, Cambridge, it has a great deal to do with everything, especially in the way people see me."

"And this is why you have not entered society as James wished?"

Emily shifted her weight slightly, just a small movement, but he knew her well enough to see it as discomfort.

"Because it is not right I do so, as you very well know. James is blinded by the fact I am of his blood, but it is not done for me to enter society. It will make life extremely uncomfortable for him, and Eden, in fact all of you, should I so much as step foot inside the hallowed walls of a nobleman's house."

It made him uncomfortable to acknowledge that maybe she was correct, so instead he said, "He wants only the best for you."

"I know."

"What was that business you and Mr. Lotus were discussing... loudly?"

"'Tis nothing." She dismissed his words.

Cam noted the arm he was not holding was behind her back.

"You said something about showing Fossett your paper," Cam remembered.

"No, I didn't."

"Tsk tsk, Emily. You are lying to me."

Reaching around her, he grabbed the hand she was hiding and brought it forward. In her fist was clutched several papers.

"You will not touch those!"

"Tell me what they are, then I won't have to."

"They are private, and mine; that alone should be enough to end this discussion."

Cam laughed. "That has never stopped me, or any of my family members. Lord, Emily, if I simply stood back and waited for people to tell me things I would be constantly in the dark."

"I don't have time for this, Cambridge. I wish to attend that lecture, and plan to do so."

He grabbed her arm again as she turned away from him, and walked her forward. After her encounter with Mr. Lotus, he couldn't discount the man refusing to admit her and he would not tolerate that. She may irritate him like a rampaging plague of ants, but he was not having her insulted by anyone but he.

"Good afternoon, Mr. Lotus."

"Mr. Sinclair." The man bowed, and shot Emily a narrow-eyed look.

"This is my sister-in-law, Miss Tolly. She wishes to attend the lecture. Is that a problem?"

"No indeed. If she is to enter in your company, Mr. Sinclair, I have no problem with that."

Cam felt Emily stiffen, but he ignored her and took some money out of his pocket. "She also wishes for these papers to find their way into Mr. Fossett's hands. Is that also possible?" Cam wrenched the papers from Emily and put the money on top. He then handed them to Mr. Lotus.

The man bobbed his head. "I shall see it done, Mr. Sinclair."

"Why will you take his money and not mine?"

"You tried to bribe him?" Cam was shocked, he'd never thought her capable of such a deed.

"Well you just did."

"Yes... well yes, but it's expected of me," Cam managed to get out.

Mr. Lotus opened his mouth, but before he could utter a word Cam had dragged Emily away.

"How dared he," she fumed. "Because I am a woman my money is not worthy of his consideration. But you wave some about and charm him with your smile and—"

"Take a breath, Emily, you are turning puce."

"He... he is a-a—"

"Small-minded imbecile?"

"The very thing."

Cam found he quite liked seeing Emily with fire in her eyes. It did not happen often, and usually only when a member of her family, or his, was under threat.

"Come along then, Miss Tolly, we shall find you the best seat in the house, then you can sit and bask in Mr. Fossett's magnificence. Should that not happen then I shall be on hand as a substitute."

"Bloody hell," Cam heard her say.

He could not muster a smile; as always, he felt like a cat with his fur rubbed the wrong way in her presence.

"Don't drag your feet, Emily."

"I am not, but your legs are longer than mine!"

He adjusted his stride as they entered the building.

"A simple thank-you will do."

She sighed. "Thank you for making him take those papers, Cambridge. Do you really think he will hand them to Mr. Fossett?"

"I hope so, but at least he now has them in his possession. Will you tell me what they are?"

"In Mr. Fossett's last journal, *The Stars Are Aligned*, he asked for submissions regarding the discovery of comets."

Her face was alive suddenly. Eyes sparkling, lips smiling, and color riding along the ridges of her cheekbones.

"So astronomy is your particular passion? Do you have another copy? I would like to read it."

"Really?" She looked shocked.

"Why does that shock you?"

"Because I did not think it would interest you."

She was looking around the room, no doubt in search of the noxious Mr. Fossett.

"And yet here I stand, awaiting an astronomy lecture, so it seems you are wrong." She was craning her neck now to see around several gentlemen who were standing in the aisle. "How long have you been interested in this?"

"Quite some time."

"You hid that well then, because until today I thought your character had the depth of a thimble."

The breath hissed from her throat, sounding like a snake, as she returned her eyes to him.

"You, sir, are no gentleman."

"Is that meant to be an insult, because if it is, you will need to put more effort into it. After all, you know who my family are."

"I shall find my own seat here at the rear."

"No you will not." Cam led her down the aisle between the seats until they were about halfway, then moved right, dragging Emily with him. He saw two spare seats. "Max and James would thrash me if they heard I let you sit in here alone with so many men present."

"Release me!"

He didn't until they were seated.

"How long have you been attending lectures?" Cam asked.

She huffed, and then twitched her skirts before smoothing them, and finally settled the little satin bag on her lap, hands now clasped neatly around the ribbons. He had the urge to ruffle her slightly.

She had fine features. A small round nose, arched brows, long lashes tipped with gold, and soft pink lips. She was vastly different from the woman he and his family had met many years ago when she had come to live with the duke. Then, she'd been a shadow of the Emily Tolly he saw today.

"I'm attempting to be polite, Emily, perhaps you could reciprocate?"

"Since arriving in London," she said reluctantly.

"And your brothers do not know?"

"Max knows, well some of it anyway."

"But not James?"

While James was a duke, Max was the bastard child of his father, like Emily. She'd never been close to James, but with Max it had been different from the beginning.

"H-he would not approve."

"I doubt Max does."

She shrugged one slender shoulder.

"What is your problem with James? He rescued you, housed you, and from what I gather he is always kind and generous to you." This too had always annoyed Cam, the fact she treated her brother like a stranger even now, after everything he had done for her.

"I have no problem with James."

"That is a lie, Emily. You keep him at a distance unlike Max, just as you isolate yourself from the Sinclairs when you can."

"Be quiet, the lecture is starting."

"This discussion is not finished."

Cam would question her again because James deserved better from her. He was a friend, and one who had saved Cam from himself. He would get to the bottom of this. Unfortunately, to do that, he had to spend time in this woman's company. The thought was not a pleasing one.

CHAPTER 2

"*S*urely you are not one of those silly women here to bat their eyelashes at Fossett?"

"Of course not, but I wish to hear what he has to say. After all, his Royal Highness the Prince Regent has acknowledged Mr. Fossett's wonderful achievements in the world of astronomy because he has been extremely successful."

"He's a puffed-up windbag."

"Then why are you here?"

"He speaks well, and I cannot fault his knowledge, for all he makes me want to gnash my teeth."

"Be quiet, he is beginning," Emily whispered.

She tried to breathe slowly. In and out. It was difficult with Cambridge Sinclair at her side, but she managed it. Damn, why was he here? She looked out the corner of her eye and saw a large gloved hand resting comfortably on a strong thigh. He wasn't as big as his brother, or hers, but he was as tall. He had a long-limbed grace that had women falling at his feet, and a handsome face that only heightened their regard.

Thick dark hair like that of his siblings tended to curl if

left untamed. He had the Sinclair green eyes, dark brows and lashes. There was also that something about him the others in his family had. An aura that she'd come to understand as almost magic. She'd seen it enough, the linking of their hands and the strength they gained from each other. The healing, the hearing; there was so much to his family that she did not understand. She'd never asked, and they'd never explained. Simply put, they knew she was family and therefore would guard their secrets.

Like James, the Sinclairs were kind and tolerated her, but unlike her, they also came from the right side of nobility.

Cambridge had questioned her about her brother, the powerful Duke of Raven. How could he think she was anything but grateful to James for saving her? Yes, she was intimidated, awed even, and of course racked in guilt where James was concerned, and likely always would be. But she in no way had a problem with him... the problem was that James was burdened with her.

"I can hear you thinking."

"That is a perfectly foolish thing to say. Now be quiet, I wish to hear Mr. Fossett's opinions."

"No, a perfectly foolish thing to say would be, what could a woman possibly know about astronomy?"

She shot him a look, and found his eyes focused on her. Emily looked away. She'd been aware of Cambridge Sinclair since their first meeting. Hated the way her heart beat a little harder when he was near, and how he provoked and teased her. Only with him did she lose control. Only he could bring out something in Emily she had vowed to keep locked away when she came to live in the duke's household.

Cam also had something Emily would never have; he was comfortable with the person he had become. He was a man who knew his place in the world, unlike her.

"I have made contact with someone who has one of the

only copies of *Our World Above*." He leaned closer, his words brushing her cheek and making her shiver.

"You haven't!" Emily forgot her anger toward Cam, and the man who spoke on the stage.

"Sssh!"

"Sorry," Emily said to the man who turned to glare at her. "Surely it is on the list of prohibited books?" she whispered.

"Yes, I believe that is the case, but I have a contact who can access it."

He glanced down at her, then back at Mr. Fossett who was now discussing nebulae. She'd always wanted to read *Our World Above*. Emily had read everything she could in James's study, and lending libraries, and she was now reading her way through Max's library. But to read that book... it would be a thrill.

"Will you be able to actually get the copy?"

"But, Emily, that would be against the law."

She ground her teeth and told herself no good would come of angering him.

"Of course, forgive me."

"Did you just say forgive me?"

"No, I said you are an annoying, irritating man, and I have no further wish to converse with you. Now be quiet."

"Much better," he said. "For a moment there I thought the sun and moon had started circling the earth once more."

Emily refused to give in to the bubble of amusement his words created inside her.

"So all this time that I believed you working on your etiquette and stitching you were reading about astronomy, Emily? You are a sly one."

"I'm not a sly one, and I like reading because it is a solitary endeavor that I need share with no one."

"And you do not like to share yourself with anyone?"

He was close enough that the sleeve of his heavy charcoal

greatcoat brushed her arm as he lifted it. Cam always spoke in gestures. He was often loud, and happy to share his opinion, even if no one wanted to hear it.

"I have no need to speak constantly and tell everyone what I did all day, like you."

"And yet that is exactly what Samantha is like."

She felt that warm ball of heat inside her at the thought of her little half sister. For so long it had been just her and her brother, who was now dead. Now she had two half brothers and a sister. Of course, there was also the guilt, but she was attempting to work on that.

"Good Lord!"

"What?" Emily rose slightly in her seat.

"Fossett just fell off the stage. All his posturing has finally been his downfall."

"Is he all right?"

"That's it, man! Shake it off, you shall be right in no time!" Cam called from beside her. His body was shaking with laughter.

"Stop that!" Emily slapped his arm. "The poor man could have seriously hurt himself."

Cam's eyes went to the hand she had on his arm, and Emily snatched it back. "Sorry."

"I like to be touched, Emily; it is you who do not."

"Do you always say every thought that comes into your head?"

"Mostly, but sometimes"—he waggled his brows—"they are not appropriate to air in public."

And this was why they argued constantly. He never missed an opportunity to unsettle Emily by saying something vulgar, or generally just annoying her. Her blood would start to boil, and the façade she had fought hard to control would slip.

"You are a...."

"Infuriating, vulgar, horrid? I believe I have had those and more from your lips before."

She felt the horrifying sting of tears behind her eyes. Her humiliation at the hands of this man would be complete if he saw her tears. So instead she found refuge in anger.

"For once, will you just shut up, you bloody horrible man!"

"Sssh!" The man turned to glare at her once more.

"And you can shut up also!"

Surging to her feet, Emily hurried down the row and away from Cambridge Sinclair. She could not sit there another minute, not with the threat of tears imminent.

"Excuse me," she said, passing a man with long legs. "Oh do forgive me," she added after standing on another's foot. Finally she had navigated her way to the aisle. Emily refused to look back at Cam; instead she stormed out. The curator scowled at her, so she glared back, but did not give in to the urge to poke out her tongue, as Samantha would have.

She was not usually emotional; in fact, the exact opposite. Calmness had helped her survive through the years with her brother, who had become mentally unstable. Yes, she did have a temper, but had learned to control it. But lately she had struggled to keep her emotions hidden away.

She could feel herself changing, and could do nothing to stop it from happening... whatever *it* was. The façade she had created around her was beginning to show cracks, and the personality she had kept hidden most of her life was threatening to be exposed.

Almost running now, she arrived at the door that led outside. A large hand reached over her head and pushed it open.

"I'm sorry."

"Go away." Emily did not look over her shoulder at Cam. She simply walked out into the icy London weather, down the path between the neat box hedges, and onto the street. A walk in the bracing air would do her good. Surely that would cool the anger inside her and help her to achieve calm before she returned to her brother's house.

Throwing a glance over her shoulder, she saw Cam was following.

Bloody bothering hell!

CHAPTER 3

*C*am had been stunned when Emily left her seat after delivering him a set down... in public of all places. Of course he was used to it when they were in private, but what he was not used to was the slight quiver in her voice.

Their arguing had never made her cry before... never appeared to hurt her. He would have tempered their verbal sparring if he'd believed even for a moment it had. He was not a complete scoundrel. In the past Cam had been glad to see some fight in Emily, even if it was at his expense, but right now he wasn't proud of himself.

He'd followed her when she left. The lecture would have been interesting, but as he'd been to several, and Fossett was not his favored speaker, he had no wish to stay when Emily was very obviously upset. Besides, he'd ruined the lecture for her, much to his shame.

She may annoy him hugely, however, she was family, and that was very important to a Sinclair.

"I really am sorry. It was not my intention to upset you, Emily."

"I have no wish to keep company with you, Mr. Sinclair. Good day."

White puffs of air accompanied these words. She reminded him of a bristling puppy. Hackles up, teeth bared, but completely harmless. Polite to a fault, Emily had tried to be everything her birth had not given her from the day she moved into her brother's house. Quiet, respectful, she never made a spectacle of herself unless he was around. Cam always had the urge to ruffle her feathers; in fact, Emily brought out the worst of him for no reason at all.... Well actually, that was not quite true. Cam always felt as if she was looking down her nose at him. It rankled, and he responded by behaving badly. There was also the matter of his chest feeling a little too tight when she was near, which confused him, so he tried to ignore it where possible.

"Come on, Em. I said I was sorry."

"I don't care if you say it a further ninety-seven times, I still don't want you in my company!" She threw the words over her shoulder.

At least she sounded steadier. He could no longer hear the tears she was choking back. Having four sisters, Cam had experienced thousands of bouts of tears in his lifetime, and where possible, he preempted or avoided them.

"Ninety-seven times? Not one hundred, or fifty-six, but ninety-seven times?"

She stopped so suddenly, he nearly barreled into her back; only by lifting her off her feet and carrying her forward a few steps did he avoid knocking her to the ground.

"A little warning," Cam said, settling her back on her feet.

She didn't answer, so he moved to stand before her. Lifting her chin, he saw absolute misery in her eyes.

"What's wrong, Emily? This is more than my clumsy attempts at teasing you, surely, as they have never bothered you before?"

"Nothing." She tried to shake free, but he held her still.

"Look, we're family, and I know we rub each other up the wrong way sometimes, but that doesn't mean I don't care. So you may as well talk to me as any of them."

Running his eyes over her face, he noted that she was no longer a thin, frightened woman. He really saw her for perhaps the first time in a long while... if ever. To his shock she was now a woman... an interesting one. She wasn't just beautiful in the conventional sense, although that was there in the silken skin and curve of her cheek; no, there was more. Almost an ethereal beauty that punched him hard in the stomach.

When had Emily gone from annoying to alluring?

The thought shocked him so much he released her, and she stepped backward, away from him.

"I don't want to talk to you, nor do I want to spend time in your company. Goodbye."

She was halfway down the road before he'd collected his wits.

"I must have taken a knock to the head," he muttered, following. He'd never thought her beautiful... surely it was a simple matter of a fever. Peeling down his glove, he pressed the back of his hand to his forehead; it felt annoyingly cool. "Malaria then?" But as he'd never been anywhere to contract it, he couldn't in all conscience blame his sudden belief that Emily Tolly was anything but a pest on that.

Crossing the street behind her, he watched her skirts swish as she stalked away from him at considerable pace. His legs were a great deal longer of course, so he was soon closing in on her with little effort. He wasn't about to let her walk about London with no escort. Her brothers would likely have several heated words to say if he did, and there were two of them.

"Come on, Em, it's freezing. We shall share a hackney home."

"I want nothing to do with you!"

Stubborn witch.

"I'm following you the entire way home, and will likely walk through the front door to James's house right behind you!" Cam roared the words at her. "In fact, we may shortly take tea together!"

She muttered something that he thought was "I hope you choke on your cake." Her shoulders then hunched and she continued walking—and ignoring him.

He was a highly sought-after member of society. Women coveted his time and attention. Just last week, Lady Shubert told him she wanted to have her wicked way with him, which, considering her husband was only several feet away, was quite a bold move. Having said that, Lord Shubert did have an ear horn.

He refused to yell at Emily again, although the urge was there. Besides, the cold air was catching in the back of his throat and making him cough. He would be the adult here, and not give in to a loud verbal tirade right here in the street, no matter how much he wanted too.

Humming to himself, as that usually calmed him, he wrinkled his nose as he passed a particularly foul-smelling puddle of something. He walked on, watching Emily's skirts twitch in fury. To his right the Thames flowed, and to his left were several buildings no doubt housing people industriously working.

He did not really know much about Emily. Only that her brother had tried to kill his sister, and nearly succeeded. He knew she'd been living in a cold, damp little house when James and Eden had called and taken her away to live at the Raven townhouse.

"There is manure up ahead, have a care!"

She veered right at his words.

Emily was a conundrum, he thought, and not a pleasant one. She was like a hair shirt, or a roll in stinging nettles.

He heard the thunder of hooves and jangle of harnesses suddenly as a vehicle approached. The carriage was coming down the street at speed behind him, which to Cam's mind was an idiotic thing to do in these conditions.

"Move to one side, you foolish woman, or it will run right over the top of you!"

She ignored him.

"Emily!"

Her feet started moving to the right, much to his relief.

The carriage passed, and Cam had to leap aside as it came dangerously close. He then watched in horror as it slowed when it reached Emily. The scent of danger filled his nostrils suddenly in a flood of acrid heat.

"Emily!" He started running. "Get out of the way!"

She turned to face him, hearing the change in his tone. Her wide eyes went from him to the carriage. Cam watched the door open, then an arm reached out and grabbed her.

"Cam!"

Her shriek pierced the air. Fear had his legs moving faster. Arms pumping, he tried to reach the carriage, but it sped up again, and in seconds was a good distance away from him.

Cupping his mouth, he roared the words "Help me!" in the hope that his siblings would hear, praying their connection would have them coming to his aid.

Dear God, they have Emily!

He had to save her. Had to reach her. His heart thumped in his chest as he tried to push himself faster. Breath wheezed in and out of his lungs as he fought to fill them with frigid air. The thunder of hooves once again drew near, and he turned to find a huge black beast of a horse; seated on top was a man in uniform.

"Hold out your hand!"

Cam didn't hesitate; he could not afford to. Taking two huge steps he jumped on the third, propelled himself upward using the man's hand, and landed behind him.

"I saw it all!"

"We have to get to her!" Cam roared.

The man didn't speak, just urged his horse on faster. They rounded the bend and the carriage was there before them. Cam pushed aside his fear and focused. She needed him to be strong, as only he and the man before him could save Emily now. If that carriage escaped, he knew deep inside him he would not see her again unharmed. The realization was a chilling one.

His eyes streamed from the cold, but he kept them on the carriage they were fast approaching.

The first shot had the rider veering right, and nearly unseating Cam. Squeezing his thighs tight, he held on. They followed it through the streets, and only when the carriage reached the outskirts of London and the houses thinned did Cam speak.

"Pull up beside!"

"Take the pistol out of my boot!"

Cam did as the man said, and then tucked it into his waistband.

They moved closer, and when he was in reach of the carriage he swung his leg over the horse and leapt, grabbing the straps on the back. Pulling himself up, he reached the roof of the carriage. A man appeared in the opening before him, carrying a pistol in one hand. He pointed and fired; Cam rolled to the side, nearly losing his grip, and the ball flew over his head. When he righted himself he took the pistol from his waistband. Aiming, he fired, but the carriage veered, and the man lost his grip, and rolled off the roof. Cam hoped the only person left was the driver.

His rescuer had pulled alongside the carriage now. He shouted something at Cam. "Traces" was all he heard, but it was enough. The driver was cutting the horses loose, which would release the carriage, and soon it would crash into something with Emily still inside.

Reaching the end of the roof, he tried to stop the driver, but it was too late and seconds later the horses veered left, and the carriage continued on.

Scrambling to retain his hold on the roof, Cam struggled his way back to Emily. Seconds later he managed to reach the opening and look inside. She was on the floor, bound hand and foot, attempting to wriggle upright.

"Emily!"

"Cam, help me!" The desperation in her eyes as she looked up at him had fear knifing through his body.

"The horses have been cut free, I must get you out now!"

Bracing himself as best he could, he reached inside to grab her, but as his fingers touched her shoulder the carriage jolted, and he had to grip the edges of the opening for support.

"Cam!"

"Try and stand!" He reached for her again, but this time his foot slipped. Cursing, he righted himself. The carriage could not roll on much longer, it would soon crash; he had to get her out now.

"You can't save me!"

"I can!" he roared, reaching for her again.

"I don't want you to fall!" She was levering herself up using the seats.

"Hurry, Em!"

She managed it, and he leaned in further, his fingers touching her shoulder.

"That's it, I have you now!" As the last word left his mouth, the carriage veered wildly.

"Cam!"

He tried desperately to hold on to her, but it was useless, and he tumbled off the roof, hitting the ground hard. Cam rolled several times, coming to a halt on the grass. He felt no pain, only the need to get to Emily. Regaining his feet, he started running. The carriage was still moving; out of control, it was heading for the riverbank. If it did not stop, it would end its journey in the icy water below.

"Dear God, no!"

He ran, heart pounding, fear driving him on. The horse and rider were closer but were as helpless as he to stop the carriage rolling over the grass and down the incline.

"Emily!" Cam's cry was hoarse as he sprinted along the road. He arrived in time to see the carriage topple onto its side and into the water. Horrified, he then watched it begin to sink.

The rider was off his horse and running down the bank with Cam on his heels.

"She's inside!" Cam roared, splashing into the water. "Can you swim?"

"Yes!"

They jumped in together, the cold seizing the air in Cam's lungs. He reached the carriage first. It had, as yet, not sunk completely. Hauling himself up on top of the side, he knew he had seconds before it was submerged completely, and that his weight would hasten things. He grabbed the door handle and wrenched it open.

"Emily!" He lowered himself inside; the water reached his waist. He couldn't see her.

"Check she was not thrown clear!" Cam roared. "She's bound hand and foot, she'll drown!"

His blood pumped, fear filled his nostrils with its vile

27

stench as he took a breath and ducked under. Moving his hands from left to right, he found her within seconds and hauled her up and into his arms.

"I have her!" Lifting her high, he turned her on her side. "Emily?"

She didn't speak. Her head lolled back, eyes closed.

"Pass her to me."

Looking up Cam saw the man who had ridden to his aid. Doing as he asked, he and Emily soon disappeared. Cam followed. He then slid back into the water below the carriage.

"Lower her to me." Taking her lifeless body into his arms he started back to the bank with the man's help. A small crowd was now waiting for them.

"She's dead!"

"No!" Cam roared at the woman who had spoken. "She will not die."

"Lay her down," the man who had helped rescue Emily said. "Is she breathing?"

Cam checked her pulse. "No."

"She's dead then," the woman said again.

Cam shut her out, and the others who were in agreement.

"She was not in the water long."

"My sister told me it does not take long to drown." Remembering what Essie had done for Samantha, he laid her on her back, then lowered his head and blew air into her lungs. Placing a hand on her chest, he felt it rise and fall.

"'Ere, what's he doing kissing that woman when she's in that state!"

"He knows what he's d-doing," Cam heard the man say. "He's breathing life back into her lungs. Now stand b-back, please."

Cam heard more noise. Horses, curses, the high-pitched worry of female voices, and the low growl of men's. His family had arrived. He didn't stop, but kept breathing for Emily until she could do so for herself. When she started coughing, only then did he turn her gently on her side.

"It's all right now, I have you."

"I will release her feet," the man said, and Cam quickly did the same to her hands. He then pulled her into his lap and held her while she coughed and spluttered up water.

"Christ, Em." He buried his face in her chilled neck when she'd stopped. "Dear Christ, you could have drowned."

"C-Cam," she managed to stutter out his name, and then her hand was in his hair, gripping it hard as she held on to him. "S-so s-cared."

"And I," he said. "I couldn't reach you." He lifted his head and looked down at her. Their eyes caught, held, and something passed between them. An understanding, a feeling... hell, he couldn't identify it, only that it rocked through him with an intensity that shocked him. It was the pressure of her hand that had him lowering his head to take her lips in a soft, achingly gentle kiss.

"You're safe now," he breathed against her lips.

"I-I knew you would save me."

Cam pulled her close then, holding her tight as relief chorused through him that he had been able to do just that.

Ignoring the voices of those watching, he simply held her close, and for now, that was enough.

CHAPTER 4

"Cam!"

Looking up as he heard his name, he saw his family on the rise above. Dev, his brother, James, her brother. Both running down to them. Behind them came his sisters, Essie and Eden.

"Our families are here now, Em."

She nodded. The hand she lifted to touch his cheek was ice-cold. "Thank you for s-saving my life."

"Cam!" His brother reached him first.

"Christ, it's Emily!" James dropped to Cam's side, reaching for her. "Emily." The name was torn from him. "What has happened?"

"S-someone tried to abduct her." Cam didn't want to let her go, but knew he must. "The c-carriage, it ended in the w-water." His teeth were chattering now. "She may need Lilly."

"She is from home, but if need be, I will find her," Dev said. "They're frozen; we need to get them warm!" he roared. "It's all right now." His brother then gripped his shoulder, and he felt the surge of power he always got when one of his siblings touched him.

"To the carriage," Essie said, arriving. "Now! We must hurry, they're in danger if we do not get them warm!"

Ignoring the questions and enquiring eyes from the curious bystanders, Emily was lifted by James, and Cam was hauled to his feet by Dev. His arm was draped over a broad shoulder, and he was half dragged up the bank.

"Th-the man?"

"There are several here." Dev looked around him.

"The w-wet one."

"He is here. Did he help?"

Cam managed a nod.

"Then he will be helped also."

Emily was being stripped of her clothes when he arrived. James wrapped her in his great coat, over her shift. Blankets were pulled out from under the carriage seats and draped over her. Propriety was forgotten in favor of survival.

"Get in and rub her arms and legs, James," Essie said. "Is there brandy in here, Dev?"

"Right side."

Cam's legs had stopped working. His brother bundled him like a pile of rags into the carriage. He fell onto the seat opposite Emily.

"E-Emily?"

She was pressed to James and he was rubbing her arms and legs with his hands.

"C-Cam" was all she could manage, but it was enough to tell him she was all right.

"Strip, Cam," Essie said.

"I-I can't, Emily is h-here."

"Dev," Essie said in that voice she used when she was treating a patient, "I insist you deal with him at once."

His brother shrugged out of his coat and draped it over Cam. He then wrestled with Cam's necktie, jacket, waistcoat, and shirt, and manhandled him into the greatcoat. He refused to remove his breeches, but the boots went. He felt the blessed relief of warmth and groaned as the cold started to ease slightly.

"Is there room in there for one more?" Eden poked her head in the doorway. "I have managed to disperse the crowd."

"Bring him in," Essie instructed. "We shall be jammed in, but will manage."

The man who had helped Cam was nudged through the door, and Dev took his arm and lowered him beside Cam. There was no coat for him, but two blankets. Dev removed his top half of clothing. The brandy flask was then pressed to his lips.

"Th-thank you," the man sighed.

"Small sips," Essie said, crouching on the floor before Emily.

"When I-I got her out of the water she wasn't breathing, Ess." He looked at his sister. "I-I did what you did for Samantha."

"And yet another Sinclair is a hero," James said, but his words held no humor, only heartfelt thanks. "Thank you, Cam."

"S-Sinclair?"

Cam dragged his eyes from Emily, who was being examined by Essie, and turned to look at the man seated beside him. He was still shaking, but like Cam, color was returning to his face.

"Yes, that is our name."

"And m-mine also."

He'd known, Cam thought. The name was not theirs alone, he knew that also, but there had been something about this man from the time he'd held out his hand to Cam.

"We are the Sinclairs of Oak's Knoll," Dev said as he rubbed Cam's legs hard. "He is Cambridge, and I am Devon.

These are my sisters Eden and Essie, and my brother-in-law James, Duke of Raven."

"I-in that case, we are cousins." The man's hand shook as he raised it to shake Dev's, but his brother tucked it back under the blanket.

"Uncle Giles's son, Christian?"

The man nodded.

"I am Captain Sinclair, but I'm known as Wolf."

They had never met his father's family, as he would not allow it, and yet now one of their cousins had found them. Cam wondered if there was more to his appearance than just fate, but now was not the time to ask.

Looking at Emily, he met her eyes.

"How do you feel?"

She managed a smile, then her eyes rolled back in her head and she slumped down in the seat.

"Emily!"

"Sit, Cam." Dev held him down as he tried to reach her.

"She is all right, brother, I can find no injuries. She is merely unconscious," Essie said.

"No one is merely unconscious," Cam ground out.

Emily nearly died today. The thought kept churning round and round inside his head as he watched his sister rouse her. He'd kissed her too, and why those chilled lips had stirred so much emotion inside him Cam could not understand. He put it down to the shock of the moment.

"Her color, Dev?" Cam asked his brother. Dev had the heightened gift of sight. He also saw people in colors. If they were pale, they were usually unwell or experiencing great emotional distress.

"Pale."

"Color?" Captain Sinclair asked.

"'Tis nothing," Dev dismissed his question.

"Do you see in colors?" The man grabbed Dev's arm, his words desperate.

Dev was silent for several seconds, his eyes on the man, and then finally he nodded. "I do."

"As do I," Captain Sinclair said, slumping back on the seat. "G-good Lord. So that was why I felt that uncontrollable urge to help you."

"Very likely," Dev muttered. "But right now we need to make sure you are warm; later we will talk more."

"Cam?" Eden was looking in the doorway, her face drawn with worry.

"I'm all right, Eden." He leaned over and grabbed the hand she held out to him, squeezing it in reassurance. Cam winced as pain shot through him. "Just cold now."

"You took quite a fall from that carriage," Captain Sinclair said.

"Fall?" Dev questioned.

"He leapt from my horse onto the carriage that held... ah, I do not know the lady's name."

"Emily. Miss Tolly," Dev added.

"When the man inside the carriage who had grabbed Miss Tolly fell from the roof, the driver realized all was lost and cut the traces freeing the horses. Your brother was thrown, and hit the ground hard."

Cam was suddenly impaled by the ferocious green eyes of his brother.

"Where do you hurt?"

Everywhere. Now that he had stopped running after Emily, every pain in his body was making itself known.

"I'm all right, Dev."

"I'll check him when we get back. For now, Emily is awake, but we must get them home to the warmth, where I can tend them better," Essie said. "James, ride with Eden please. Go fast, and have baths drawn."

The duke wanted to protest, but one look at Essie held him quiet. Reluctantly he released his sister after murmuring something into her ear, and then stepped from the carriage.

"I must see to my horse." Captain Sinclair went to follow.

"I will ensure it accompanies us," Dev stepped from the carriage. "He is the large black one standing beside the carriage I gather?"

"Yes," their cousin nodded.

Cam looked at Emily; her eyes were on him. She lifted a hand and he took it in his, squeezing it gently. He wanted to retain it, keep her close, but his family would think that odd, so he let her go. But their eyes caught, and held, the entire journey home.

CHAPTER 5

*E*mily opened her eyes, and then slowly moved her body. She was sore and bruised, but considering what she had endured four days ago, well. Her head no longer hurt from the knock it had taken, but she still felt several twinges. Something warm was pressed to her side, and she knew what it was, because Emily had woken with the same feeling every morning since she'd been abducted. Looking down, she saw a fair tousled head of curls.

The hand she lifted to touch them shook. Her darling little sister lay along her side with one arm thrown over her waist. The thought that she could have been taken away and never seen her again was a terrifying one.

"Em?"

"Here, Samantha." She brushed the curls as the girl turned to face her. Sleep softened the blue eyes that sat in a pretty pale face.

"Are you well today?"

"Very well, and I have you to thank for nursing me back to good health."

Samantha and James were the late duke's only children

born in wedlock, and raised by the tyrant. Because of this she held tight to those she loved. When one of them was injured she panicked, fearing they would be taken from her. Her father had beaten and locked her in her room constantly, and then brought a governess into the house who was little better. James had not known Samantha existed until after his father's death. They had since forged a bond that was only strengthened by what they'd endured as children.

"You were the color of porridge the day James carried you inside. I was scared."

"And yet here I lie, talking to you, and now the picture of health, so there is no longer a need for fear."

"You do look better."

"I think I slept better having you close." Emily cupped a soft cheek. "I really am all right, Samantha."

Samantha was Emily's half sister, they shared a father, but Emily's mother had been a servant at Raven Castle.

"I love you, Em."

"And I you, my sweet little sister."

Samantha rose to her knees and leaned over Emily. The hug brought tears to her eyes, as did the kiss that was placed on her cheek.

"Why did those men try to take you away from us?"

"I have no idea, but you can be sure that Max and James will be searching for that very answer, and in the meantime I shall be safe here with you."

Samantha smiled, her mind eased.

"Shall we go to the breakfast parlor this morning, Emily?"

"Oh most assuredly. I find I am quite famished, and have no wish for invalid's food any longer."

Samantha bounced on the bed, and Emily fought the wince that followed. Her muscles were still very sore.

"All right, but I don't think we can go to the park today, as you will not be up to it. So we shall read in my rooms."

"Yes, your majesty, but to be honest I think a walk in the sun will help me a great deal."

"There is very little sun to be had today, so we shall see what Essie has to say on the matter."

"Very well, but first I must ask how is Cambridge, Samantha?" Worry had gnawed at her over his condition. He'd fallen from that carriage and surely hurt himself while trying to save her. Was he all right, or had her family not told her the truth due to her condition?

"He was in bed for a day, then rose. His back was sore, but Warwick told me Lilly healed him while he slept."

"Did she?" She knew Lilly had magic in her hands, had seen her heal with just a touch, although it was never spoken of.

"She can do that you know, Em. Take the pain away with just a touch. She checked you also, but said all you needed was rest."

She wasn't sure how to respond to that. Emily knew that the younger Sinclairs also had special senses, but wasn't sure just how much Samantha knew.

"I know the Sinclair family is different, Em, but they're also special, don't you think? I always feel better when they're around."

"Yes, they're good people." In fact they were so much more than that. The Sinclairs seemed to fill the air with energy when they were nearby.

"Well, I'm going to get changed because I'm hungry." She bounced again, this one accompanied by a sweet-sounding giggle. Samantha then got off the bed and ran from the room. "I shall see you soon."

"Oh, to be so resilient," Emily said, throwing back the covers. Moving slowly to the edge of the bed, she took a few seconds before standing.

Bracing a hand on the end of the bedpost, she stood there

inhaling and exhaling. Her body was still one big ache, but at least she was warm now. There had been times in her life when Emily was cold with no means of warmth, but what she'd felt that day had eclipsed all those memories.

She remembered the blissful warmth of the bath water they had lowered her into, and Essie forcing her to drink something bitter, and then she'd slept. It had been wonderful to fall into the oblivion of darkness after the terror of the day.

Cam saved my life.

Emily wasn't sure she would ever be able to describe what she'd felt seeing him above her on the roof of the carriage, knowing instinctively that he would save her. Relief had given her strength to rise, and fear that he would fall had urged her on, and then the carriage had swerved, and he was gone. She'd had no idea if he lived or died, and then as the carriage crashed into the water she'd believed she would never know, as surely she could not survive her plunge into the water, especially bound hand and foot. She was right, she had died, but Cam had brought her back to life.

"I am now indebted to Cambridge Sinclair," Emily whispered. How was she ever to repay him?

Looking around the room, she saw it clearly for the first time in days. She and Samantha had picked the colors and furnishings. Her bed was large, and when she'd first lain in it, she'd spread out her hands and legs and barely been able to reach the sides. A cover of jonquil and cream matched the curtains. She had a comfortable chair before the fire, and rugs to keep her feet warm. Emily had placed a writing desk beneath the window, and spent many happy hours there. A vase full of blooms sat on a side table, which Samantha had told her James insisted on.

Someone had tried to take her from all this. The safe haven that was finally her home. This had been her fear, that suddenly she would be plunged back into the life she had once been forced to live.

"But they did not succeed," she reminded herself.

Emily had dreamt over and over again of Cam roaring her name as that man had grabbed her off the street. Felt his hands forcing her onto the floor as he bound her hands and feet. She'd known fear before, but not like that.

Death had stared her in the face that day, and the biggest surprise to Emily was how hard she'd fought against it. Suddenly survival had been paramount, and she'd fought against the water dragging her under. Fought with every-thing she had, but then despair had gripped her as it covered her head. She hadn't known just how much her life meant to her until that moment.

"Miss Tolly, should you be out of bed?"

Her maid entered the room.

"I wish to wash and dress please, Belinda. I have bed sores on my sores from lying about for so long."

Having a servant at her beck and call had also taken Emily some time to become accustomed to. She had once been the servant, doing everything for herself and her brother.

"I can do this," Emily said, making for the door thirty minutes later, after her maid had departed. She was tired and sore, as this was the most activity she had done in days, but dressed and determined to at least eat with her family today. Hopefully walking should ease some of the stiffness in her limbs.

The Duke and Duchess of Raven's house was large, as it should be for a man of her brother's status. Unlike when she'd first moved here, after her brother's death, it was no longer austere. Eden had seen to that. The duchess had placed color everywhere. It was in the furnishings and paint-ings. Floors held rich rugs, and dressers delicate ornaments.

She often had to pinch herself to ensure that she was no longer living in poverty and fighting to put food on the table.

Reaching the room she wanted, Emily placed a hand on the door and pushed it open.

"Emily!" James rose from his place at the table. "Should you be out of bed?"

"I could not lie there another minute."

"And yet you are still pale, and breathless. The walk here has obviously taxed your strength. Come, sit."

She sat in the chair he held out for her.

"I am fine, thank you, James, and it is time for me to get back on my feet."

He took his place across from her, a frown marring his brow.

"Would you like tea?"

"I can pour it, James."

Emily was not entirely comfortable with this brother, a fact Cam had spoken of at the lecture. She wondered if anyone else had noticed.

"I can pour my sister tea."

His words were brusque, surprising her. James rarely used that tone with Emily.

"James?" The silence stretched as she waited for him to speak. "Are you all right?"

His gray eyes held hers for long seconds, and she saw the worry then, etched deep in his handsome face. Was it worry for her, or was something else bothering him?

"Someone tried to take you away from us. How do you believe that made me feel, Emily?"

"I am sorry for that, James. The thing is—"

"Was it your fault, then?" He cut her off.

He wasn't like the James she'd come to know. The calm, patient one. This one was tense, his words clipped.

She shook her head.

41

"I didn't think so. More tea, thank you." He nodded to the maid as she brought in a rack of toast.

"I'm sorry you were worried."

"Did you think I wouldn't be?"

"James, what is wrong?"

He exhaled loudly, but before he could speak someone else entered the room.

"What the hell are you doing out of bed!"

Emily turned in her chair to watch Cam stalk to her side. Her heart did not race faster seeing him; she was just still recovering from her walk.

"Well?"

He had bruises under his eyes. His hair was unbrushed and his necktie slightly crooked, as if he'd been tugging it. Emily felt it again, the ache of longing. She pushed it aside. She was good at that, hiding what she really felt.

CHAPTER 6

"*I* should be asking you that." Emily watched as he pulled out the chair next to hers and eased himself into it. Cam rarely lowered himself sedately, which told her he was not feeling as he should. "You look in no better state than I."

"I was not abducted."

"However, you were thrown from a carriage, and Samantha tells me you hurt your back."

He waved a hand about, dismissing her words. "I am well."

"Yet you lowered yourself gingerly into that chair," she persisted.

He stopped slathering butter on a piece of toast to send her a sharp look. Nothing was wrong with his eyes, it seemed.

"Lilly fixed me. I am merely a bit stiff. You, however, have been sleeping and bedridden for days."

"I was not bedridden, but tired."

"Yes, Essie said as much, but you looked pale."

"You came to my room?"

"Just to see for myself that everyone was not lying to me. I promise, I did not step over the threshold and into your maidenly bower."

"Cam," James cautioned. "Behave yourself, Emily is still unwell, as are you. Now if you will both excuse me briefly, I need to collect something from my office."

Emily watched James leave the room, unsure how she felt about being alone with the man who had brought her back from the dead.

"Are you really all right?"

Cam's hand settled over the one she had on the table. Warmth traveled up her arm and down the other one—which was ridiculous and not possible, Emily reminded herself. His eyes held hers, the green depths filled with concern.

"I am, thanks to you. Cam, I—"

"Don't." He squeezed her fingers gently. "No good can come of thinking about that day, Emily."

"How can I not," she whispered. "You gave me life."

"As you would have me were our positions reversed."

Her eyes ran over his face. Yes, she would have done anything to ensure this man lived were it in her power to do so.

"Why was I taken, Cam? What did they want from me?"

"I don't know, but we will find out, I promise you."

"But you know something?"

He shrugged.

"Not really, but we will understand more when you have told us exactly what happened. James would not let anyone question you before you were ready."

"Is he all right, Cam? James seems upset."

His eyes ran over her face. His expression, like her brother's, was suddenly tense.

"Can you really not understand why?"

Emily frowned.

"Why do you struggle to comprehend how your brother feels about you?"

"I don't struggle with it. I understand the way of things." Emily pulled her hand free.

"No, you don't. In fact, you are oblivious."

"I am not!"

"Totally oblivious."

"I wish for you to be quiet, as you have no idea what you are talking about."

"James is important to me, and a friend, and your continued restraint toward him is causing him pain, Emily."

"I don't know what you mean." Surely his words were not true? How could she hurt the powerful Duke of Raven?

"We discussed this at the lecture, Emily. I know you remember that, because you just lowered your eyes."

"You saved my life, therefore, I had thought for the next few days at least I should make an attempt not to insult or argue with you."

His snort of laughter had her looking up. The smile made him seem younger suddenly. The tiredness was still there, but when he smiled his face came alive.

"Do you really believe that is possible?"

"We are adults, so yes I do."

"Emily, Emily, Emily." He sighed. "Whatever the hell this is between us is not going away because you choose to play nicely for a few days."

"Wh-what do you mean... between us?" Emily could not believe he had said those words. Surely the only thing that lay between them was animosity... wasn't it?

"Do you ever give thought to why we argue constantly?"

"No, and neither should you, so desist in this foolish conversation at once!" She hadn't meant to raise her voice, but it had happened anyway.

"One question?"

"What?"

"You get to ask me just one question, Emily, which I will answer, but I get the same right."

"No." She shook her head. There was no way she wanted this man to ask her anything personal, which he surely would.

"Not curious about anything?" he teased. "No burning question you've always wanted answered about me?"

"You flatter yourself that I would even have you in my thoughts," Emily lied.

He clutched his chest. "You wound me."

She rolled her eyes.

"You can go first."

Dare she? The opportunity was almost too much to resist.

"Have you ever loved?" The words came out before she could stop them. "Don't answer that, I'm not—"

He held up a hand, his face serious.

"You asked, and the answer is yes. My family of course, but I once loved a woman called Miss Louisa Grossley. She was beautiful right down to her dainty feet, and had a heart as cold as a lump of ice. She liked to have many men dangling after her, and I was one. She broke my heart when she turned down my proposal."

"I'm sorry, that must have been painful for you."

"It was, but I got over it quickly." He smiled.

"Which would suggest you didn't really have your heart broken."

"Or I'm shallow. And now for my question."

Emily exhaled slowly. She'd given him this right because she'd asked him the first question.

"What is keeping you from allowing a bond to form between you and James?"

She looked away from him to give herself time to think.

"Guilt," she whispered, realizing she could not lie to this man, not after what he had done for her.

"About what?"

"That is a second question, so I'm not answering."

"You can't just say guilt!" His brows drew together as he glared at her, attempting to intimidate her into explaining.

"You should have formed your question better."

"Damnation, Emily—"

"Don't speak to me that way!"

"They are already fighting, and to the best of my knowledge Em has been out of her bed only a short time." The voice carried in through the open door.

"I will have my answers," Cam whispered.

Not if I have any say in the matter.

Relieved, Emily watched Max walk in with Essie. Everything was slightly off-balance between her and Cam at the moment. Yes, they were still arguing, but there was something else simmering between them since they'd shared that kiss.

"Are you feeling better?" Max kissed her cheek.

"Much. Thank you."

He was different from James. There was a toughness about this brother, a wildness that had never quite been tamed, even though he appeared everything that was civilized, from his clothes to his manners. Yet life had imprinted itself on his face, the hard life of a boy abandoned by his mother and thrown into the hands of a cruel sea captain. It was Essie who brought him back into the light. Their love was a wonderful thing, Emily thought, watching the look he threw his beloved.

"What are you doing?" She looked down at the plate of buttered toast Cam had just placed before her.

"I may be angry with you, but you need to eat. You're thin and pale."

"I'm always pale," Emily protested.

"However you have not been as thin lately," Cam said, filling her teacup. He then added two teaspoons of sugar.

"I'm perfectly capable of doing that for myself, Cambridge, and I can hardly help that I am naturally thin... or pale!"

"Now, Emily—"

"She should still be in bed," Cam interrupted his sister.

Emily glared at him. "Just because you are a man, Cambridge Sinclair, does not mean you are stronger than I, and thus able to rise from your sick bed sooner."

"Yes it does." His words were accompanied by a small smile. It wasn't the usual one he gave her laced with menace; this one was gentle, and it unsettled her.

"That will do, both of you."

Emily tore her eyes from Cam and looked at James, who had just returned. Was Cam right, could her behavior be hurting him?

Emily acknowledged that she did treat him differently to Max. Max was like her, a child born out of wedlock, and she did not feel alienated from him like she did James.

"Eat up now." Cam nudged Emily's plate closer.

"Yes, in this I agree with him. You must eat to regain your strength, Emily."

"I will, thank you, James."

"If you are up to it, Emily, I have asked Dev and Lilly and the others over to hear your story, as I think it best we all understand what happened so we can find who is responsible."

Emily shivered at the thought of recounting that day, but she simply nodded. James was right, they did need to know if the culprits were to be caught.

After the meal had finished with no more arguing, Emily

followed James and the others to his office, a large room where the family spent a great deal of time.

The ceiling was high, with the farthest wall holding floor-to-ceiling windows that streamed in sunlight—when there was sun, that was—making the room a wonderful place to sit and idle away a few hours with a book, of which there were many. Lining two walls, high enough that a ladder would be needed to reach the top ones, there were enough books in here to appease any interest. The furnishings were of rich, deep reds and blues with woven patterned rugs scattered on the polished wooden floors. It was a room that Emily secretly loved, but she did not spend a great deal of time here, as James was usually occupying it.

Soon the room was full of Sinclairs and Ravens. Dev sat beside his wife, Lilly, who looked lovely with her fair locks and beautiful smile. In her arms was Charles, their son, a happy little boy who had the Sinclair coloring. Eden was holding Isabella, who had brown curls and showed signs of being a beauty like her mother. James, Cam, Max, and Essie were also seated throughout the room. Everyone was here to listen to Emily recount what had happened the day of the abduction.

"Give me that child," Cam said. He was seated in a chair to her right. Lilly handed him Charles, and the boy settled back happily against his uncle's chest. A comfortable place to be, Emily remembered.

"I have told them what happened until you stormed out of the lecture," Cam said. "So start your story from the moment you were abducted, Emily."

"I did not storm out. I had no wish to spend another minute in your company, therefore I left the building... discreetly, and with great composure."

He let out a great big bark of laughter. Cam didn't do anything quietly.

"Now, where was I?"

"I told them about the paper you wrote."

"You didn't!" She glared at Cam. "You had no right."

"He had every right," James snapped. "Why did you not tell us of this interest you have in astronomy, Emily?"

If only they knew all of it.

"I—ah, well as to that, I did not want to bother you."

"Why would you studying astronomy bother me? In fact, had you told me I would have been delighted, as it interests me also."

"Does it?" Emily wasn't sure what to make of that.

"Me, however, it bores witless, so don't even try and tell me about it," Max said, smiling at her.

"I would like to read this paper."

She nodded to James, but said nothing further. She had educated herself where possible, and since coming to live here had continued with that, but James had been educated at the best school, by the best scholars; she would not feel comfortable with him reading her paper. Of course there was every possibility he had read her work without realizing it. Every morning in the newspaper.

"Drink this tea please, Emily," Essie said, handing her a cup. "I've had it brewing for you. It will continue to help with bruising."

She heard the collective group sigh. They had all been subjected to Essex Sinclair's potions and tinctures.

The cup was warm as she cradled it.

"Bottoms up."

Ignoring Cam, she took a sip, and found it surprisingly sweet. There was the earthy taste of herbs, and whatever else had been brewed in there, but it wasn't unpleasant.

"I put some honey in."

"How come she gets honey?" Cam said as he pulled a funny face at Charles. The little boy gurgled with laughter.

The picture was an appealing one, she could not deny that. The handsome man and his nephew. He'd be a wonderful father when the time came. She pushed aside the depressing thought that she'd never have children, as it had been her choice to make; no one else had influenced her.

"I like her. Now be quiet, and hopefully Emily will be able to get through her story without interruption."

"Highly unlikely," James stated.

"I was walking—"

"On that matter, Emily," James interrupted. "I do not approve of you gadding about London unescorted. Or slipping out of the house without first notifying any of us where you are going."

"Two seconds, that has to be a record even for us," Max said. "However, in this I agree fully with James."

Emily glared at Cam, who had obviously told her brothers about the lectures she had attended.

"We will come back to that. Now continue, Em," Essie said gently.

She told them everything she remembered, which surprisingly was quite a bit.

"He spoke a language?"

"The man who grabbed me did I think, Max, but I could understand very little. I did not get a look at his face, as I was forced facedown on the floor at first, and when I turned, he was climbing through the roof to get Cam."

"You must have been terrified," Eden said.

She had been, and wondered if she'd ever see her family again.

"Do you have a feeling they were targeting you deliberately, Emily, or was it random?"

"Random!" Cam roared at Max's words. "How the hell can you suggest it is random?"

"Calm down, Cam," Dev said.

51

"James and I spoke with our friendly Bow Street Runner," Max continued. "Mr. Brown told us concern is growing, as three women have been abducted and disappeared entirely without a trace. They believe they are being sold, and put on ships, heading for God knows where to be enslaved as concubines."

The thought made Emily queasy. There could be no worse fate as far as she was concerned. To be enslaved to a man... or several, for their pleasure for as long as they wished it.

"Christ!" Cam's face paled even more.

"Quite," James added. "And that is why Max asked the questions he has."

"I'm not sure," Emily said. "I don't remember the man mentioning my name."

"There are a few options." Max looked grim as he continued. "One is what I have just mentioned; the other is that whoever took you knows the money and power your brothers have and has decided to ransom you back to us."

"Lord, I hope it's the first one," Essie said. "I could not bear to think Emily was still in danger."

"We must all be diligent," James said looking grim. "We have employed the services of Mr. Spriggot, and he will be looking into the matter for us. It is hoped he can track down the man thrown from the carriage, or the driver first, as it is likely they were just hired help. We have told him to use the manpower required to get a result, Emily. Whatever this is, we want it dealt with immediately. I want to reassure you, however, that no further harm will come to you."

"Ouch, you little blighter," Cam said, shaking a finger. Charles had just bitten him, and it was just the moment for him to do so. Everyone laughed, but inside Emily felt cold, because while she hoped this was a random act, something inside her said it was not.

CHAPTER 7

*S*he'd just said the one word, *guilt*, which left him no wiser and a great deal more frustrated. What the hell was she guilty over, and what did it have to do with James?

Cam watched Emily gather Isabella into her arms and hug her close. She was scared that the abduction had not been an isolated incident, just as they all were.

Several days had passed since Emily's abduction, and the anger inside him still raged on. His body had yet to recover fully, even though Lilly had healed the worst of his pain. But it was his head that had not returned to normal. He was struggling to push aside the thoughts of Emily being taken right off the street in front of him. He would wake, cold with sweat, at the memory of the carriage rolling into the water, and he unable to find her.

He saw her terror as she looked up at him through the roof of the carriage. The desperation to reach her, save her, that he'd experienced that day was fresh in his mind. He wondered if he would ever be completely free of those memories, the consuming fear that she would drown before he could get to her. He prayed, fervently, that whoever grabbed her had been working randomly; the other possibility was not one he wanted to consider.

"You must show caution now, Emily, until we have this matter resolved," James said to her. "As must we all."

She wouldn't look at her brother, looked instead at the child in her arms. Isabella was smiling at her, her hands reaching for a wisp of hair that had come free of the simple bun Emily wore at the back of her head.

Guilt. The word could mean so many things. But whatever it was, it stopped her from getting close to James.

Her white dress was a simple style with no adornment, and around her shoulders was a thick rust-colored shawl to ward off the cold. He watched as she muffled a yawn; he had seen her wince several times as she moved. Twinges that, like he, she felt after what they had endured. Her pallor told him she needed her bed, but he wasn't about to suggest that again, because as was often proven, she would seek to do the opposite.

"So, just to clarify, she is not allowed to leave the house again."

"Pardon?" Emily turned her eyes on him as he spoke. "I will not be made a prisoner in James's house."

She'd said he was pale, but he doubted it was anything when compared to her. Emily was a walking ghost, fatigue written in every line of her face.

She could have died. The thought turned him cold.

"It is your house also, Emily."

She turned from him to James.

"Of course," she said in that polite little voice that annoyed Cam. She never used it on him, only when the others were near.

"We are not about to make you a prisoner, Em," Max said, stepping into the conversation.

Cam had come to love the man like a brother since his marriage to Essie, but there had been a time when, like James, he had been closed off to the world. It had taken his sister Essie to find the key to unlock his darkness and pain.

"However"—Max raised a hand as Emily smiled—"you will not leave the house without a maid and a footman."

"Oh now, that is ridiculous."

"Ridiculous how?" Cam said. "Someone took you from beneath my nose and I could do nothing to stop them, Emily. For pity's sake show some sense and acknowledge you are in danger, and for once let your family care for you, at least until we understand what is going on."

"Wh-what do you mean for once?"

At least she had color in her cheeks now, even if it had been put there by anger. Anger directed at him, which of course was nothing new. However, today, Cam realized, there was something else simmering between them. A tension brought about from what they had endured... and the kiss.

"That will do." James tried to step in; Emily ignored him.

"I demand to know what he means."

If she wanted the truth, Cam was happy to supply it, because her family sure as hell would not.

"That you are secretive and contained, and rarely let anyone watch over you. You walk about in silence, as if a loud noise will have you scuttling back to your room. Do you believe that speaking your mind will have you tossed out of the house?"

Her mouth fell open. Soft pink lips, Cam noted. *The perfect lips for kissing.*

"Enough, Cam."

Max did not raise his voice, but there was strength behind the words.

"Very well." Cam rose to his feet. "You may all dance about her, but I will not. She has been with this family long enough now to feel one of us. Equal in every way that matters, as Max does, and yet she still acts like a visitor. The only time she raises her voice is when I'm around."

"H-how dare you!"

"How dare I speak the truth?" Cam glared at Emily. "How dare I say what they are thinking, but are not brave enough to voice?"

He walked out then, leaving a stunned silence behind him. For the first time in his life, he wished for his sister Eden's gift of hearing. He could then listen to what was being said in his absence.

The front door opened as he reached it. "Thank you, Buttles. It is my fondest wish that your day is going better than mine." He acknowledged the Raven butler.

"I have just polished the silver, Mr. Sinclair, and anticipate a meal in my immediate future."

"The silver I could forgo, however the meal shall be splendid, I am sure."

Cam walked out into the gray day, the frigid air slapping him hard in the face.

"Excellent. I left behind food and hot beverages," Cam muttered. "My impetuous nature once again strikes."

Pride had him walking out the gates. He could find plenty of food in his aunt and uncle's house, or even his own, should he need it.

The street housed the Raven and Sinclair families—all of them, at least the ones important to him. It was an odd thing, but through a myriad of happenstance they had all landed here, housed within minutes of each other, and Cam had to say he did not mind. It certainly made things neat and tidy, and he was not forced to travel long distances to visit his loved ones. There was also the fact that he could wander from house to house and receive a meal at any given time.

It also gave members of society no end of amusement. In fact the Earl of Hamner was heard to say that someone should have the street renamed the Clan Close. As he was not the most intelligent peer of Cam's acquaintance, the man had done remarkably well there.

"Hello, Cam!"

Turning, he saw his little siblings, accompanied by their maids. A long green ribbon was tied around Myrtle's collar. The Sinclairs' shaggy dog was walking obediently at Warwick's side, likely because the boy had a treat in his pocket. The tension in Cam's shoulders eased as he watched them skip toward him. Like their elder brothers and sisters they were also named after the places in which they were conceived. Not an easy thing to grow up with, but they had handled it by abbreviating them.

Dark hair and green eyes, like all but Eden, these three would be variations of their elder siblings as they grew. They were growing up fast, he realized, no longer the little siblings he had carried about on his shoulders or tucked into bed at night. The thought was a sobering one. Change, Cam knew, was inevitable. He saw it everywhere he looked, but today it felt harder to see in these three.

"Hello, my heathens, what has you out here on such a day?"

They were wrapped in bonnets, hats, and gloves with scarves up to their ears. Dorrie and Somer were ten-year-old twins, a fact their brother constantly lamented, as at nine years he was often the butt of their mischievous natures.

"We are going to collect Samantha, and then go to the

park," Somer said. "If we're good we can go for tea and cakes, Dev said, and as we always are—"

"No you're not," Cam scoffed, cutting her off.

"We are going," she continued as if he had not spoken.

"Your nose will grow if you continue telling tall tales, Miss Somer, and your ears will fall off if you stay out here too long. Are you sure you wish to go to the park?"

"The problem is, Cam, as you are hurt, and Emily too, Dev said we weren't to bother you, and he is doing something with James that may not be concluded in time. So we may just have to stay and play with Samantha." Dorrie looked at him, her little face screwed up with concern. These three knew exactly how to get him to do as they wished, and even as that thought entered his mind, he was opening his mouth to agree.

"Shall I take you then?"

The whoop of joy was deafening.

"I'll take that as a yes."

Cam took a hand each of the twins; his brother was now supposedly past holding his hand, or so he'd told him last week. This week could be an entirely different matter.

Walking with his little sisters skipping at his sides, and Warwick striding out in front, he felt the fiery emotions inside him shrivel to a small, tight knot.

He had been wrong to say what he had, but for years he had watched Emily act like the poor relation, sitting in silence through every family occasion. The only time she truly came out of herself was when she was with Samantha or his little siblings. Or when he challenged her.

Why does this bother me so much now? Because suddenly he was very aware of Miss Emily Tolly, which was a discomfiting thought on a frigid, bleak day.

"Are you all right, Cam?"

Warwick was walking backward now.

"Of course."

"I heard what happened to Emily, and that you saved her. But you were thrown from that carriage and—"

"You should not have listened, Warwick." Releasing the twins, he stepped closer and grabbed his brother. Lifting his hair, he noted the plugs of wax in his ears. Like Eden, Warwick's strong sense was hearing.

"I have them in."

"I see that, and I'm sorry you heard what was said, but I assure you all is well now, and both Emily and I are unhurt."

He nodded, then faced forward once more. It was a burden they carried, because Cam remembered when he was aware of the difference between him and others. It had not been a happy moment. It would take time to adjust, but with the help of he, Dev, Essie, and Eden, they would get through it.

"That man is riding his horse without holding the reins!"

Looking to where Dorrie pointed, Cam found Captain Sinclair approaching. He was indeed riding without holding the reins, and the horse was magnificent. Huge, with a long dark mane, he had hooves the size of ham hocks. Cam had first seen the animal the day Emily had been abducted.

Man and horse stopped beside them without the rider issuing the horse a command.

"Captain Sinclair," Cam acknowledged. "I hope you had no adverse effects after the rescue."

"Wolf," the man said, dismounting. "And no. It took a while to warm up, but other than that I am well, thank you, Mr. Sinclair."

"Cam." He held out a hand. "As I was not myself that day, please allow me to thank you again on behalf of Miss Tolly." Those eyes, Cam remembered, saw like his brother did. They too were piercing in their intensity. Just how much they saw was yet to be determined.

The horse stood still as a statue now. Still enough to intrigue Warwick, who instantly went to pat him.

"Apollo will not harm him."

"I can see that." Cam watched his little brother stroke the soft muzzle.

"Apollo! He is god of so many things," Somer shrieked.

"Yes, music, poetry, and medicine just to name a few," Dorrie added.

"Very good, girls. Please allow me to introduce you to your younger cousins, Wolf. Girls, this is Captain Sinclair, but he is known as Wolf. Master Warwickshire Sinclair, Miss Somerset Sinclair, and Miss Dorset Sinclair."

The captain bowed, and when he rose his smile showed off a row of white teeth.

"How wonderful, I have little cousins as well as big ones."

"And you, Wolf. Do you have sisters?"

"Yes, two actually; they reside in Dorset with my mother," he said, smiling at Dorrie. "Both are younger."

"Would you like to come and meet your cousins properly. All are inside," Cam added.

"But we are to go to the park!" Somer squealed.

"You forget your manners, Somer."

The little girl hung her head.

"Sorry, Cam."

"No apology necessary, Miss Somer. I love the park also."

"Come with us then, Captain Sinclair!" This time it was Dorrie who squealed. His sisters rarely spoke in gentle voices.

"Wolf." He smiled at the children.

Cam raised a hand to quiet them. "We shall introduce our new cousin to everyone first, and then go to the park. Captain Sinclair is of course welcome to accompany us, but you will not force him to do so."

"Cam?"

He turned to find Essie approaching. She'd likely come to find him and talk about what had just happened, but he didn't want to discuss it, because he wasn't sure what the hell was going on—only that something had changed since Emily's attempted abduction, and now he was aware of her as he'd never been before.

CHAPTER 8

"*My* sister, Wolf, Mrs. Huntington. I believe you met her the other day."

"Yes I did, but we were not formally introduced. A pleasure, Mrs. Huntington, and thank you for your care. I took the tonic you sent around to my lodgings and felt much better for it."

"Wolf is coming inside, Essie. So let's get along, as my extremities are freezing," Cam said, nudging the children forward. He wondered at his reception from everyone when he returned. His words had likely shocked them all.

"We shall hand Apollo to a groom upon arrival, Warwick. Don't fuss," he told his little brother, who was showing signs of not moving.

"We are very bright," Somer said.

"Somer, I have told you that makes you sound like a braggart to anyone but family," Cam said.

"But Wolf is family."

"She has you there," the captain said.

"Look at Myrtle, she is pressed to Wolf!"

Cam looked at the dog, and as Dorrie had said she was indeed pressed to the man's leg.

"How strange, she rarely likes people she does not know," Essie said.

"Animals like me."

"It sounds like you will fit right in, Wolf, as we have peculiar talents also."

Cam felt it again, a gentle stirring of the air around them, like one force meeting another. It seemed their strength was about to grow again.

"Ask us something, Wolf. Anything, and we shall answer it!"

Cam rolled his eyes as Somer skipped to his side, grabbed his hand, and swung it several times. Cam picked her up and threw her in the air. She squealed, as he'd known she would.

"When was Julius Caesar assassinated?"

"44 BC," Warwick said before one of the twins could answer. "You need to try harder than that, Cam."

"I'm easing you into it."

"What does *in hac causa mihi aqua haeret* mean?"

"Your Latin is very good, Cam."

"It has to be, these three challenge us constantly, Wolf." Behind them, Cam could now hear the twins and Warwick conferring, their fertile brains working through the answer to his question.

"And I am Essie. How did your name change from Christian to Wolf, cousin?"

"I was born Christian, but my father called me Wolf from a young age, as I used to howl like one, and I have used it ever since."

There was something of Dev in him, Cam thought. The way he tilted his head and walked.

"The Romans say that the water stopped for them," Somer

said. "It is when you can no longer go on, and reach a point when your muse has stopped, or you are at a stand."

"Good Lord," Wolf said, looking at the children. "You are indeed very bright."

They smiled.

"How many ribs does a horse have?" he then asked.

"That actually may stump them," Cam whispered. "I'm not sure they've studied animals overly."

"Eighteen pairs," Warwick said slowly, and Cam could almost see his mind working. "But some have been found with nineteen."

"Of course, occasionally I'm wrong."

"Very good. How many teeth?" Captain Sinclair questioned.

The twins were not pleased their brother knew the answers and they did not. They would be requesting more literature to read.

"Forty," Warwick said.

"And now we have arrived." Essie urged everyone through the front door, a door Cam had not long exited.

He felt it again, the tension at seeing Emily. He hoped this settled down, because it would be bloody annoying if it did not. There was also a question over how everyone would treat him after his outburst; he guessed he would soon find out.

"Are the families still in the duke's study, Buttles?"

"No, Mrs. Huntington, they are now taking refreshments in the cerulean parlor."

"Blue," Somer whispered to Captain Sinclair. "Cerulean is a big word for blue."

The children ran on ahead, knowing this house as intimately as they did the others the family owned on the street.

The adults followed at a slower pace. The cerulean parlor was indeed full when they entered, and Cam found Emily seated with Samantha and his little siblings. Before them was a large tray of food.

"While I think you could have chosen a more private setting for your words, Cam, I believe they were accurate," James said, coming to meet him and drawing him to one side.

"I'm sorry for speaking them in the manner I did, but not for the content. There is something riding Emily, to make her behave the way she does. I just don't know what."

"Why does Emily's behavior concern you so much?"

Why indeed.

"Perhaps you need to give that some thought, and I shall consider what you have said."

"Ah—"

"We shall let the matter rest for now, Cam."

Relief had him exhaling loudly. He wasn't going to give the matter any thought, because he didn't care about Emily's behavior, he cared about the way she treated her family. Cam felt better after thinking it through.

"James, this is Captain Sinclair. He is known as Wolf," Essie said, making the introductions.

"Another one." James sighed. "Just when I thought we were gaining on them."

"Pardon?" Wolf looked confused.

"The Ravens have fewer numbers than the Sinclairs, Captain. Seeing as I have recently found a brother and sister, I had hoped our numbers were gaining on them, but with your arrival, I fear that hope is now dashed."

"He has two sisters," Essie said.

"I suggest we are beaten, brother," Max added, coming to shake Captain Sinclair's hand. "I am Max."

"Of course our intellect far outstrips theirs, so it is not too much of a concern."

"Tsk tsk, James, we all know that for a tall tale. Why,

marriage to my sisters increased the intelligence in your family tenfold," Cam added.

"And where are you staying in London, Wolf?" Dev asked.

"I have lodgings, but am seeking new ones."

"You can move in with me if you wish?" Cam said.

His cousin looked shocked. "I-I.... You can't possibly want that. We barely know each other."

"You are blood, Captain, and if that were not the case, then your actions the other day would have assured me of your character. The bed is yours should you need it."

"But surely you wish for your privacy?"

Dev snorted.

"You have met my family. As you can see, privacy is not something I am used to."

"I should be obliged, just until I find other accommodations, Cam."

"Excellent. Move in when you wish."

"I will, and thank you." He and Cam shook hands, and soon he was deep in conversation with Dev.

"Tell me about your vision, Wolf? You can speak freely here, everyone is aware of what we have."

Cam moved closer to be part of the conversation, for now putting distance between him and Emily.

"It is not easy to speak of, as before today, only my two sisters would understand."

"Of course, it is not an easy burden we carry," Dev said. "But it is something that we have learned to live with. I am sure you used your senses while doing your duty to your country?"

Color flushed Wolf's cheeks.

"Many times. But my strongest sense is the affinity I have with animals. I can feel what they feel."

"This I have witnessed," Cam said, and explained to Dev

how Wolf's horse had moved without his guidance on the reins.

"Myrtle certainly seems to like you." The dog was still pressed to his side.

"I see well at night, and long distances. The colors come in flashes, but I cannot control them. Usually when I am near a sick person, or someone gripped by a fierce emotion."

"And your sisters, Wolf? Do they have a developed sense?" Eden came to her cousin's side. No doubt she had heard everything anyway.

"One has a developed sense of taste, the other hearing."

Eden clapped her hands together in excitement. "How wonderful, another like me."

"There is no one like you, my darling," James said, joining her.

They talked about their senses, and the uncle and aunt that they did not know, and began to acquaint themselves with Wolf Sinclair.

"He is like Dev," Essie whispered as she drew Cam to one side. "In mannerism and demeanor."

"Very much."

"Are you all right, Cam?"

His sigh wasn't loud, but she heard it.

"What happened in James's study is not like you, Cam. Yes, you can be loud and demonstrative, but usually it is in fun, or a verbal debate. Rarely have I seen you angry, at least not in a long time."

They both knew when he had been angry. His behavior had nearly destroyed the family he loved. He would never, ever forget that.

"I am tired, Ess. My body still hurts, and I am not myself."

She rose to her toes and kissed his cheek.

"Yes, you are all those things, my dear brother, but there is also something else bothering you. Something to do with

Emily. But I will not push; you will talk to me when you are ready."

Essie left his side to go to Max, and Cam found his eyes searching for Emily. She was laughing, her pale face suddenly alive as she played with the little ones. It hurt his chest to see it, and he hoped like hell that was because he had consumed two macaroons in quick succession upon entering the room.

What had she meant by saying the word guilt?

CHAPTER 9

$\mathcal{E}$mily would not look at Cam, in case she stormed across the room, which would be extremely painful given the state of her body, and fired a volley of insults at his head, which would achieve nothing except cleansing her spleen and shocking everyone else in the room. How dared he say the things he had... even if there was some truth to his words, she admitted silently.

"You may all dance about her, but I will not. She has been with this family long enough now to feel one of us."

When had he realized how she felt? Him, of all of them, had cut to the core of her insecurities. Emily had never voiced her thoughts, because they would have been selfish and ungrateful, but she'd felt them.

"Equal in every way that matters, as Max does, and yet she still acts like a visitor."

It had been her own private battle, something that waged silently inside her. A feeling of being inferior, of being a burden to James, and then Max. And that she would continue to be so into her old age as she had no means of support. Not exactly true, as she was earning some money, just not a great deal.

James insisted on giving her money, but she rarely spent it on anyone but Samantha.

"You are secretive and contained, and rarely let anyone watch over you."

Cam had left the room after speaking these words, and the silence had been loud enough to make Emily wince. No one had spoken for several long, drawn-out heartbeats, and then everyone had talked at once, as if Cam had not just exposed her with those words. Emily had left the room on the guise of collecting Samantha to take tea with them all, but in truth, she'd needed to escape before they all started asking her questions about what Cam had meant.

She'd felt their eyes on her when she left, and Max had opened the door, his hand lingering on her shoulder.

"Are you all right?"

She'd managed a nod, and may even had said "yes," but the truth was she had been shocked.

"I hope you are feeling better today, Miss Tolly?"

Emily got to her feet as Captain Sinclair appeared before her.

"Thank you, Captain, I am much better. And I must also thank you for helping in my rescue."

His smile was just like Cam's, although a touch more somber.

"I'm afraid I can only take credit for the transportation. It was Cambridge who took the risks. He leapt onto your carriage, and then dived into the water to save you. It was an act of incredible bravery, and I'm just pleased you are both here today to speak of the matter."

Emily looked to where Cam stood a few feet away. As if sensing her regard, he turned and their eyes caught. She pulled away first. He was the reason she was alive today; it was a sobering thought, and shriveled her anger toward him.

"Yes, it was a brave act indeed."

"May I have a word, Captain?"

"Of course. Excuse me, Miss Tolly."

Emily watched him walk at Essie's side. The two of them were soon talking to Eden. The rest of the family were scattered around the room. Had they all treated her gently... different from each other? Not confronted or questioned her because they feared she would not cope? Had her behavior allowed them to see her as weak and vulnerable? If so, then she had misled them, because she was neither. Shy, yes, guilty, definitely, and also intimidated. She was the baseborn child of a duke and a maid; her life before coming here had not been spent in a grand house, eating with the best silver service with servants to see to her needs. She constantly feared she would disgrace herself, and in doing so had portrayed herself as timid.

"I call Roman gods. In French."

Emily turned at Warwick's words, glad to have something else to occupy her thoughts. She was well used to the Sinclair children. They played word games continually, and their siblings were constantly tossing out words for them to spell or mathematical equations for them to solve. They were not a normal family, she knew this, and knew there was much to them that she had yet discovered; or perhaps it was fairer to say she had never asked. Was Cam right, should she try harder to show this family she felt one of them? Did she feel that way? Was she to live in the shadows of its members her entire life?

Her head ached from all the conflicting emotions. She needed her room, and the quiet solitude it offered, but then wasn't that where she usually ran?

"I shall take Roman," Emily said before she could stop

herself. Her French was better and she'd been studying Roman gods with Samantha.

"And I shall take gods," a deep, familiar voice drawled.

Of course he had said that. Emily made herself look at Cam as he sat on the arm of the chair opposite. The one where his twin sisters and Samantha were all wedged in, like peas in a pod.

"We shall need a shoehorn to get you out of there," he teased the little girls, who giggled.

He was good with children, she'd give him that.

"Take your time, Emily, we are in no rush."

Did he think she could not do it? The look in his eyes was unreadable. Not mocking, nor angry... just blank.

"Rupert of Mars applauds Neptune." Emily then repeated slowly in French.

"Well done."

She ignored Cam, while the children clapped her performance.

"Genius orders Dover sole."

His French was of course fluent and flawless... the cad.

"Your French is much better, Emily."

"I have been practicing." She made herself meet his eyes.

"It shows."

"Thank you." She could be polite if he could.

"Gunther's ices," he then said, holding her eyes. "In Latin."

"Gunther's," Somer squealed.

"Ices," Samantha shrieked.

He moved to take the seat beside her, then leaned in to whisper, "I'm not going to apologize for speaking the truth, Emily."

"You had no right to say what you did in front of everyone."

"Who has that right then? Your brothers? Samantha? Should I have spoken it only before them?"

She got to her feet, her instinctive reaction to run.

"Running away like you always do, Emily?"

"What do you want from me?" she whispered. "Why are you being... being—"

"Mean?" he said for her. "Honest, because I'm the only one who is actually brave enough to speak the truth. But you know that already, don't you."

"Shut up!"

"Be honest with yourself at least. And then try and be honest with James. He deserves better from you."

"G-go to hell." There was not a great deal of strength behind her words, as she'd whispered them, but she could feel the heat of anger wash through her. She'd never spoken in such a way, and especially not in company.

"Already been there, and have to say it is not a place I wish to frequent again."

"When did you go to hell?" she asked before she could stop herself. "No, never mind, I don't want to know."

"I'll tell you if you really want to hear."

His eyes were serious on hers. Cam was rarely serious.

"I don't, and I've been to hell myself, and would not wish that upon anyone else."

He caught her hand as she started to leave her.

"When?"

"It matters not. What matters is that you and I avoid each other, as no good can come of us conversing anymore. So please keep your distance."

"Because I make you think, Emily. I force you out of hiding, and because I make you feel, that scares you."

She walked away. Fighting her first instinct, which was to leave the room, Emily instead conversed with Eden, and lastly Max. Only when she was sure she'd stayed long enough so that no one would think she was fleeing—most especially Cambridge Sinclair—did she leave. His words had annoyed and shocked her, but also made her aware of her behavior, and while she'd never admit that to him, Emily was determined to stop hiding in her room and running away.

Looking over her shoulder, she found Cam watching her, his green eyes intent on her face. And that was another thing that would change from this moment on. She would no longer shiver, or be aware of that man, and in fact she'd do whatever was necessary to ensure they put their relationship back on its previous footing. Well, perhaps not exactly that, as arguing with him was exhausting.

CHAPTER 10

*T*he adults had decided that today they would take the children to visit the insects and butterflies on display at Sidley House. This would offer them entertainment and keep them warm and dry inside. Plus, stop them from tormenting each other.

"Warwick painted Mrs. Wattle's face, Cam."

"I'm sure it will wash off, Dorrie." Mrs. Wattle was her favorite doll.

"And he tried to break my dolls' house," Somer added.

"I did not break it, I merely wanted to test how much weight the roof would hold."

"That will do," Cam said as Somer prepared to launch herself at her brother. "We will turn the carriage around if you three do not behave."

They had meant to go several days ago, but had decided to wait until Emily was recovered enough to accompany them. This Warwick had demanded, as Emily had once confided in him that she envied butterflies as they appeared so weightless, and able to flutter about wherever they wished.

A telling statement that for Cam just added weight to what he already believed. Even after four years, she was still not settled in her new life. She had adapted in a way that ensured she made no scenes, created no conflict, which as far as he was concerned was not healthy for anyone. It was certainly not the Sinclair way. If a thought came into their heads, it usually came out their mouths. He doubted she could keep it up indefinitely; one day she would explode, as her brothers had when his sisters picked away at them.

"Take your finger out of Warwick's ear, Dorrie."

"I just wanted to see if he could hear what was being said in the carriage behind out of one ear, Dev."

"Yes, well it is not done, so don't."

"Emily is telling Samantha about butterflies," Warwick said, unfazed by his sister's finger.

"Somer, leave your ribbons, please, or they will be hopelessly tangled and I will be called upon to work them free."

"Yes, Cam."

Cam's morning business meeting had been cancelled at the last minute, which had left him free to accompany his family to Sidley House. The fact that Warwick had told him Emily was to come also did not have any bearing on the situation.

Riding was not an option as it was raining, so he was jammed in the carriage with Dev and his three little siblings. Lilly had stayed home with Charles due to the weather. Behind them rumbled the Raven carriage with Eden, James, Samantha, and Emily. Essie was looking after Isabella.

"Cam?"

"Yes, Dorrie?"

The twins wore cream, which to his mind was a disaster waiting to happen, knowing their love of investigating everything. Sweet in their chipped bonnets, they looked like little angels. Warwick wore white trousers and a green jacket; by day's end they too would be brown, and streaked with mud.

"Why do you not like Emily?"

Christ.

"Of course he likes Emily. What a silly thing to say, Dorrie," Dev said, smiling at his sister and then shooting a scowl at Cam.

"He's always arguing with her, and she with him."

"Yes," Warwick said. "With everyone else she is gentle, and barely speaks, just sits quietly, but with Cam she's different."

"I'm sure you're wrong." Cam tried to brush off the words.

"No, we're not," Somer said in that direct way children had which he usually found endearing—when it was aimed at anyone but him.

"Perhaps we are just destined to argue," he said, because he had nothing else. "Like you and Samantha, Warwick, and like you two were with that Pillock girl... what was her name? Her mother was the seamstress in Cranston Cliff."

"Oooh, Jenny Pillock!" Somer shrieked in outrage. "She had two front teeth missing and used to whistle when she spoke."

"Nice deflection," Dev whispered as the twins launched into a discussion about all Jenny Pillock's defects. Warwick offered up a few of his own.

"I thought so."

"They were bound to notice, Cam. I'm just surprised it's taken them this many years to comment."

"They haven't before now." Cam looked out the window and wondered how long it would be before he could get out of the carriage.

"That business in James's study the other day, what prompted that?"

"I was tired and sore. Perhaps I was not myself."

"I'm sure you were, as you're rarely anyone else, plus there is the small matter of your avoidance, which is a sure sign of discomfort on your part."

"Avoidance?" Cam wrinkled his brow to appear confused.

It was fair to say that Cam had been avoiding his elder siblings since that day in James's study, because he'd known they would want to discuss the matter with him. Eden had paid him a call, and he'd rushed out the door citing an urgent appointment he did not have. Essie had asked him to eat a meal with her and Max, but he'd declined, and gone to his club alone. Dev had attempted to ride with him in the mornings, but Cam had ridden during the day.

"Yes, avoidance, and you cannot lie to me, I have known you longest."

Cam grunted.

"I thought about what you said, and discussed the matter with Lilly."

"Of course you did." Cam sighed.

"She is my wife, and loves you, as do I."

"You always use the *L* word when you're trying to bring one of us to heel."

"Only on you does it not work."

Dev's face was serious.

"Somer, there is no need to speak that way, thank you," Cam said as he overheard his sister shrieking that Jenny Pillock was a pudding-faced simpleton.

"James and Max bear no grudge, Dev, so let the matter lie. I apologized to them the following day."

"Because they know your words for the truth, Cam, as do we all. But it was not your place to speak them."

"Then whose?"

"Her family—"

"Don't want to upset her. I have no problem doing that, as

with me she usually just fires something back. We have always communicated that way."

Dev's eyes took on a speculative glint.

"I wonder why?"

"Why what?"

"She is a Raven, after all."

Cam felt color fill his face as he took in his brother's words.

"What the hell does that mean?"

"Cam said hell."

"Thank you, Warwick, I heard."

"Apologies, I should not have done so." Cam glared at his eldest brother. "I don't care for where your thoughts are leading, Dev, and will thank you to never raise them again."

His brother shrugged, then pulled the twins off each other as they began to wrestle.

Dear Christ, he could not actually be serious! Cam and Emily. Just the thought made him shudder. They would kill each other in days.

"When does Wolf come to lodge with you?" Dev asked, changing the subject, much to his relief.

"Next week. He sent word yesterday."

As the carriage was finally slowing, Cam put the ridiculous thought of any connection with Emily from his head. His brother had said it to annoy him; there was no more to it than that.

Urging the children from the carriage, they hurried into Sidley House and out of the cold. The occupants of the Raven carriage followed. Emily's face was, as usual, devoid of expression. Just looking at her made him feel as if he was standing on his head, but Dev was wrong. No way could he ever marry such a woman. The idea was absurd.

"Look!"

Following Warwick's hand, they saw a wall completely

covered in butterfly paintings. A door to the right opened, and out walked a man and woman.

"We are Mr. and Mrs. Flutterby."

"Are you really?" Cam asked.

Mrs. Flutterby wore a dark brown dress with white shoes, gloves, and bonnet, and her husband wore a bright blue jacket with white trousers and gloves.

"They are dressed as the Blue Adonis," Warwick said. "The male is bright blue, and the female brown."

"Are you reading by candlelight again at night, because I've told you that's dangerous, Warwick," Dev said.

"No, Mr. Lineus loves butterflies. He has a collection."

"Ah, that explains it all," Cam said. Their tutor was a man of many collections, the elder Sinclair's had come to learn in the years he'd been schooling Dorrie, Somer, and Warwick.

"Is Mrs. Flutterby your real name, because it's very pretty," Samantha said, moving forward to wedge herself between Dorrie and Somer, as she usually did.

"Well thank you, my dear, and yes it is."

"I think I'd like to marry a man with a name like that," Dorrie said. "Do you have any young sons?"

Cam chuckled, Dev blanched at the thought of his little sisters wed, and then they started the questions.

"Do you catch the butterflies yourself?"

"Where is the horridest place you've been to catch one?"

"They really should be loaned out for interrogation purposes," Cam whispered to Dev as they entered the first room, which held rows of glass cabinets with colorful insects and butterflies.

"My money would be on them lasting less than a day before driving someone mad," Dev replied before he moved on to act as intermediary.

Cam wandered behind their party, happy to bring up the rear and observe. The fact that most of his time was spent watching Emily was annoying, but every time he tried to drag his eyes away, they returned seconds later.

She wore a pale rose coat, buttoned to the chin. The sleeves were puffed at the shoulders and straight down the rest of her slender arms. The bodice was fitted, and buttons ran down to her waist, the rest was open to reveal a cream dress with matching rose trim around the hem. The style suited her, Cam thought. She looked elegant and beautiful. He had to acknowledge that, because he'd come to realize lately she was that and more.

Her scent had always been there, the orange blossom mingling with a thousand other ones, but now, for some reason, it seemed to rise above them, as if it had lined his nostrils and he would need to scrub them to remove it.

"How are you feeling?" He fell in beside her, determined to at least try for a modicum of harmony between them. He was an adult after all; this should not be a difficult task. They had not spoken since that day, and while he hadn't been avoiding her precisely, he had definitely not sought her out.

"I am well, thank you."

Her words were rigidly polite.

"And have you heeded your brothers' advice and left the house only in company?"

Her eyes narrowed, and Cam wondered why he felt the need to ruffle her feathers. Harmony, he'd wanted, but instead the first words out of his mouth had been ones that would achieve the opposite. He watched as she inhaled a deep breath before speaking, something she often did when addressing him.

"Mr. Brown and Mr. Spriggot, along with my brothers, whose opinions I of course respect, believe now it is likely the abduction was a chance thing, and connected with several women who have been abducted off the streets lately, as they can find no evidence to state otherwise."

"As opposed to my opinion, which you do not respect?"

Her lips tightened.

"It is still wise to show caution, Emily."

"I am not a fool, contrary to what you believe, Cambridge."

"Fool, no; stubborn, yes."

Her chin lifted.

"Please worry about your welfare and that of your family, and I shall worry about mine."

"But I have already saved you once, so your welfare does concern me."

"Thank you, I am of course grateful—"

"Be sure you don't choke on those words."

"Desist!" she hissed softly.

"Forgive me," Cam whispered, knowing two of his siblings had acute hearing. "It was not my intention to speak to you that way, but I fear it just happens."

Her slender shoulders rose and fell on a sigh.

"I-I know what you mean, as it is no different with me. Therefore, I think we should make an effort to at least try to be polite to each other... for our families' sakes."

Surprised she was agreeing with him and taking a portion of the blame, Cam found himself smiling.

"The effort will be herculean, but I shall try if you will."

Her lips rose, the smile like sun peeking through a cloud. *Where the hell did those words come from?*

"Cam!"

"Yes, Warwick?"

"They have a Pontia daplidice, Cam!"

"Good Lord, do they really?"

"Come and look."

"I'll be right there," Cam said, dragging his eyes from Emily to find his little brother, who now had his face pressed to the glass. When he looked back she'd moved away.

"Is her color good now, Dev?"

"Who?"

His brother was bent over a display.

"Emily's."

"Yes, I checked when she entered. She is back to full health."

"What are you doing? Surely you of all people have no need to get that close."

"No, but when I do it's rather spectacular. The colors are quite something."

"Really?" Cam bent to look also. He couldn't see as well as Dev, but the detail on some of the wings, this close, was amazing.

"So, why did you ask me about Emily's color?"

Their faces were close as they studied the display.

"I thought she looked a bit pale."

"It's winter, she's a lady, therefore she is pale. Or we could go with my earlier theory—"

"I'm leaving." Cam rose and walked away with his brother's laughter following him.

They walked through the floors, looking in each cabinet and discussing what they observed. The children were as always tireless in their enthusiasm.

"If you'll come this way, we have another display on the lower level," Mr. Flutterby said.

To his credit, the man's smile had not slipped, even with the constant barrage of questions.

"Where is Emily?"

Looking around at Warwick's words, Cam felt his pulse kick when he did not see her.

"I shall find her. You all go on."

James started to follow, but Eden grabbed his arm and dragged him down the stairs, which Cam thought odd. To the best of his knowledge his sister had no interest in butterflies.

He searched two rooms, and it was in the third he found her. He took a moment to get his breathing back under control before approaching. She was safe; no one had abducted her again.

"Problem?" She was crouched on the floor looking at her shoe.

She shot him a look, then back down to her foot.

"My boot lace is knotted. Please go on, I shall be with you shortly."

Cam dropped down beside her.

"The ends came free," she said, sounding irritated, "and I bent to retie it, but it has knotted."

"Allow me."

"Thank you, but I do not need your assistance." She batted his hands away. "It would not do for someone to see us this way."

"Yes, because we have bumped into several hundred people already since arriving. Let me see, there was Mr. and Mrs. Fluttersby, and I'm am still dubious about that name, and the sum total of no one else. It seems butterflies are not the rage in London this November."

"I don't care. Please return to your family, and let go of my laces."

"Don't be dramatic, Emily. This is the new me, attempting to help the new you. Remember, we are to be civil to each other from now on."

Her face was close to his now, so close he noticed a dusting of freckles on her cheeks. Her gray eyes had a sprinkle of white under the iris on the right one. They were really rather beautiful.

"I am quite good with laces and bonnet ribbons, just ask the twins."

"I have seen you, but I am sure I can work this free on my own."

Her eyes were doing their own study of him, and Cam felt wherever they landed.

"Please, Cam, let me go."

He hadn't realized his fingers had wrapped around her upper arms until she said that. Instead of doing as she asked, he leaned in and kissed her softly, so soft that it was barely a touch, just as it had been after he'd carried her from that water. His head was instantly full of her, his senses heightened, and he wanted more... a great deal more.

He was in serious trouble.

"Stop that!" Emily tried to regain her feet, but simply fell backward onto her bottom.

"You have a lovely mouth. I just never realized it before, because it's usually firing a volley of insults at me."

Cam elegantly got to his feet, unlike her, and held out his hand. Emily ignored it and scrabbled to hers with more haste than grace.

"Do you go about kissing every woman you believe has a 'lovely mouth'?"

"No, pleasurable though that would be, it would likely get me into serious trouble."

"Well, don't do it again to me."

He was frowning now, his eyes locked on her face with an intensity that was unsettling. Studying her as if he had not seen her before.

"I don't know what possessed you to kiss me." Emily brushed out her skirts as she spoke, giving herself the perfect opportunity to look away from Cam.

"Strangely, neither do I. You were there, and it happened."

"It shouldn't have."

"You kissed me last time."

"What?" Emily looked at him again. "I-I did not."

His hands were in his pockets, and he rocked back on his heels as if he had nothing greater to do than discuss kisses with her.

"You grabbed my hair when I saved you, and tugged my lips down to meet yours. I remember the moment clearly, as I do everything about that day."

Lord, she remembered it too. The feel of his cold mouth pressed to hers had touched her soul.

"Yes, well, neither of us were ourselves that day."

"We were ourselves today, however."

He rocked back on his heels again.

Emily battled the flood of emotion still humming inside her from just that small contact with Cam's mouth. She'd always believed that to kiss a man would be disgusting. Now she had to revise that opinion, although she was certain that with the wrong man it would not be a pleasurable experience... not that Cambridge Sinclair was the right man... *oh God*!

"Don't ever do it again... ever," Emily reiterated, in case the first "ever" was not clear. "I have no wish to be handled in such a way." She tried not to look at his mouth.

"You wanted me to kiss you."

"I did not, how can you say such a thing?" She took a large step backward. "Now let us forget that... ah"—she waved a hand about—"silliness, and attempt once again to observe the truce we discussed earlier."

He followed, mimicking her movements, making her uncomfortable.

"Stop that!" Emily looked around to check no one was near and had seen what they did.

"I am merely following you, Emily."

His face wore an innocent expression; unfortunately, she had seen it all too often and knew it for the exact opposite.

"Why are you doing this?"

"Something changed between us the day I rescued you, and I'm not entirely sure I can change it back."

His face lost its former expression and was now starkly open. He'd felt what she had that day, and in the days since, and was as confused as she by their reaction to each other.

"Well, try harder! Nothing has changed. We... we must simply put distance between us and try to be civil. Soon everything will be as it was."

Dear Lord, let that be the case.

CHAPTER 11

*O*ne month after her abduction, life appeared, thankfully, to be returning to normal for Emily. Well, as close to normal as she could make it while avoiding Cambridge Sinclair. So far she had been successful in seeing him only a handful of times, briefly. She'd pleaded three headaches, an upset stomach, and offered to stay home with Isabella to avoid him, and as yet no one in her family had noticed.

Her brothers had come to the conclusion that her attempted abduction had been a random thing, but were still uneasy. She was unable to leave the house unless she had the company of a maid and a footman. She was also not to walk anywhere, which was most vexing, as Emily liked to walk. But she did as they asked, and hoped that given time, these restrictions would ease.

She'd left home early this morning, after James, Eden, Samantha, and Isabella had gone to visit an old acquaintance of the duke's who lived a distance from London. The invitation had included Emily, but she had declined, as this was the perfect opportunity to run some errands. She had her maid and a footman, and one of the household's carriages, so that if her family returned they would not be worried, and had left word she was to visit Max. Not actually a lie, but she had a few stops to make on the way to his warehouse.

London was experiencing one of those ice-cold days, but the sky was clear blue. It was bracing to be outside in such weather, even if her cheeks were soon numb.

Her first stop was the large bookstore in Finsbury Square. Several stories high, it was a wonderland to explore, and she usually brought Samantha with her, as her little sister loved the place. Emily tried to visit at least twice a month, and usually on a Monday or Tuesday, as it was often not busy and she could browse at will.

"I shall not be long today, John. Please stay with the carriage and we shall return shortly."

Emily and Belinda entered the building. Inhaling, she breathed in the wonderful smell of books.

"I need to get Samantha the second story in the Miss Rose Petal novels, and I will then have a quick look to see if there is anything new in the astronomy section, Belinda. If you wish to browse, I shall find you shortly."

Leaving her maid, Emily located Samantha's selection, and then was soon lost in hers.

"Good day to you."

Emily offered a smile to the man browsing beside her. In his hand were several books. The titles on the spines he held were both ones she had read.

"They make excellent reading."

He smiled. "Thank you, I have read most of the books in here."

"As have I, but I come in the hopes there is something new."

The smiled widened. "That is the exact reason for my visit here also."

"Well then," Emily returned to looking at the books, "if that is the case I am sure I shall see you again."

"Excellent. Good day to you."

After the man had left, Emily found a book she had not read and made her purchases. Back in the carriage minutes later, they were heading to her next stop—that was, after she had purchased hot roasted chestnuts for herself, Belinda, John, and their driver.

Stepping from the carriage, she looked at the tall brick building that housed *The Trumpeter*, a small daily newspaper, and felt the usual jolt of excitement.

Leaving John with the carriage, Belinda and Emily walked through the entry and started up the stairs. She knew the way, as this was not her first visit; in fact, far from it. The man she sought was seated in his office when she arrived.

"Good morning, Mr. Ledbetter."

"Miss Tolly." He rose, motioning her into a seat.

Short with hair the color of a pumpkin, Mr. Ledbetter had a sharp face made up of harsh lines, and an equally sharp intellect. He wore his burgundy scarf wrapped to his ears, and small circular spectacles. Emily had made contact with him last year, and he'd been publishing her works once a fortnight since. It had not worried him that she was a woman, and in fact he had created an alias just so her work could be published in the Beginners Guide to Astronomy section of *The Trumpeter*.

"I received your note that you wished to meet with me, Mr. Ledbetter. Is everything well?"

Usually she had the articles delivered to him by a footman, but his note had said he needed to speak with her personally.

"It is, but there are changes afoot here, Miss Tolly. Your last piece was excellent, but unfortunately I am unable to print it."

"I see." Emily took the paper Mr. Ledbetter held out to her. "May I ask why?"

"It is not because I have no wish to, you must understand. It is merely that *The Trumpeter* has been sold, and until the new owner tells us how he wishes to continue, we cannot acquire anything. In fact, I'm not even sure he'll keep the astronomy for beginners section going, Miss Tolly."

"Oh but surely he must! I have heard many speak of it, and what they have learned."

"As have I." Mr. Ledbetter took off his glasses and cleaned them. "It would be a terrible shame to see it gone, but my hands are tied, I am afraid."

"If you could notify me when you have word of what is happening, I would be grateful." Emily rose, feeling dispirited. She'd enjoyed writing for *The Trumpeter*, and the money her articles received.

"Of course, and I have enjoyed your articles immensely, and will ensure to put in a good word for you, however, I would advise all contact be made in writing from now forward, as I'm unsure how receptive he will be to a woman submitting articles to his paper."

Emily bit back her instinctive need to defend herself and a woman's right to do as she wished, and instead tucked the paper back in her reticule.

"And your job, Mr. Ledbetter, is that secure?"

"Thankfully, yes it is, as are all the staff here at *The Trumpeter*."

"Good day to you then, Mr. Ledbetter."

"Good day, Miss Tolly."

She would have to find someone else to print her articles if the new owner did not. It would take time, but she was determined to continue. People enjoyed her articles, and she enjoyed writing them.

Taking the stairs back down, Emily listened to the

familiar sounds of the printing press. Often she would step inside the door and watch it operate. The men bustling about working did not seem to mind, as long as she kept her distance. Perhaps one last peek, if she was not to return.

"I shall return shortly, Belinda. Go to the tea shop and I'll join you when my business is done," Emily said to her maid. "And take John with you." Opening her reticule, she passed over some coins.

"Very well, Miss Tolly, and I shall order for you."

Opening the door, Emily was bombarded by noise, and her pulse quickened. It intrigued her how the press worked. The clatter, clatter, and chug chug of the machine, the noise and bustle, it never failed to stir her senses.

She saw two men, heads bent, watching the press work, but it was the taller man who made her stiffen. Surely it was not him... here of all place? Just as she decided to retreat, in case, Cam straightened, and his eyes found hers almost as if he'd sensed her.

"Emily!"

CHAPTER 12

*H*is bellow galvanized her into action. She quickly raised a hand, because she didn't know what else to do. Waggling her fingers, as if the fact she was here, at *The Trumpeter*, was a daily occurrence, she backed toward the door, hoping to get out of the building before Cam reached her. Because she had no doubts that he would follow, none at all. She got the door open, and even stepped a foot over the threshold.

"What the hell are you doing here?"

Large fingers wrapped around her elbow and urged her out the door, shutting it behind them. He kept walking, taking her with him, until they'd reached the small reception area, which was thankfully empty. She was then turned, and both shoulders gripped.

"Answer me!"

He was angry, which was nothing new. He was always angry with her it seemed, and if not, then he was teasing, or *kissing* her. The man was exhausting, Emily thought. Exhausting and handsome, her treacherous mind acknowledged.

His greatcoat hung open, revealing a deep green jacket, white shirt, and necktie. The black locks were, as usual, ruffled. Green eyes were narrowed and focused intently on her.

Anyone who looked at this man and saw only the teasing, demonstrative facade was mistaken. There was a great deal more to Cambridge Sinclair than he often exposed. Emily knew this as she had observed him for years. He was extremely sharp-witted, like his siblings.

"I don't have to answer that."

Nobody knew what she had been doing. Emily wasn't ashamed of her articles, but she hadn't been sure how her family would respond, and so kept them private.

"But you will."

"No, I won't."

"Fine, then we will stand here all day, with me holding your shoulders. I'm sure no one will notice."

She hadn't been in his company for a while, and refused to admit she'd missed it... him, and the sparks he set off inside her. Distance was the best way to deal with whatever this was between them, she needed to remember that.

"Why are you so consumed with knowing my business? Do you not have enough people's lives to meddle in that you must also do so in mine?"

"You"—he lifted a hand and pointed one finger at her rudely—"were abducted a few weeks ago by God knows who, and are not allowed to wander the streets alone, as you bloody well know."

"I'm not wandering the streets! My maid and footman are nearby, as is the carriage, and I left word that I was visiting Max."

"I don't see Max anywhere here." He made a show of looking around that had her wanting to slap him.

"Of course he is not here, I am on my way to him. Why are you here?"

"I just purchased this building and the business within it, so I have every right to be here, and ask why you are standing inside it. Plus," he added when she opened her mouth, "you are, for better or worse, family, and therefore it is my duty to ensure you do not, *again*," he added with heavy emphasis, "rush foolishly into danger."

"It is hardly my fault whoever was in that carriage abducted me!"

"The point is you were walking the streets alone." He made a great show of looking about him again. "I see no one with you."

Emily took a second to swallow down her anger. Losing her temper put her on the back foot with this man, because she lost all reason with it.

"I've just told you my maid and footman are waiting for me next door in the tea shop."

"I am relieved, however, they cannot protect you from there," he said in a cold, flat tone that told her he was not relieved at all. "Do your brothers know you are out and about?"

"Of course," she said quickly... too quickly, it seemed.

"Liar."

"I've just told you that I left word I was meeting up with Max."

"But he does not know you are coming here on the way?"

"Let me go, and I'll leave your property."

"No. I want to know why you are here."

"Have you really bought it, *The Trumpeter*?"

He nodded.

"How wonderful," she said, feeling a tug of jealousy. She would love to own the paper.

"I'm waiting."

Emily looked down at the reticule dangling from her wrist. Dare she tell him?

"Still waiting."

"Oh for heaven's sake. I don't have to tell you," she said, sounding like Samantha.

"No you don't, but I will be speaking with your brothers if you do not."

"What? Why?"

"Because I want to know why you are here, and if you will not tell me, then I'll ask them."

"They don't know."

His smile held no humor. "That I already knew."

"Oh botheration." Emily exhaled. She did not want to tell him, but it seemed she would have to. "Do you read this paper, or did you purchase it on a whim?"

"I rarely make business decisions based on whims, Emily, and as I purchased *The Trumpeter*, I can assure you I also spent a great deal of time reading it beforehand."

"A simple yes would have sufficed."

His lips twitched but he did not smile.

"Have you... do you like the section, Beginners Guide to Astronomy?"

His eyes narrowed. "I do, very much. In fact I think adding that section eleven months ago was inspirational."

A slow flush of heat spread through her body. Cam had read her articles, and what's more, he liked them.

"You'll keep it then?"

He nodded.

"I am E. Nivers."

"I beg your pardon?"

"I thought you told me you had excellent hearing."

"You are E. Nivers, writer of all those wonderful little articles that led hundreds of people into discovering the world of astronomy?"

She wanted to smile, but instead said, "I am. I came here to hand over my next piece, but was told the new owner may not wish to keep the section."

Gone was the anger and in its place was a wide smile, which had its usual devastating effect on Emily's insides.

"Emily Tolly is E. Nivers, who would have thought."

"Yes, well no one knows, so please keep it to yourself."

"Max and James would be proud of you, as would Eden. Why have you not told them?"

Emily looked away, feeling uncomfortable. She should have told them by now, especially considering her attempts to come out of her room and be part of the family now, but the time had never really been right.

"Still hiding, Emily?"

"I have to go, as I am meeting Max."

"Excellent. I was just on my way to his warehouse, you can come with me."

"I have the carriage."

"We shall send it on its way."

"No," Emily hurried to keep up with his long strides as he headed out the front door, "we will not."

He stopped suddenly, and she barreled into his back.

"Ouch," Emily grumbled, stepping back with the help of a large, steadying hand.

"We shall discuss your next article, and those thereafter."

"You really wish for me to keep writing for you?"

"Of course." He frowned at her. "Why wouldn't I?"

Why indeed. "Because I'm a woman."

He made a tsking sound in his throat. "I have four sisters and one sister-in-law, you and Samantha, plus there is Isabella, who is already proving her lungs are healthy, and my aunt. I dare not discriminate against a woman for fear of retribution."

Emily snuffled. "Not all believe as you do."

"Forward-thinking is what I am, Emily. Now come along, don't tarry." He grabbed her arm once more. "Go and collect your maid and footman, then we will send the carriage home."

She did as he asked because she wanted to, not because he'd told her, Emily reassured herself. Once she was back on the street with her maid and footman, she found Cam waiting for her.

"Please take the Raven carriage home. Miss Tolly no longer has need of it, or your services today," he instructed her driver and footman.

"And yet you did not ask me if these arrangements suited," she muttered, "simply ordered."

"Be quiet, Emily," Cam said as his carriage rolled to a stop before him. "Get inside, it's cold out here."

She could find no way to argue with him as he'd sent her carriage away, so she got inside, again because she wanted to, plus he was correct, it was cold out there.

"What is your name?" Emily heard him asking her maid.

"Belinda."

"A very pretty name it is too. In you get now."

Belinda's cheeks were flushed as she joined Emily.

"What?" Cam gave Emily an innocent look as she rolled her eyes at him, but she did not reply.

"Now, show me this article you have written," he said, settling himself across from her and taking up all the leftover room and air in the carriage.

"Please."

"Pretty please," he said, holding out one hand.

She did as he asked, and then sat back as he read it. This one was titled, What Do You See Up There In The Night Sky, and she thought it one of her better ones. She sat nervously watching his eyes move back and forth across the page until he'd finished.

"Clever girl."

"Thank you."

He tucked it into the inside pocket of his coat.

"I believe that belongs to me."

"Do you not want it printed?"

"You'll do that?"

His brows lowered. "I've just told you I would."

"No, what you said was 'clever girl,' it is not the same thing at all."

"I will make sure it is printed. Now, I want to set aside some time with you to discuss writing more of these, so we increase the astronomy for beginners to weekly."

"Really?" She could not help but smile. "I would love that above all things."

"Surely not all things. After all, there are those little cakes with the sugar sprinkles on the top."

"I concede they are good." For the first time in... well possibly forever, Emily and Cam had a discussion that did not involve argument, teasing, or just general annoyance, and she found she liked it very much indeed. It was riveting. There was still that little charge of tension in the air between them, but she could deal with that if they were discussing her continued writing for *The Trumpeter*.

"We will get more in-depth at a later date, but now I want to ask why you've been avoiding me."

And just like that she was tense and unsettled once more.

"I-I have not."

"Yes, you have."

"I've been busy."

"Doing what?"

"Things," Emily said, shooting Belinda a look. Some people discussed anything in front of their staff, but she was rarely comfortable doing so, as it had only been in the last few years she'd acquired a maid. She had no wish for Belinda to be privy to what went on between her and Cam... whatever that was.

"What things?" His expression was polite, but she knew better; he was like a bloody tiger waiting to pounce.

"Things. You can't expect me to remember all of them surely?"

He leaned closer, and Emily tried not to inhale, because then her senses would be filled with him.

"You're not telling me the truth, Emily."

"I don't want to discuss this now."

Cam sat back. The carriage rolled on for another twenty minutes while they sat in awkward silence, and then he rapped on the roof, and it stopped.

"Why are we stopping here?"

"It's only minutes to Max's warehouse and I thought you'd enjoy the walk."

"It's freezing!"

"It's bracing," he said, "and the exercise will do you good. After all, it would not pay for you to become a layabout. I like my employees to be clearheaded and spritely."

CHAPTER 13

"*I* am not your employee!"

Cam opened the door and stepped down. "Come along." He held out a hand to Emily, ignoring her shriek. The look she gave him suggested she wished to sink her teeth into it, however, she could do little but comply, as Belinda was watching avidly, and unlike most of his family, Emily was not one for making a scene, a fact he'd counted on. Taking his hand, she joined him outside.

"Take Miss Tolly's maid home, then come back to Mr. Huntington's warehouse please, Brian."

"Right you are, Mr. Sinclair."

"I don't want my maid to leave."

"You will be in the company of your brother."

She pressed her lips into a small, tight line, and struck out ahead of him.

"I believe the excuses for avoiding me were headaches and a sore stomach."

He'd realized what was going on when Emily did not appear at the third family gathering, but until today had had no opportunity to question her. The hell of it was, he'd missed her. Missed sparring with her, touching her, and dear Christ he'd missed the opportunities to kiss her. This should have disturbed him a great deal more than it did, especially as the prospect of any future with this woman made him feel like he was wearing a hair shirt.

"I had all those," she said as he drew level with her. "Now, shall we discuss your new acquisition?"

"Emily, you cannot go on avoiding me. Our families will notice soon enough."

She sighed. Her slender shoulders rose and fell.

"All right, and I'm sure the madness has now passed."

"What madness?" Cam took her hand and placed it on his arm. He liked to feel Emily close to him, but he wouldn't tell her that, just as he wouldn't tell her he'd dreamed about her several nights in a row. Heated dreams that had him waking painfully aroused.

"You know perfectly well what I mean."

He'd felt her presence in that printing room with an awareness that was usually only reserved for his siblings. Another strange occurrence had happened when he looked at her; he'd been unable to smell anything briefly.

Odd.

"Ahhh, the kissing."

She sniffed.

She once again wore the rose coat, with matching bonnet, and it suited her soft, pale skin and gray eyes. She was like an itch he could not quite reach at the moment. Constantly there, slightly annoying, but worthy of attention.

"It will never happen again, therefore there is no reason to discuss the matter further. We shall move on and return to what we once were."

"Angry with each other?"

"Yes."

"Perfect."

Cam saw Max's warehouses up ahead; he sniffed the air and smelled the herbs and medical supplies he knew lay in one of them.

"Why did you purchase *The Trumpeter*, Cambridge?"

"Printing has always interested me, so when my uncle told me about it, I went and took a look."

"It's an intriguing world, isn't it? I think *The Trumpeter* could be turned into a thriving paper, equal to others with some work and planning."

Her words surprised Cam, because Emily rarely ventured an opinion. He made an agreeing noise to see what came out of her mouth next.

"I think a children's section would be wonderful. Something for them to read weekly. They would then ask their parents for the next edition. Perhaps an ongoing story?"

"That's actually a good idea."

She stopped suddenly and turned on him, eyes sparking with irritation.

"I can have good ideas!"

He loved seeing her face like this, so animated.

"Did I say otherwise?"

"No." She exhaled softly. "Forgive me." She started walking again.

"I think the earth just moved beneath my feet, because Miss Tolly asked my forgiveness."

"It won't be a habit."

He wished her family saw this side to her nature, but often she kept it hidden. Emily had a sly sense of humor that peeked out when provoked.

"Would you like to help me with the paper, Em?"

"Pardon?" She stopped again.

"Would you like to help me with the paper?" he said again, patiently. Unlike other noblemen, he and his family owned businesses, ships, and other investments. Max, of course, had his fingers in multiple pies, which had made him one of the wealthiest men in the United Kingdom. However, he was not a nobleman, thus it did not sully his name—not that Cam cared overly, but still he did not talk about his business interests among those who did not share his views.

"You would really let me?"

He'd never seen her so excited. Her face was alive, and the gray of her eyes darker.

"Of course."

"Truly?"

"If I say of course again will you believe me?" he teased. "But you have to tell your brothers everything."

That deflated her.

"What is this guilt that you spoke of regarding James?" Frustrated, Cam felt his good humor of seconds ago abating. Only this woman could do that to him, make him feel several emotions in the space of a few minutes.

"As I have told you before, I have no problem with him."

"That's another lie. You're becoming quite adept at those."

They now stood toe to toe, glaring at each other.

"You told me about your guilt, just not what it was. James is simply a man like Max, but one who had the misfortune of being born with a title hanging over his head. Why do you struggle with that?"

She dropped her eyes first, then muttered something before walking away. Cam was sure he heard the word "brother," and "disgrace," but couldn't be certain.

"Does your guilt stem from your brother, and what he did to Eden and James?" Cam had given this a great deal of thought.

"I won't discuss this further with you."

Her expression could only be termed mulish.

"James does not blame you for that."

"He is a duke!" She turned on him. "I am the baseborn

daughter of one. I was raised in squalor, and with no airs and graces. How do you expect me to feel?"

Now they were getting somewhere, Cam thought. All he needed to do was push a little harder.

"I expect you to understand that your brother loves you, and wanted you to live with him and Eden. I want you to understand that to him, you are important, and that your past has no bearing on that."

Her color was high, breathing rapid, and she was past tempering her reactions. Cam had struck a vein, and she was about to vent.

"I am inferior to him in every way, and if that were not bad enough, my brother's acts nearly killed Eden and James. How can he forgive me for that? H-how can he not look at me and see?"

"Emily—" He tried to grab her arms but she stumbled backward.

"Damn you, why will you not let this alone! I know he tolerates me because he knows his duty, but nothing more. For the love of God, please stop this incessant probing, Cam, and leave me in peace!"

"No, that is not the truth." He started after her.

"No more, Cam. Leave it alone!"

He walked behind her, letting her calm as they approached. Max appeared, striding toward them.

"I could hear you two from inside. What are you arguing about now?"

"Nothing," they both said. Cam did not want to discuss this here... now. He would bring the matter up again, but not until he felt the time was right. He knew she was wrong and that James loved her, he just needed to work out how to get Emily to see that.

"Excellent. Then do you care to tell me why you are walking down the street on this icy day and not riding inside a carriage? Better yet, why are you keeping each other company?"

Emily shot him a look, but Cam kept his mouth closed. He wanted to see how she handled this. It was not his place to tell Max what his sister got up to when he and James were not looking.

"I, ah, well I was coming here, and on the way I stopped somewhere, and Cam was there, so we came together."

Max's brows lowered. "Where did you stop?"

Emily looked at Cam, pleading now for him to come to her aid. He remained silent. It was time for her to stop hiding. God's blood, he had no idea how she kept all the secrets she did inside her head; it must play hell with her peace of mind.

"I went to *The Trumpeter.*"

"Why?"

She sent him another pleading look, and Cam relented. "You know I recently acquired the paper, Max, don't you?" Idiot that he was, he didn't like to see her upset, which was odd as he was always upsetting her.

"I do, and although I find the name ridiculous I think it will be an excellent acquisition."

"Well, Emily is writing some articles for me on astronomy."

"Is she, by God? How wonderful." Max smiled.

Cam saw the guilt in Emily's face that she was deceiving him.

"I have been writing for them for some time," she rushed to add. "Mr. Ledbetter, he's the man I deal with, set up the astronomy for beginners section for me, and I write the articles for it."

The silence was loud as Max absorbed these words. Hatless, he stood like a large, solid piece of wood, unmoving, just watching his sister.

"I'm sorry," Emily whispered, making a fist clench around Cam's heart. The woman was wringing far too much emotion out of him. It really must stop.

"Did you think James and I would be ashamed to hear this news, Emily?"

She nodded, and Max shook his head.

"My past is blacker than most. I've sworn, shot people, and done things that even Essie is not aware of, and you think that you writing an article for a paper would shame me?" Max snorted. "I'll add to that, James is no saint either."

Max urged Emily in for a hug, and she went willingly. She could do that with this brother, it was the other one she held at arm's length.

"My sister the writer," Max said, testing the words. "I hear your new employer is something of a clodpoll, Em. It will take some getting used to."

Cam muttered something rude, and followed them into the warehouse where a man was waiting for Max to return.

"Mr. Jackson, allow me to introduce you to Mr. Cambridge Sinclair and my sister Miss Tolly."

Tall, with wispy brown hair, the man had a pleasant smile on his face.

"Good day to you again, Miss Tolly." His eyes passed over Cam and settled on Emily.

"Again?" Cam said.

"We share a love of astronomy, sir, and met at the book-store. Miss Tolly and I discussed a book selection."

Cam had the sudden urge to gnash his teeth at the man and did not know why.

"You did not tell me you had a beautiful sister, Mr. Huntington." Mr. Jackson took her hand and kissed the back of it. "It is a pleasure to be introduced formally, my dear Miss Tolly."

Emily removed her hand as soon as it was polite to do so,

and the man left after several more compliments that clearly left her uncomfortable.

"I don't like him," Cam said.

"Jackson's an odd sort, but harmless," Max replied. "He has been at me for months to let him invest in my latest consortium, but I trust my instincts, and something tells me he is not good with money."

"Excellent instincts," Cam said. "I didn't like him."

CHAPTER 14

"*How* ow is Wolf settling in?"

Emily walked at Max's side as he questioned Cam, and tried to rein in her rioting emotions.

"Very well. He is quiet, unlike my siblings, makes little mess, again unlike my siblings, and is rarely there. When he is, I find him a great deal like Dev, only without the need to lecture constantly. He is the ideal person to share a house with."

"I'm sure with exposure to you, and time, he shall come about," Max drawled.

"Very likely."

Only Cam could make her speech unguarded. He had provoked her into sharing part of her past she'd shared with no one, and that was disturbing. Why could he not just leave her alone? Why the constant poking at her, as if she were an onion that needed peeling, one painful layer at a time.

Hearing a loud sniff, she glanced up at him. His head was thrown back and he was sniffing the air.

"You look like a hound," she muttered.

"This place has more smells than an evening out in the company of two hundred of society's finest members."

"What do you smell first?" Intrigue overrode her anger at him.

He shot her a look, then away again. They had never discussed this, the strange abilities his family had, but she knew, and they knew she knew.

"The thyme...." He then went on to list every other herb in the warehouse, and there were considerable.

"Very impressive." Emily walked to the first long table and stripped off a glove. Picking up some dried lavender, she crushed it, sending the pungent scent into the air. She loved this warehouse for the blend of smells.

"I shall pass out if you continue to do that."

"Really?"

Cam smiled. "It would take more than that, but very strong scents can make me nauseous and unstable."

"The children are waiting, Em," Max said, touching her shoulder. "Essie, Dorrie, Somer, and Warwick are there also. But before you go to them, I wanted to remind you once more about the fund-raising event coming up. Do you still wish to attend?"

"Of course," she said when inside she wanted to decline. It was for his charity, so she could hardly refuse. It was not a society event, so she could attend, even considering her birth.

"What are the children waiting for?" she heard Cam ask, but did not wait to hear her brother's reply. Climbing the stairs, she heard loud chatter as she reached the room she wanted. Entering, her eyes ran over the children assembled.

"We have come to help today!" Somer Sinclair said in her usual excited little voice. Beside her sat Dorrie and Warwick, and lastly Essie.

"Excellent. I'm sure the boys will enjoy that."

There were ten of them, all boys Max had rescued off ships, and not one of them looked happy about the prospect of girls teaching them anything. Warwick, however was accepted, and seated beside Silver, who was blind.

Max had procured books, so pages were opened, and the lesson progressed with few issues until it got to the point where someone was to read out loud.

"I wish to," Dorrie said.

"But you know how to read. The boys do not, so one of them can do it."

"But if I read first, that will show them how, then they can do so after," the little girl said with a logic Emily could not fault.

"These boys have devilishly good memories, Dorrie, and would remember your words, and we do not want them cheating, now do we?"

"Warwick cheats," Somer said, she then smiled at Ben, one of the boys. The smile a hundred women gave a hundred men every evening within the hallowed walls of society.

"I do not cheat!"

"You cheated at cards just last night," Dorrie said, backing up her sister as she always did, no matter if she was right or wrong.

"I'm telling Dev you lied!"

The boys watched eagerly as the Sinclair siblings erupted into an argument. As Essie had just slipped out of the room, it was left to Emily to attempt to rein them in, but it was no easy task.

"Hello, my heathens, what appears to be the problem?" Cam appeared in the doorway.

"Somer said I cheated." Warwick glared at his sisters.

"That was harsh, my sweet, and thoroughly uncalled for

given your penchant for the same thing. Apologize at once, or there will be no treat for you."

"Sorry."

"With more feeling, if you please."

"I'm very sorry for calling you a cheat, Warwick. Please forgive me?"

Emily wanted to laugh at the meekly spoken words, but swallowed it down. The elder Sinclairs were masters at controlling their siblings, and it was a wonderful thing to observe.

"Warwick," Cam then said in a tone that asked something of the boy.

"I accept your apology," he said begrudgingly.

"Harmony is restored. Now please continue, as I am in need of a refresher in how to spell. Just yesterday I spelled peg incorrectly. Who in this room, who does not have the last name Sinclair, can help with the correct way to spell it?"

Emily watched as Silver raised his hand.

"Go ahead, Silver," Cam said.

"P-E-G," the boy said.

"Excellent, how about 'and'?"

Emily sat quietly while Cam took over the lesson. She did not mind. He was very good at this, and soon had the boys involved, their usual reticence gone in their excitement to participate.

Max had asked her to help him educate the boys he saved from the ships. Most had been mistreated, and he was giving them a chance to make something of their lives by educating, housing, and looking after them until they could do so for themselves.

One of the boys, Peter, had been gravely ill, unable to breathe with ease when Essie got hold of him, but now he had color in his cheeks and smiled often. He still wore a thick scarf that he breathed into when the weather was cold or thick with fog.

"I'm sorry for taking over your lesson." Cam came to where she sat as Warwick took over throwing out words.

"No, that is quite all right. They love this, especially the interaction with you and your siblings. What is that look for?" she questioned him as he looked at his little sisters and brother.

"They are growing up; it is hard to take. They no longer wish to sit on my lap or let me cuddle them."

"They will always want that, I'm sure. You are very important to them, and have such a bond with your family I doubt it could ever be severed."

He looked at her, his eyes filled with sympathy.

"You sound wistful. Did you not have such a bond with anyone before you came to live with James?"

"I don't wish to discuss that, and should not have done so earlier."

"I provoked you."

"What a surprise."

"What was your brother like? I'm asking as a friend, and for no other reason."

"I believe you met him," Emily said in a stilted voice that she loathed, but could do nothing to stop. Speaking of Edward was not easy.

"I did, and he could be charming, so surely he was not always unstable?"

Emily shrugged as she felt a fist close around her chest.

"A shrug is not a response, Emily. So let's try that again. What was your brother like to grow up with?"

"We moved about a lot, there was little time for fun, or... or that."

"That being?" How could a pair of green eyes change expression so rapidly?

"'Tis of no matter." Emily managed to exhale.

"I beg to differ. It matters to me if it matters to you, which by the rather pained expression on your sweet face it obviously does."

Emily refused to blush at his use of the word sweet. He was just speaking, complimenting again as he always did. He was a master at that, making people feel good about themselves. She'd often wondered why.

"Why do you do that?"

"What?" One dark brow rose.

"Compliment, deflect, always the happy, funny man who makes everyone laugh."

She'd surprised him. His eyes widened.

"I cannot help how I am natured, Emily. My family is large, and we all have our place within it."

"I understand that, but you seem—"

"We were discussing you, not me."

"But I have no wish to discuss me."

"One question," he said, looking around them.

"Pardon."

"You get one question again, as do I. Are you game to ask it?"

The look in his eyes challenged her.

"Oh, they have left," Emily said, surprised that she had not noticed the children filing out.

"Max came in to herd them down for a meal."

Emily didn't move. "Who goes first?

"You, and I will know if you lie."

"How?"

"Your face goes perfectly blank."

"It's always blank."

"Not completely."

How did he know that about her too?

"All right, let's begin before we start arguing," he said. "I will go first."

Emily braced herself; he would not make this easy on her, as he hadn't last time. But then, she would be sure to do the same.

"Have you ever loved someone who is not family? I mean the heartrending, I cannot live without you kind of love that can be shared between a man and woman?"

He was asking the same question she had. His eyes held hers steady, all mockery gone.

"Ah... well."

"The truth, Emily."

"Yes," she whispered. "I once believed I was in love, but I was a young girl, and soon realized it for what it was."

"Which was what, exactly?" His words were gentle.

"You said one question, and now I must see to the children."

"Do you not wish to ask me a question?"

The lure was too much to resist. "What is your deepest fear?"

Unlike her, he answered without hesitation.

"To wake and find myself alone. To rise and have no one who loves me, or cares if I do not come home for my meal. To realize that I walk this land alone, and am bound to no one. That, Emily, is my deepest fear."

She sniffed, then pressed a hand to her nose. "That would indeed be a terrible fate."

"Although," he raised a hand, "I must own to wishing for solitude often when my family is around."

He'd said it to make her laugh, but she knew him by now. Knew he was doing what he always did, and trying to make light of the situation.

"No, Cam. Don't lessen what you said. It was honest and

true, and came from your heart. Thank you for sharing it with me."

His smile was gentle, and so sweet Emily's toes curled inside her boots.

"I wish I'd thought of asking that one first, but perhaps next time."

"Will there be a next time, then?"

"Oh yes, there most definitely will."

CHAPTER 15

The carriage carried the women into Bond Street. Eden, Essie, Lilly, and Emily. All going to have their final fitting for new dresses they would wear to the Winslow charity ball.

"The evening will be fun," Eden said. "I always find these kinds of things more enjoyable than a traditional society event."

"Yes, and the women are not quite so uppity, and willing to discuss things more candidly," Essie added. "Of course there will be some peers there, the more forward-thinking kind."

They were so beautiful, these sisters-in-law of hers, and Lilly. Confident, capable, and more importantly, born on the right side of the blanket.

"Madam Blanchard will have just the perfect style and color for you, Em. Don't worry, you are in the best hands. She has your measurements, so we are to see the finished product."

"I'm looking forward to it," Emily lied.

They chatted and laughed until the carriage pulled up in

Bond Street. Then they were stepping down and heading for the boutique.

"Don't tarry, Em."

"Your brother says that to me," she said to Eden as she stepped from the carriage.

"Which one."

"Cam."

"Ah well, his aim in life is to annoy people, so I can imagine he says it often."

"Why do you think he does that?"

"What?" All the women turned to look at her.

"Jokes and makes light of all situations?" Emily wished she'd kept her mouth shut, as Eden and Essie frowned. It was not her place to speak this way.

"I have no idea. He has always been that way," Eden said. "Annoying."

"But loyal and the best of brothers," Essie added. "I have never actually thought about his behavior before."

"I should not have said anything—"

"You have as much right to speak as you wish as any of us, Emily. Perhaps it's about time you realized that."

Lilly said the words, her eyes steady on Emily's.

"Yes she does, but only she can come to that realization, and as we are on limited time today, perhaps she can think about it once Madam Blanchard is treating her like a pincushion."

Eden had not been exaggerating. In fact, she was pinned, draped, and tweaked for some time, until finally they were done. She stood through it thinking about what Lilly had said. They believed her an equal, and yet she did not, and doubted she ever would. But perhaps she could be less of a mouse when she was in their company.

"How do you cope?" Emily felt exhausted as the fitting finally drew to an end. Yes, she'd been fitted before, but it had not been as laborious as that. She was relieved when they were once again back on the street.

"You get used to it, and there has to be a price to pay for looking beautiful. It is my life's work to make Dev's jaw drop and his eyes narrow. I love it when he roars at me to get upstairs and put the rest of my dress on." Lilly laughed.

The others agreed, and Emily thought it must be nice to love someone as much as these women loved their husbands.

"Miss Tolly."

Turning, she found Mr. Jackson behind her.

"Good day to you, Mr. Jackson."

"My dear Miss Tolly, may I say how beautiful you look today."

"Ah... thank you." Emily fought the blush as she introduced him to the other women.

He only glanced briefly at them before looking at her once more. It was disconcerting to have a man stare at her in such a way.

"Will I have the pleasure of seeing you at the Winslow event?"

"Yes, we are to attend."

"Wonderful. I hope you will save a dance for me?"

"Of course," Emily said, flustered.

He bowed once more and left.

"That man seems to be popping up all over the place." Essie was frowning. "I believe you saw him at the bookstore and Max's warehouse?"

"He likes you, Emily. Very much is my guess," Eden added. She too did not look happy about that fact.

"Oh, I don't think so."

"Emily, dear, he does, but because you are not used to male adoration you can't see it for what it is. Now just accept it, and let us get into the carriage. The children are waiting for us," Lilly added.

Emily believed Mr. Jackson a nice enough man, but she had not thought of him in any other light but as her brother's business acquaintance.

"Come along now, we are late and the show is due to start shortly. Cam will have eaten all the candy, and the children will be arguing if we do not make haste."

Cam watched the carriage roll up with his sisters, Lilly, and Emily inside.

"Finally," Dorrie said loudly. She was swinging Cam's hand in boredom while they awaited the womenfolk's arrival. "We have been here an age."

"Surely you exaggerate. It has only been ten minutes."

"An absolute age," Somer said from where she leaned on Dev's long legs. "I'm quite exhausted."

"Yes, because your life is extremely taxing," Cam drawled. "Rising whenever you wish, someone helping you bath and dress, and then supplying you with an endless buffet of food."

"It's a hard life," Max agreed. He had Warwick attached. The boy stood at the man's side quietly, watching as he always did. But close enough that he could lean in every few minutes and feel Max's presence, who in turn had his hand resting on the boy's shoulder. The man had come a long way since marrying Essie. Before he would have done anything to avoid contact with people.

Warwick was raised with two loud, rambunctious sisters who tended to talk and do everything for him, which for the most he handled. It was rare that he rebelled, usually with a curt word that brought the twins into line. He was more and more like Dev every day.

"At least it has not started without us," Samantha said. She held James's hand.

The adults always took charge of a child each when in

company, as they had a habit of running away or causing mischief if left to roam free.

"Hello!"

Cam smiled as Eden waved from the carriage doorway. Lilly followed Essie and Eden. They were three extremely beautiful women, and the beauty was bone deep. Happiness also contributed to that, a happiness they had not always felt.

"Hello, you're late," Cam said, because it was expected of him by the little sister currently hanging off his hand. "Dorrie wanted me to censure you."

"We were waylaid I'm afraid, by one of Emily's admirers."

Emily appeared in the doorway after these words, and Cam battled the fist that wrapped around his chest, cutting off the supply of air to his lungs. *This has to stop.*

It annoyed him that she would have put herself deliberately last getting out of the carriage. Annoyed him that she believed herself beneath the other woman.

"Admirer?" he heard Max say.

Emily immediately moved to the back of the group. He wanted to shake her.

"Yes, Mr. Jackson. He was quite taken with our Emily."

"What?" Cam dragged his eyes away after cataloging everything she wore, from the chipped bonnet down to her small black leather boots. "Who has an admirer?" he said, suddenly recalling his sister's words.

"Emily." Eden came forward to kiss her husband and slip her arm through his. "He is quite taken with her, and wants her to save him a dance at the Winslow event."

The only word for what he was feeling was rage. It was swift and fierce, and only because he'd had lots of practice in his lifetime hiding his emotions from his family was he able to do so now.

"Pardon?"

"Mr. Jackson was on the street when we left the dress shop, and he stopped to talk with Emily."

"Did not so much as glance at us," Lilly added. "Only had eyes for Em."

Emily blushed. "He was just being friendly."

"Oh no, dear, it was more than friendship I saw in his eyes."

"I don't think I like the idea of a man looking at my sister in such a way," James said, winking at Emily.

She in turn reacted predictably and went into herself, as she always did when he addressed her. It was damned annoying, Cam thought—now that he could think, that was.

"Jackson is a fair enough man, but I don't believe he is a man I want showing interest in my sister."

"Who is standing right here," Emily said, surprising Cam with her forthright words.

"I will marry Emily one day, so now that is settled could we go inside."

Warwick's words made everyone laugh, and Emily hurried over to hug the boy. He allowed it because she was one of his people, and he also understood that she was vulnerable in many ways. Warwick had always been aware of such things.

"I have tickets. Children must remain attached to an adult—"

"Must we have this lecture every time, Dev?"

"Yes, Somer, because if you will remember, last time we went to something like this you pulled that lever and stopped the entire platform from rotating, thus causing that woman to topple onto me. A rather large woman."

The little girl offered her big brother a contrite smile.

"Please continue, Dev."

When the lecture was finished they began to file inside Mr. Roland's Circus of Strange and Ridiculous Curiosities.

This was an annual event for the family, because the first time they had attended the twins had been abducted right there in the street. What followed had been terrifying for all concerned. To eradicate that image, they had come back every year since.

It was softly lit inside, the stage illuminated from beneath. It had not changed, even slightly, since they had first attended several years ago.

"Oh, you're back?"

Mr. Roland, the proprietor of the show, saw them coming and his smiled dimmed. He still wore a battered top hat and bright red jacket. His mustache was waxed to curl up on the ends and covered the upper half of his mouth.

He had yet to forgive them for the lever-pulling incident, or the incessant questioning from the children. James had thrown some money at him, and only this had stopped them from being barred. There was also the small matter of a fire that they had had nothing to do with, but he blamed them for. This had also cost them money for repairs.

"No bowing and currying favor today then, Duke," Dev drawled as they moved to take their places. "You've lost your power."

"I'll always be several rungs higher on the ladder than you, Sinclair."

The teasing continued as they took up their positions. Children in the front, adults at the rear, close at hand if need be, and then the lights were lowered.

"Excuse me, Cam, I am unable to see clearly," Essie said. "And you are standing between me and my husband."

"You saw him two minutes ago!"

"I may get scared and require him."

An elbow was applied to Cam's ribs. Winded, he did as he was asked, and found himself beside Emily.

Bloody, bothering hell.

CHAPTER 16

*E*mily kept her eyes on the stage as the music started. Today's show was to be a production on the mythical centaur, half man, half horse. She had been lectured about the creature by Samantha this morning.

"So, Mr. Jackson thinks you're beautiful?"

The whispered words came from Cam as the first centaur rose onto the stage.

"Sssh."

"And do you think he's handsome?"

"I'm not sure I would ever think a half man half horse handsome, but there is a certain something about his look. Samantha told me that there are many myths surrounding centaurs. That they, the offspring of King Ixion, mated with the cloud nymph, Nephele, whom a jealous Zeus created in the likeness of Hera."

Cam snorted softly. "You have been spending too much time with people under the age of twelve. It's my belief that this particular centaur is named Joseph from Peckham, and he has a wife and four children."

"Surely not?"

"You did not answer the question, Emily. Do you find Mr. Jackson handsome?"

"That is none of your business."

His breath brushed her cheek, and she fought the responding shiver.

"I am curious, nothing more. The man did not strike me as someone worthy of your interest."

"How can you know that when you barely conversed with him?"

"Emily." Dorrie turned to shush her. "Please temper your excitement, we shall miss something otherwise."

"Forgive me, Dorrie." She sent a glare at Cam through the dark, to find his face very close to hers.

"I know men, and I have met him a few times at Max's warehouse. He seems untrustworthy."

"You cannot know that either," she whispered furiously.

"You are not used to male adoration, therefore I feel I must caution you—"

"That is not your place to do so." Emily cut him off.

"I disagree. I know men, and you don't."

"Shut up," Emily hissed. "I have no wish to discuss this further."

"You say that a lot to me."

Pressing her lips together, Emily vowed not to speak with him again.

"One question?"

She stilled at his words.

"Yes."

"Your turn."

"Why do you hide behind humor? Why are you rarely serious?" Emily looked at Cam, wondering if he would answer something so personal.

He was silent, his eyes on the stage where a kaleidoscope

of images was rotating, and yet she doubted he saw anything as he thought about her words.

"Because they deserved more from me when they needed me most, and I did not deliver, so I am redeeming myself now."

"I don't understand, what could you possibly have done?"

"That's two questions."

Frustrated, she stood in silence contemplating what she had learned. There had been a time in Cam's life when he had not been a good person, and his family had suffered because of his actions? The thought shocked her.

"What is your deepest fear?"

The words made her shiver. He'd asked the very question she had.

"I-I do not know how to answer that," she said truthfully.

"Only you know what is inside your mind, Emily. Think, and you will find the answer."

She stood there in the darkness as her mind whirled. No one had asked her such a thing before, and she rarely considered the matter herself.

"That all this will one day be gone and I will return to the life I once lived."

She felt his hand in the middle of her back, and the warm presence chased away the cold that Emily had felt saying those words. The dark memories of a past she'd been forced to live.

"You know deep inside that will never happen, Em. Allow yourself to live today, as you will every day. Allow yourself to embrace it, and the darkness will fade. Let them, your family, see the real you."

Could she?

"I know my family deserve more of me, Cam, your words have shown me that." Emily decided on honesty.

"James certainly does."

Emily searched for her brother. He stood with Eden leaning on him, and Samantha before him. One large hand was on her shoulder. She knew he was a good man; could she forgive herself for something she played no part in, and treat him as she did Max?

"Will you at least try?"

She managed a nod around the lump in her throat, but said nothing more. They stood there, she and Cam, his hand on her back, and watched the performance, and she'd never felt more aware of a person in her life before than she did the large disturbing man to her right.

She was aware of the breath he drew, the small movement of his body, and it had to stop. He was Cam, her nemesis, the man she'd often wished to maim. Emily believed it now, believed that since he'd saved her that day everything had changed between them. She'd fought it, but could no longer deny the truth. Something stirred inside her when Cambridge Sinclair was near, and it must stop. There was no future in feeling this way.

"What?"

"What?"

"You made a noise," Cam said.

"Clearing my throat."

"Only you would clear your throat with a soft moan."

"I beg your pardon, but I did not just moan... in public!"

"Emily." Dorrie faced her again. "You are my friend, and my older siblings tell me I am not allowed to be rude to friends."

"Forgive me, Dorrie, for raising my voice. I promise to refrain from further discussion."

The little girl studied her, then her eyes went to Cam, whom Emily could feel shaking with laughter.

"I'm sure some of the blame could be laid at Cam's door,

as he could provoke a nun who has taken a vow of silence, to speak."

The only suitable response to that, to Emily's mind, was a solemn nod, which seemed to appease the girl as she turned away once more.

"I pity the poor men who end up with my twin sisters."

She heard the pride in Cam's voice, and found a smile, but this time refrained from saying anything. He did not remove his hand until the show ended, and fool that she was, Emily missed it.

"And now we have a surprise for you all." James said the words as they reached the carriages, and suddenly all eyes were on him.

"I want mint!"

"We are not going for an ice, Warwick," Dev said, and the boy's face fell.

"It's not educational, is it?"

"I thought you enjoyed learning."

"Mostly, but I enjoy fun too."

"I'm growing old here, and it's cold, so stop tormenting us and speak, brother," Cam said.

"We are going to the park to watch the balloon ascent," James said.

"No!" Warwick cupped his face as color filled it. "Are we really?"

James nodded. Warwick, Emily remembered, had a fascination for ballooning and had been plaguing his family to take him to watch an ascent for some time.

"The conditions are perfect, as the day is cool and clear, with very little wind."

"I want to fly in a balloon."

"No, absolutely not," Dev, Cam, Eden, and Essie all said as one in response to Warwick's words.

"Why not? People do all the time, and I'm a person."

"You are a young boy, and what's more, our younger brother. We have no wish to watch you floating many feet above the earth, with the prospect that at any time you could plunge down into it at speed," Dev said.

"I still want to," Warwick grumbled. "Did you know that the first person to fly in a balloon was Vincenzo Lunardi in 1784?"

Dev look pained as he urged his little siblings toward the carriage, and Emily knew that those traveling with Warwick would be deluged with facts about ballooning.

The journey was not a long one and undertaken with Samantha giving them an overview of what they had all just seen, which Emily did not mind, as it gave her time to think.

Perhaps she should leave London for Raven Castle, and stay there until she no longer felt anything but annoyance for Cambridge Sinclair once more? Just a brief break would surely do it?

No it won't.

Bloody bothering hell!

CHAPTER 17

The park was full of people and carriages. The day was brisk, but lovely, and everyone wore warm clothing to ward off the chill.

Cam had Somer by the hand and was inspecting the balloon with the rest of their party. His eyes constantly strayed to Emily, who had Samantha attached. The little girl was asking her questions, to which she responded patiently.

Sweet, he thought. Sweet and far too disturbing.

"Good day to you, Miss Tolly. How fortuitous it is to have chanced upon you once more this day!"

Cam was fast coming to the conclusion that Jackson had designs on Emily. He had appeared first at the bookstore, then the warehouse. Today there was the dressmaker's, and now again here. Once was a coincidence, twice perhaps, but his appearance here was not, which suggested he was following them. Locating Max, he left Somer with Dev and went to speak with him.

"That man needs to be warned off."

Max looked at Emily and Jackson.

"Why?"

"He is not right for Emily, you said so yourself. God's blood, you only need to look at him to see he is not worthy of her. There is also the matter of his effusive behavior. It's nauseating."

"Jackson is harmless, Cam. Yes, I've had a time or two to question his business dealings, but for the most he is respected and tolerated. I must own that he would not be my choice for her, but Emily has her own mind, and should she be receptive to any approach from him—"

"What?" Cam actually shook his head. "You cannot be serious, that man is not good enough for her!"

Max studied Cam with a look that was not entirely comfortable.

"That is for her to establish, not you, and as it is likely she will not have many eligible men falling about themselves to marry her. If she chooses Jackson, there will be little I can do to stop the union."

"She deserves more from you and James. That man is not the right one for her."

Cam refused to be intimidated by the look Max gave him, or curl his toes inside his boots. He had said too much and alerted Max to the fact Emily unsettled him. So he retreated... for now. But Jackson would not be approaching Emily in any capacity if he had a say in the matter. Which granted he would likely not, but still, he could put a word or two in James's ear.

"I am in awe of your beauty and knowledge, Miss Tolly."

Snapping his teeth together as he heard Jackson's effusive words, Cam moved to stand beside Emily. Too close, but it forced Jackson back a step.

"Good day, Mr. Sinclair."

"Mr. Jackson."

"I was just telling dear Miss Tolly that she is to be commended on her knowledge of ballooning."

"You sound surprised that she is knowledgeable on such a matter, Mr. Jackson."

The man's condescending smile was enough to have Cam itching to wipe it off with his fist.

"Well now, we know that a woman need only certain skills to make a man happy, don't we, Mr. Sinclair? A woman's beauty and refinement are all that counts to the man she will one day marry. Her sole purpose can surely be in attaining those qualities, for what use is there for anything else?"

Emily made a choking sound, but a look at her face showed nothing. She was composed, as she always was, but those eyes told a different story. They were the icy gray of the skies on a stormy day.

Excellent. Jackson had put his foot firmly in his mouth; Cam just needed to make sure he choked on it now.

"So you believe a woman's place is to devote her attentions entirely on the man she marries. She can have nothing else to occupy her but that single purpose?" He leaned in slightly, feigning interest. Jackson took the bait, delighted to be able to impart his knowledge to Cam, and of course Emily. *The fool.*

"Oh indeed, for what other purpose can they have?"

"I think that a very narrow viewpoint, Mr. Jackson."

Of course it was Eden who arrived first to defend her kind. She'd heard every word, and her eyes were blazing. Jackson looked stunned at her words. Cam simply folded his arms and prepared to enjoy the next few minutes.

"Your Grace." He bowed deeply, his nose nearly touching his knee. "Forgive me, I had not meant to offend you."

Jackson looked panicky now, his eyes going from Emily to Eden, then lastly Cam for support. Cam gave him a pained look to suggest he supported the man, hoping his foot would become wedged so tight inside his mouth, he'd choke. He knew enough about the women in his life to understand that Mr. Jackson would soon leave with his ears blistered.

"Do you believe a woman can offer nothing but excellent household management skills, and that her main focus is to ensure her husband's every comfort is met?"

"Is that how it's meant to be?" James asked Dev. Both had approached to enjoy the moment.

"Well, it's news to me if it is. Perhaps I should have a word with Lilly," Dev said, smiling as his wife joined the fray. "I wouldn't mind my every need met," he added.

"The wait will be a long one, my lord," his wife said, but her eyes were focused on Jackson, who was now surrounded by women. The men, Cam included, were standing a few feet back with the children, enjoying the situation hugely.

"Oh, well, of course there are indeed different marital situations, but I have always found the man to be in charge." Jackson battled on gamely, although now his face was parchment white.

"Jackson, run now while you have everything intact. It will not be pretty if you do not," Max suggested.

"I did not mean to offend," he said stiffly. Obviously he was used to men who enjoyed the power in their households, which was of course the norm in most marriages. Cam's family, however, had always been slightly different. Strong women were a source of pride to their husbands... and brothers.

"Perhaps I could prevail upon dear Miss Tolly to walk with me awhile."

"Thank you, but no, Mr. Jackson," Emily said, much to Cam's relief. He'd feared her kind heart may have her sympathizing with the man. "I am here with my family, and should not like to leave them."

He bowed, and when he rose the expression on his face showed his frustration. *Good riddance.*

"We must retreat now, as the balloon is about to leave," Cam said as he saw the preparations had begun. He was feeling quite happy with the Jackson outcome, and once again at peace with the world... well as peaceful as he could be with his tormenter standing a few feet away.

"Trouble," Essie said softly. "Something is wrong."

The Sinclair's were suddenly alert. Sniffing the air, Cam sensed it too. Something was stirring, but he could not see the cause.

"Dev?"

"I feel it, but see nothing."

"I hear nothing," Eden said.

Something made Cam turn to the right, and he saw Emily running.

"Emily!"

"Warwick!" she screamed, but did not turn.

Cam sprinted after her, but she had distance on him, and reached the balloon before he could grab her. He then watched in horror as she lunged at the basket as it started to rise with her gripping the edges.

"No!" He stopped, heart pounding, looking up at her. "Let go, I'll catch you!"

Instead, he watched her legs disappear as she was pulled inside the basket.

"Emily!" Cam watched her head appear.

"Warwick is inside!"

"What?"

"She said Warwick is inside!" Eden arrived, breathless.

"Dear Christ!" Cam stood with his head back watching the balloon rise higher into the sky with his little brother and Emily inside, and could not think of another time when he'd felt more helpless. He was sure that later, when they were safe, something would come to him... but not now.

"She just said she will keep him safe."

"But who will keep her safe?" he said, watching her floating away from him. He felt as if part of him was up there in that basket. A very, very important part of him, and that if it was not returned he would no longer be able to exist.

"I can't breathe." His whisper was ragged as he dropped to his knees.

CHAPTER 18

"*I*t's panic, Cam." Essie was there beside him. "Slow your breathing down and focus on my voice."

She placed a hand on his stomach and he forced himself to listen to her calming words. Forced himself to breathe, and slowly the tightness began to ease.

"Push my hand in and out."

He did as she instructed and finally the tightness eased.

"They will be okay until we reach them, brother, have faith."

He managed to stagger to his feet, and pulled Essie to hers. He then hugged her hard.

"Easy, Cam." He gripped the hand Dev put on his shoulder.

"I am well, just had a moment. Carriages!" he rasped.

They started running. His nostrils were filled with the stench of fear, and blood pumped through his veins. The thought of his little brother and Emily up there was a terrifying one.

"Essie, take the children home, and we will follow the balloon!" Dev yelled. "We need Lilly and Eden with us."

"I want Warwick and Emily back!" Somer cried.

Cam scooped her up, squeezing her hard.

"They will be safe, sweetheart, but you have to be a good girl and go with Essie. We will bring them home as soon as the balloon lands, I promise."

His heart thudded, and his skin felt tight. Thoughts of death and destruction as the balloon crashed taking Emily and Warwick from him made his chest heave once more, but he pushed them aside.

"Promise?"

"Promise." He hooked fingers with his little sister, then handed her to Essie.

"We have Lilly, should we need her, and then you will be waiting when we reach home. I promise we shall bring them to you safe, Ess."

She nodded, but said nothing, her face pale. Max hugged her briefly, whispering words of reassurance. She then bundled the three terrified little girls into the carriage and left.

"Follow that balloon, Bids," Dev told his driver. Minutes later they were inside, traveling in the same direction. Grim-faced, James, Dev, and Eden sat across from him; Max and Lilly were to his left.

"God's blood, that boy is staying in his room for two months," Cam growled.

"A year," Dev added. "And I'm feeding him gruel."

"Can you hear anything, Eden?"

Pale and shaking, Eden gripped her husband's hand as she moved to the window and leaned out. She shook her head. "They are too high now, and the wind is strong. Perhaps when we leave the city, and I can stand under them?"

Cam sat with his hands clenched in fists on his thighs.

"How is your breathing?"

"All right," he told his brother.

"I have never seen you like that before."

He felt their eyes on him, but his were out the window.

"I thought she was going to fall right there before me, and I would not be able to save her."

"But you would have," James said. "Just as you have before."

The absolute belief in his words surprised Cam.

"But you hate that we are your protectors."

"No, never that." He shook his head. "We Ravens are blessed to have the Sinclairs in our lives. To know that whenever danger presents itself, you will do what needs to be done to protect us, no matter the cost to yourself. I feel the great burden this task has placed upon you by some greater force, but I could never believe it was anything but a blessing for us."

"We would be dead were it not for you," Max added. "And our sister lost to us."

"I make light of it because that is our way, but never doubt that to me, you are the most wonderful people I have ever encountered," James said.

Humbled, Cam nodded, unable to find words. He had never understood how the Ravens in his life felt until that moment.

"Thank you." Dev's words were thick with emotion.

"I fear for them up there in the cold," Eden said. "They do not have enough clothing on to keep warm."

"The man will have a blanket, I'm sure, love." James lifted his arm, and Eden burrowed into him. "He will also land as soon as he is able."

"We can do no more than follow them." Max was the voice of reason. "That balloonist is experienced, and has done many, many flights, bringing each down safely, and with passengers."

"My heart cannot stand this," Cam gritted out. "First she

gets abducted and then throws herself recklessly into a balloon."

"May I remind you, that selfless act she just did was to save your brother."

"I know, Max, but I'm scared."

"As are we all." Eden took one of his fists and held it tight. "But we have to believe they will be safe."

"Do you have anything that smells nice on you?" He questioned her. "The scent in my nostrils is noxious."

Eden dug into her reticule and found a handkerchief. She thrust it at him. "This has scent on it."

Taking it he inhaled deeply; the relief was acute.

"What's it's like?"

"What?"

"The smell?" James asked him. "Is it only when someone you care about is in danger?"

"No, I can smell most things near or far all the time, I've just got used to it. But it's worse when danger is approaching. When Emily was abducted, I knew something was about to happen. The stench made my head swim."

"Which is strange as she's not your family, don't you think?" Max said, watching him closely.

"Firstly, she is a Raven, and secondly she's part of my life, therefore someone I am aware of," he said, choosing his words carefully.

"That must be it then."

Cam looked out the window again, but he had a feeling all kinds of silent signals were being thrown around the carriage. Right at that moment he didn't care. What he cared about was getting Emily and Warwick home safe.

Emily was cold. She wore her coat, hat, and gloves but it was not enough. Warwick too was shivering.

Mr. Hailmaker was most displeased that they were on his journey, as he had not calculated for the extra weight, nor did he have supplies to cater for them.

"To have thrown yourself at my basket in such a reckless manner shows extreme foolishness or incredible bravery. I'm not sure as yet which it is, Miss Tolly."

He wore thick woolen trousers and jacket. Two scarves, and a woolen hat pulled low over his ears. Emily envied him that. Her bonnet was no barrier against the cold wind.

"E-Emily is br-brave, not stupid, sir."

Unwrapping her scarf, she took off Warwick's cap, and wrapped the wool around his ears and head.

"Th-thank you."

Emily then moved in behind him, and wrapped her arms around Warwick's body. The boy allowed it, which told her just how cold he was.

"What can you see?" she bent to ask him.

"How v-vast it all is. There is a c-castle, and it's surrounded by so much land, a river also. The trees seem like dots, and the animals the same. It is as if they were drawn on a piece of p-paper."

"We shall have to land as soon as I find a suitable place," Mr. Hailmaker said, and Emily could only be grateful that she would not be up here for too much longer. She was not overly fond of heights, but had not truly had that fear tested until this moment.

"Your family will be very cross with you, Warwick, you do realize that?"

"I don't c-care, it's worth it."

Warwick was as stubborn and defiant as Cam. Even though the boy had realized the error of his actions not long after the balloon had risen high in the sky, he would not admit it. She'd seen his fear and worry. Watched as his excitement had moved into trepidation.

"No it's not. You're cold and miserable," she said. "But you have your brother's pride, so that will carry you until we land, I am sure."

"I-I'm sorry, Emily. I do not usually do impulsive things, like the twins. But I wanted this, and I did not think through the consequences."

He was solemn now, thoroughly chastened, and she could censure him no further.

"Well, as this is the first and last time I will ever fly in a balloon, shall we enjoy it, and attempt to locate landmarks?"

"Here." A flask was handed to them. Taking a tentative sip, Emily enjoyed the burn of the brandy as it slid down her throat. Her second mouthful was larger.

"Can I have some?"

"No!" both she and Mr. Hailmaker said in unison.

"Thank you for risking your life by hurling yourself inside the basket when you realized I was hiding in it, Emily."

"You are welcome. I can think of nothing I'd rather do than be up here, freezing my ears off, terrified, with you."

He snuffled then leaned back into her.

"Do you like Cam, Em?"

"Of course, just as I like all your siblings." But there was so much more to what she'd felt when she'd looked down into Cam's terrified face. His fear had ignited hers. She'd wanted to jump and have him catch her as she'd known he would. But of course his fear was for his brother as well as her, and the little boy was the reason she was in this basket, miles above the ground.

"But do you like him more?"

Emily wasn't sure where this was going, but didn't think she'd like its eventual destination.

"No more than Dev."

The boy was silent, and Emily was relieved the conversation was over. Her relief was short lived.

"I think you should marry him, and then you'll always be with us."

Stay calm. "I will always be with you anyway. I have no need to wed Cam for that. Besides, we would not live in harmony, as we are continually arguing."

"He likes you, I can t-tell."

"You are cold. Here, let me warm you up." Rubbing her hands up and down his arms, Emily tried to dismiss his words. The problem was that lately she had come to the realization that she liked Cam too... a great deal more than she should.

CHAPTER 19

*W*orry gnawed at Cam's insides as he watched the balloon. The panic that had robbed his breath had eased slightly, enough so he could inhale and exhale, but only slightly. Inside that basket were two people who had the capacity to destroy him should anything happen to either. Emily had crept inside him somehow. The woman who had always been like a persistent pain in his side had become something more, he just had no name for it yet.

On and on the carriage rolled for God knew how long, and the tension inside ratcheted up with every mile they traveled. Fear was so thick it nearly choked Cam, and he knew his siblings fared little better.

Dev was pale, and his pupils big, eyes focused out the window with an intensity that would be unnerving to anyone who did not know him. He could see the balloon clearly.

"Move to the middle, Dev."

"What?" He tore his eyes away from the window to look at Cam.

"James, move and put Dev on the other side, between you

and Eden. He can see the balloon clearly, and it's making him ill," Cam added.

"No!"

"Yes." Lilly leaned forward, taking her husband's chin in her hands. "It is for the best, my love."

Between them, they moved him along the seat. He did not fight them, but the urge, Cam knew, was there. Dev then gripped Lilly's hand, and slowly his pupils began to retract.

"Eden, do you have your earplugs in?"

She shook her head at Cam's words.

"Replace them now."

James dug about in the pocket of her coat and found them, then helped her push them in.

"We can do nothing until they land, therefore there is no need to become worked up to the point of panic, until they do," Cam said as calmly as he could.

"And you, brother." Dev's voice was gruff. "What can be done for you?"

"Very little. I have the handkerchief and will inhale that when the smell is too strong."

"I was often envious of your closeness, but watching you all now," Max said softly, "it is a kind of hell I never wish to experience."

"I feel it, but not as strong. Most of the sensations I feel come from touching the sick or injured," Lilly said. "I pray to God my skill is not needed this day."

They all agreed silently.

As the sun began to lower in the sky, Cam watched the balloon closely.

"It's coming down. Dear God, please let it come down gently," he prayed.

"Find a place to stop, Bids!" Dev roared at his driver. "As close to the balloon as you can get!"

The carriage traveled for a while longer, and then stopped.

"It's landing in that field, my lord, near them trees," Bids said as they got out. He then crossed himself, which did nothing to ease the panic inside Cam.

"Be prepared to leave as soon as we reach you, Bids. Get the blankets out and ready."

"At once, Lord Sinclair."

The driver was right, the balloon was heading for the trees. Cam climbed the fence into the paddock, then turned to help Eden, whom James was lifting over. Lilly was next, and then he started running with his family on his heels.

"It's slowing!"

The wind was carrying it away from the trees, Cam noticed as Dev shouted the words. His heart was thudding so hard it hurt.

"Warwick just told Emily he wanted to see his family again!" Eden cried. "We're coming, darling!" she shrieked.

Cam's gut clenched for his little brother and the fear he was feeling.

"Be strong, Warwick, and hold Emily tight!" Cam roared, hoping his little brother would hear.

"We love you!" Dev roared.

"Emily is soothing him, trying to distract him with questions now. He just told her that he heard us. There is another male voice, the owner of the balloon who is reassuring them all will go well, and that he has done this many times."

Lilly would heal any injuries; Cam just prayed she was not needed. They often said that between them all they would be the perfect medical people to have on a battlefield. He hoped again that those skills were not required today.

"Hold hands," he said suddenly. "Give them our strength, see if there is anything we can do to get this balloon down safely!"

He felt the surge of power as Lilly gripped his fingers. It intensified as Eden and Dev joined. On they ran until they were directly under the balloon. Only then did they stop and complete the circle. The power rose.

"Look up!" Dev roared. They did as he asked. "I can see them. Emily has Warwick in her arms, surrounding him, keeping him warm. They're both pale, but it's from cold and fear, not injury."

"Warwick said he can feel us, he just told Emily that we are below, and that everything will be all right."

"We're here," Cam said, talking to his brother.

"Emily is singing now."

Cam's gut clenched as the balloon sank lower. She must be terrified.

"Is... is it going too fast?"

"Not according to the man inside who Warwick just called Mr. Hailmaker. He said they are descending at the correct pace," Eden reassured them.

Cam held his breath as it got lower, and then it landed with a thud, tipping on its side. Breaking the circle, they started running again.

Arriving first, Cam dropped to his knees beside Emily, who was on her side with Warwick in her arms.

"H-he's all right," she stuttered.

"You kept him safe," Cam managed to get out. He reached for his little brother and lifted him out.

"It's all right, you little heathen, I have you now." Cam kissed the top of his head, squeezing him, then handed him to Dev.

"You next," Cam said. Emily was attempting to crawl out, not easy as she was burdened with skirts. He grabbed her around the waist and helped her, settling her between his knees.

"Thank God, you're safe." He whispered the words into

her hair. Her hands clutched his coat, while his arms held her in a ferocious hug. He needed to let her go, or crush her, but he couldn't make himself.

"Thank you, Emily." He heard Dev's heartfelt whisper from behind him. "I am going to kill you," Dev said slowly. "Warwickshire Sinclair, you will be paying for this act of stupidity for days... weeks, make that months. You have aged me ten years this day."

Emily was burrowing into Cam's chest, and he had his face pressed into her hair. Her scent calmed him. He wanted to hold her until her tremors eased, and even then he wasn't sure he would let her go.

"Emily?"

James touched her head, and she lifted it. Her eyes went to Cam first, and then her brothers. Reluctantly he released her as she gently pushed against his chest.

She was then held by her brothers, and Cam managed to stagger to his feet. He took Warwick from Dev, and held him tight.

"Apologies, sir, my brother's actions have inconvenienced you hugely," Cam heard Dev say.

"Your brother is a very intelligent boy, sir. I would be honored to take him up again, and teach him more about ballooning."

"I don't think so" was all Dev said. "But thank you again for returning them to us safely."

"There now, there is no need for tears, Warwick," Cam said. His little brother was shivering and sobbing softly into his coat. "We would never let anything happen to you."

"I-I'm sorry."

"I know," Cam soothed. "And there will be plenty of time to discuss that, but for now let us get you warm."

They walked to the carriage, and soon all were inside. It was a squeeze, but Lilly sat on Dev's knee, and Eden on

James's. Emily was pressed between her brothers, directly across from Cam, while Warwick sat between him and Dev. They were covered in coats and blankets, and Emily given a flask to sip from. Which she did; in fact, she was gulping down several large mouthfuls.

"She had some of that in the air," Warwick grumbled, "yet I was allowed none." He was getting his voice back now he was warming up.

"Because you are reckless enough without any inducements. Emily, however, is not," Dev said. "She is polite and behaves rationally, so a few sips will not harm her."

Cam watched Emily swallow down more brandy. As if she felt him looking at her she turned, offering him a sweet smile, perhaps the sweetest he'd ever had from her. Coughing to clear his throat, he reached for the flask. "You have to share that, you know."

She lifted it out of his reach, shaking her head. "I n-need it most."

"And what of the torture we went through thinking about you up there? Do we not deserve some fortification?"

Her eyes narrowed as she studied him.

"I'm sh-sorry for your pain. I sh-saw it in your eyes as we rose in the air."

"Did you?"

Her nod was vigorous, and had her bumping shoulders with Max. Had the circumstances been different, Cam might have enjoyed a foxed Emily, but his emotions were still too raw.

"So, there will be punishment, Warwick, but firstly, what was it like?" Dev said as Cam continued to watch Emily. She'd be legless by the time she reached London, but no one seemed terribly worried about that fact, so he left the flask in her possession.

"It was wonderful, but terrifying, Dev." Warwick yawned,

but no one rebuked him for not covering his mouth. "Especially for Emily, who does not like heights."

"Don't you?" James looked at his sister. "I never knew that."

"There is mush you don't know about me," she said, attempting to focus on him but failing. She tried to stretch up to get a better look, but when that didn't work, she gave up, slumping into her seat and sipping from the flask.

"She's going to have a hell of a headache in the morning," Cam said softly.

Max reached for the flask, but she clutched it to her chest, so he left it there.

"Yes, I know that. Perhaps one day you could tell me," James said.

She shook her head. At least color had crept back into her cheeks, making her look less like a ghost.

"My p-pasht... past," she corrected, "h-has too many demons to share, brother. I would not wish to burden you."

"Your brothers have broad shoulders, sister." James's words were gruff as he looked down at her. Cam could see the emotion he battled to suppress. "We would be more than happy to carry some of your burdens."

The others were quiet, listening to the conversation. It was probably not the place for it, but the fact that she was talking, and acknowledging her past, was an opportunity too good to miss. Warwick, Cam was pleased to note, was now dozing against Dev.

"I try to sh-shut them out." Emily squeezed her eyes closed.

"Of your head?"

Her eyes sprang open as she nodded. "They are too p-painful."

"We are here to listen when you are ready, sister." Everyone heard the pain in Max's voice. "Remember that

149

we all carry demons; some are just more heinous than others."

She thought about that as her eyes went slowly around the carriage. It was perhaps the first time he had ever seen Emily truly unguarded. Her defenses were down; brandy had driven them away briefly.

"You are all very nichhh people."

"Thank you," Dev said solemnly.

"And you"—she pointed the flask at Cam—"you f-force me to be a lioness, not a mousshh."

Her eyes then began to close and she fell sideways onto the duke's shoulder. Seconds later, like Warwick, she slept.

James inhaled deeply.

"What the hell was that supposed to mean?" Cam asked the carriage.

"Your continual poking and jabbing at her makes her be the person she wished she could be all the time, is my guess." Dev shrugged.

His brother's words eased some of the tightness in Cam's chest.

"What did she suffer?" James looked devastated.

"We don't know, but it's a start that she spoke of her life before us, brother." Max gripped his shoulder.

It was, Cam thought as the carriage took them back to London. Today he'd learned something about himself. Learned that Emily Tolly had come to mean a great deal more to him than any woman before her. The thought of losing her had told him that.

I turn her into a lioness. Why that thought made him smile he didn't know, but smile he did.

CHAPTER 20

*E*mily walked into the Winslow charity ball on
James's arm, one week after her balloon adventure.
She rarely, if ever, attended social functions, but this was an
event to raise money for several of their family's charities.
Lilly looked after children who lived on the streets, and often
needed medical care or a place to hide. Max ran several
houses for children who had been mistreated also. Both were
hoping to raise awareness tonight for the plights of those
children, and so all the family was in attendance.

Emily had agreed to come purely to support them, as she
had on two previous occasions. She often attended the
theatre with her family, and other places members of society
would be, but never a society ball or event.

"Relax, Emily."

James whispered the words in her ear. She nodded, but
could still not draw in a deep, steadying breath. A few
noblemen would be in attendance, those who owed their
support to Max in return for his help in various ventures.
James was one, but he was also family, and came to support
his brother and Lilly.

She has been with this family long enough now to feel one of us.

Cam's words often circled around inside her head since that day he'd spoken them. She had not seen a great deal of him since the balloon incident, but when she had, he acted as if nothing between them had changed... but it had, they both knew that. She'd told him that he turned her into a lioness, and he had not used that against her... the old Cam would have. In fact, he was a great deal nicer to her, which in itself was unsettling.

"Breathe in and out, that's it."

"Thank you, James, I know how to breathe."

She remembered it all, the brandy she'd consumed, and how it had loosened her tongue. She'd told them her past held demons, and since that day, her brothers had spent a great deal of time in her company, even coming to her room should she be hiding in it. They were slowly getting to know each other better, and Emily had to admit she was very happy about that. She was trying harder to speak openly, trying to be the woman she wanted to be.

"I read your article in *The Trumpeter* today."

"Really?" She looked up at James.

"It was extremely illuminating and well written, Emily. I enjoyed it very much, as did Samantha."

She felt ridiculously happy about that. She'd told him the day after the balloon trip about her writing, and he had been proud of her.

"Thank you."

He patted her hand.

Cam had spoken briefly about *The Trumpeter*, and asked her to write as many articles as she could. He'd told her there would be more discussions, but until he knew intimately how the place ran, they could wait.

Warwick had written her a letter of apology and delivered it in person, and she was pleased that the little boy had shown no ill effects from his adventure.

"Smile, Emily."

"Yes, Eden."

Her stomach clenched as they walked through the crowds. The evening was a cold one, with a light dusting of snow on the ground. Fires roared in the two large hearths in the ballroom, and branches of candles were dotted everywhere, while candelabras hung suspended above the guests.

"You look lovely, Emily."

"Thank you, James."

She felt his eyes on her face.

"I mean those words, sister."

Emily looked at him. His frown had drawn a line across his brows.

"I'm sorry, James." The words came out before she could stop them.

"For what?"

"Everything." Emily exhaled. How did she begin to explain her behavior to him, when she'd struggled to understand it herself? But lately, she'd thought it necessary to at least attempt to try. Especially as he was trying so hard to forge a relationship with her.

Emily was changing, and with that change she had begun to see herself as others did. Cam's words had triggered that change when he accused her of hiding away from her family, and life.

"I'm fairly sure you did not chew Eden's new satin slippers. That was the fault of that beastly Whiskers. For a small animal, he can cause a large amount of trouble," James said.

She laughed, as he'd wanted her to.

"Our relationship is progressing, Emily, but there is still much to speak of. We are long overdue for a talk, but it will not take place here, for all these people to witness."

She did not say anything further, simply nodded, and then before she lost her courage, rose to her toes and kissed his cheek.

"Thank you, James."

Eden was on James's other arm, and Dev and Lilly walked behind them. Max and Essie beyond them. Cam, Essie had told her, was running late.

Emily found the blank expression she had perfected for just such an occasion... or any time when she felt out of her depth. She could do this if for no other reason than her family deserved her support.

"Duke."

"Lord Howe."

James bowed perfectly, and Lilly dipped into a curtsey that was elegant and spoke of years doing just that. Emily exhaled slowly and followed suit.

"Relax, Em."

"Yes, James."

"If you make a mistake it will not matter here, you know. Those from society that are in attendance do so knowing they walk among people in trade, industrialists, and those that have made their money from investing, like Max."

"I understand that, James, but I have no wish to embarrass you."

"You have never embarrassed me, and I doubt you could," James whispered. "Besides, when I first entered society, I tripped on the stairs halfway down to the ballroom and rolled to the bottom, where I landed on Lady Walters. She screeched, and fell backward into the arms of her husband, and as she is not what you would call a delicate woman, he was forced to stagger backward, standing on Mr. Grislow's gout-swollen foot. The results, I assure you, were not pleasant, and all parties are still not speaking to me."

"Is that actually true?" Max asked.

"Absolutely. It was, and always will be, the single most embarrassing moment of my life."

"So even dukes are subject to censure... illuminating," Max drawled.

"Brother, I may be a duke, but let me assure you I still get my share of censure from many people who do not like my beliefs or the stances I take in the House of Lords."

"That is hard to believe," Emily said. "I-I mean, most people appear to bend over backward to appease you."

"Some, yes, but not all, and there is the matter of all that simpering and fawning that makes me shudder. Believe me, it is not all pleasant."

"I had not thought of that," Max said. "We, your minions, just enter a room as part of your flotilla, basking in your magnificence. I had no idea that you were not universally adored."

"I don't universally adore him," Eden said.

"Nor I," Essie added.

"I never have and likely never will," Dev drawled.

James snorted.

"You would be even more arrogant were we to do so," Eden added. "We mere mortals keep your large feet solidly planted in the soil."

"Thank you, Duchess." James kissed his wife's cheek.

They walked, and were often waylaid by those wishing to discuss business with Max, James, and Dev.

"Good evening." Wolf Sinclair joined them, looking handsome in uniform. "May I have this dance, Miss Tolly?"

"Captain Sinclair." Emily sank into the curtsey. "It would be my pleasure." *As long as I remember the steps and do not trip over his feet.*

He led her onto the dance floor where others were assembling.

"Cambridge was waylaid in the hallway by two men. He is a popular man."

"Yes, he has many friends I am sure, Captain."

"Please call me Wolf."

"And I am Emily."

He was as tall as Cam, with the Sinclair looks. Emily wondered why her heart did not beat a little harder when he was near, as it did with Cam.

"And are you enjoying lodging with him?"

"Oh indeed. He is an interesting man, with a great depth of knowledge. I have already learned so much, and with his help hope to make a few business investments."

"I am pleased you have settled in so well."

The dance was one she knew, and while she counted the steps under her breath and kept her eyes on those opposite, she managed to acquit herself well enough.

"I heard about the ballooning incident, and am glad you have recovered, Emily," Wolf said, escorting her back to her family.

"May I have this dance, Miss Tolly?" Mr. Jackson stepped into their path.

Her hesitation was brief, but Wolf felt it.

"Miss Tolly is tired. I am escorting her back to her family."

"And yet we are friends, are we not, Miss Tolly. She will surely not refuse me?"

Emily felt the muscles under Wolf's jacket stiffen, and knew she must take action before he said anything further. She doubted he would make a scene, but still she did not wish for heated words to be exchanged when one dance would cause her no harm.

"Of course, Mr. Jackson, it would be my pleasure to dance with you."

"Excellent."

She left the captain's side, but felt his eyes on her as she returned to the floor. Why she suddenly felt uncomfortable with Mr. Jackson, Emily had no idea, but she did. Since that day at the balloon event, she had come to realize his views on the role of a woman in the marriage were not to her liking, which in turn meant she had no wish to be in his company.

He moved to take his place across from her in the line, and Emily forced herself to return his smile.

Mr. Jackson was as different as night is to day from Cam and the other men in her life, and Emily knew that if ever she married, it would not be to someone like the man across from her. She would want a man just like those in her life.

Like Cam Sinclair.

CHAPTER 21

"Care to tell me why you look like you've eaten something vile, Lilly?"

Cam moved to his sister-in-law's side after leaving the two men who had wished to discuss his acquisition of *The Trumpeter*.

He and Wolf had arrived late after a large meal that then led to a glass of port. He liked his cousin very much, and was enjoying tutoring him on investments and other aspects of London life.

"Do I? Forgive me?"

"Of course, but you still have yet to answer my question."

He located Emily dancing with Mr. Jackson, which annoyed him because he'd thought for sure after the incident in the park that he'd scared the man away.

He tried to not catalogue every inch of her as she moved through the steps of the dance. She danced well, seeing as he didn't think she'd been in such a setting more than a few times, or danced those steps in public often.

"That dress is a trifle low," he growled to Lilly before he could stop himself. Emily wore a deep, rich cream, almost beige, with an overdress of matching lace that was trimmed on the edges with satin, and the bodice was low enough that he could see the creamy swells of her breasts. The lace appeared as if it was wrapped around her, because one side curved from the hem, up and across her hips on a diagonal, and disappeared around the back. Cam swallowed as he imagined exploring where that end went.

"Emily's dress is fine. Now concentrate, Cam."

"On what, Lilly?" He couldn't drag his eyes from her. Her hair was bundled on top of her head and secured with two cream satin bands, and no doubt a card of pins.

"I want to know why you behaved the way you did that day with Emily. Just after she had been abducted."

"That happened weeks ago. Why does it now have you looking like you've sucked lemon?" He should walk over there and plant his fist in Jackson's face; the man was entirely too forward with Emily. Cam could see his eyes roving over her body. The fact that his eyes had done the same had no bearing.

"I have not had a moment to discuss the matter with you, and while I did not agree with the way you approached the matter, Cam, I cannot fault you for your accuracy."

Dragging his eyes from the subject of conversation, he looked at Lilly.

"That look was severe, Lilly. Surely there is more bothering you than something that happened many weeks ago?" Cam had no wish to discuss Emily with anyone seeing as he had no idea how he felt about her yet.

She tapped his arm. "That is merely my resting face. Dev tells me I often look as if I want to cause bodily harm; I fear there is little I can do about it. Now back to you and Emily, and that day in James's office."

"I was tired and sore; clearly I was also not thinking

straight. Forgive my rudeness, I should have kept the words inside my head."

"Perhaps, but then perhaps not."

"Well, which perhaps is it?"

"I think it is perhaps not. Because I think you are correct. Since that day I have noticed a thawing in Emily, and that pleases me greatly."

"Good Lord do you really believe I am correct?" he teased. Cam rather liked his sister-in-law, not especially because she'd brought his brother back from the dead. He could never thank her enough for that. He may not openly show his brother how much he cared, but the thought of having his large presence gone from their lives was not something he ever wanted to contemplate until he was old and gray.

"Occasionally you can be."

"Just occasionally? You wound me."

"Do you really believe her life before coming to live with James was awful, Cam? I have thought endlessly about what she said in that carriage after the balloon landed. I ached for the pain I saw in her face."

"Emily?" Cam said, knowing exactly who she meant.

"Yes Emily, as you very well know." Lilly accompanied these words with another slap to his wrist. "I understand you two have this ability to irritate each other by simply breathing the same air, but I have a theory on that too; however, Dev told me I had to keep it to myself."

"Not easy for you, but my brother has my gratitude," Cam said. He could feel his necktie tightening at her words. "However, let me put you straight, darling sister-in-law, and assure you there is nothing between Miss Tolly and myself other than an ability to irritate each other."

"Something he specializes in," Dev said. He immediately moved to his beloved's side, placing a hand on her back.

"Surely it is not my specialty alone, brother?"

"No, we are all rather good at it to be fair. But what I want to know, my love," Dev looked at his wife, "is why you believe he is being irritating tonight?"

"Emily."

Just her name, but it was enough to have Dev rocking back on his heels and nodding in that superior way older siblings had that annoyed their younger ones excessively.

"Ahhh."

"Ah what?"

"Ah, Emily and you." Dev looked at him. "Two bristling dogs... and yet."

"Yet nothing!" Cam snapped slipping a finger inside his collar. "Whatever was about to leave your mouth, keep it there."

Dev rocked back on his heels again at Cam's words.

"Ahhh."

"Stop doing that!" Cam snapped.

"What?"

"That rocking thing accompanied by that very annoying ah. It's irritated me since I was old enough for it to do so, and it has not alleviated any with time."

Dev gave him a slow smile, his piercing green eyes impaling Cam to the spot. "Ah," he said, slowly rocking.

When a Sinclair got the chance to irritate a sibling, it was a sure thing he or she would take it.

"Good Lord, that bloody windbag Evermore just brayed in my ear the entire dance. I should simply pour hot wax into my ears and seal them up. That would solve the problem!"

Eden stomped to their side and wedged herself between Cam and Dev. Sinclairs knew no personal boundaries. Should they wish to wedge themselves between siblings, they did so.

"No please, tell us exactly how you feel," Cam said.

"'Tis all right for you, you simply have to smell things, I have to hear every inane comment and... and supposed hushed word."

Eden wore red tonight and looked beautiful, as she always did. The Sinclair dark hair was primped and piled on top of her head, and dotted with something sparkling. He'd heard people call her beautiful, some even said exquisite, but when he looked at her he saw his younger sister who he loved very much, but who had spent her childhood listening to his every conversation, and been hell to catch while playing hide-and-seek.

"Yes, because I love the scent of foul-smelling unwashed people all in one place. Or," he added as she opened her mouth, "the overperfumed women who think the more scent they put on the better they smell."

"Oh please." Essie forced her way into the Sinclair circle, looking equally beautiful in deep forest green. The circle, Cam noted, Lilly had stepped out of. She stood behind them with Max, looking amused. "I can taste nothing without breaking it down to each individual ingredient. And do not get me started on eating something that is off. Plus, there is that hideous taste I get when one of you is in trouble."

"Pfft," Dev said. "I can see everything, night or day. I see distances, I see what people have no wish for me to see, and that which I have no wish to see. I can tell if each of you are troubled or sick."

"He always has to win." Essie sighed.

"Yes, 'tis most vexing," Eden agreed.

"Lady Hinderly has bad breath," Cam muttered, "and Lord Bexley has an onion in his left boot; why, I have no idea."

"If I may interject, I believe I am now part of this conversation." Wolf Sinclair nudged his way into the circle. "I watched a man fall overboard and sink as he wore a heavy coat and boots. I tracked him with my eyes, but could not save him; by the time I had dived in, he was dead."

"Oh how horrid!" Essie cried.

"Do I win?" Wolf looked hopeful.

"You made that up." Cam's eyes narrowed.

"Perhaps, but I can actually track things when they do start to sink. Plus, there is the small matter that every animal, no matter its state, wants to be near me. If you look about you now, there will be a few mice lurking."

"You are indeed a true Sinclair." Eden smiled. "They will do anything to best another Sinclair."

They laughed then, as they often did. Sinclairs argued passionately, but rarely held grudges. They were demonstrative people, and the surprising thing about that was the ones who had married had wed their exact opposite in personality.

"But we digress. When I first joined Lilly, she and Cam were discussing how irritating he can be."

"Really, Dev, surely you are not speaking about our brother in such a way. We all know he is never irritating."

"Yes, thank you, Eden. You who are everything that is sweet and agreeable," Cam said. "And on that note it is time for me to dance. The young ladies are growing restless with so much masculine beauty before them."

Dev snorted.

"As this is not my usual setting, I'm sure these women have yet to experience the wonders of dancing with me."

"These women are far sturdier than your noble ladies, Cam. Daughters of industrials and the like. They will not fall at your feet so readily," Lilly added.

"We shall see." Cam walked away to the sound of his family's laughter. There was no chance of getting a swollen ego around his siblings.

He partnered Miss May Swindon in the first dance, the

daughter of Mr. Louis Swindon, an astute and wealthy businessman with his fingers in many investments including textiles. They discussed satin, and how it was the finest silk a person could fashionably choose for a Regency gown, to which Cam had replied appropriately while searching for Emily.

He found her dancing with another gentleman; she did not look happy, a fact he knew as her face was blank. Strange, how he now knew so much about her.

When the dance finished and he'd returned Miss Swindon to her mother's side, he headed straight for Emily. She was in conversation with Jackson. How had the man intercepted her again?

"Good evening, Jackson," Cam said, taking Emily's hand and placing it on his arm. "My dance I believe."

"We were talking," Jackson said, looking displeased.

"And now you are not," Cam replied, walking away with Emily on his arm. "Come and dance with me."

"I don't think so, but thank you, Cam."

"Too late." He directed her back to the floor. She had to follow or make a scene, and he knew Emily would never do that.

"I did not want to dance!" she hissed. "I'm weary."

"Yes, you being so old and infirm, this must be a struggle for you."

"Fiend!"

Cam pretended to ignore her and simply smiled as a waltz struck up.

"I-I have not danced this." She looked a bit frantic as he swung her into his arms.

"You've had lessons, Eden told me."

"Yes, but... oh dear, I must count."

He watched her lips move.

"Take a breath, Em. You're dancing with me, and you know these steps, so relax and enjoy them."

"Easy for you to say," she muttered. "You were born to do this type of thing, I was not."

"Actually I wasn't."

"It's in your blood."

"You're a duke's daughter; it's in yours too."

"A duke's illegitimate daughter."

"You trot that out when it suits you."

She gasped, her chin rising so she could glare at him. "I cannot believe you just said that."

"Yes you can, and by the way, your last article for *The Trumpeter* was excellent. I was wondering if we should start up that children's section you mentioned."

"Oh!" Her eyes widened and the anger was suddenly gone, replaced by excitement. "Yes, there are so many wonderful things you could fill it with."

He had come to realize she was beautiful no matter how she dressed or wore her hair, but here, in that gown, she was exquisite.

"Our young ones are a wonderful source of information, Cam. I was thinking we could put a quiz in each paper, with ten questions, and they would get the answers the following edition."

She talked, and he listened. Her excitement lit her face and made something heat inside him, an ache he was struggling more and more to control.

"Emily, you need to tell Jackson you are not interested." He said the words as they started back to where their families stood.

"Pardon?" The excitement fell from her face, but that did not stop him from continuing; the words needed to be said.

"Jackson wants you for his wife. You need to dissuade him."

165

Her expression changed back to anger once more.

"That has nothing to do with you."

"Are you interested in him?" He battled the need to roar at her.

"I am not having this discussion with you. Mr. Jackson has not made an offer for me, nor is he likely to considering my birth."

"Don't be ridiculous. You have a duke for a brother and the other one has more money than anyone in England. Of course he is interested in you."

He'd hurt her, he saw it at once.

"I did not mean to say you are not worthy of his attention, Emily—"

"I have nothing further to say on the matter." Emily pulled her arm from his grasp. "Now I am leaving, before we draw more attention and I give in to the impulse to slap you... hard!"

Before he could stop her, she'd walked away. Cam didn't follow, feeling like he needed time away from her. Time to calm down. If he stayed it was likely he would find Jackson and threaten him, and that would never do. Cam was not usually the jealous type, but he was now. That man would not have her, he vowed silently.

Finding Wolf, he then left, dragging him to his club where he would drink himself into a stupor in the hopes that when he woke, his head was once again sitting straight on his shoulders.

CHAPTER 22

*E*mily wandered down the hall after leaving the ladies' retiring room. She could not delay her return to the ballroom much longer, as soon someone would come looking for her. But she'd needed a few minutes to calm herself after her argument with Cam. Jackson meant nothing to her, but it was not Cam's right to point that out.

"Beastly man," she muttered. What was she to do about him?

"Miss Tolly, are you lost?"

Emily turned to find Mr. Jackson behind her. *Jackson wants you for his wife, you need to dissuade him.*

"Thank you, Mr. Jackson, but I am just on my way back to my family."

"You are going the wrong way, Miss Tolly. Let me direct you."

"Oh dear, am I? How silly."

"Come, I shall escort you."

He held out his arm, and she could do little but take it.

"Thank you."

"Your beauty captured me from the beginning, my dear,

and my admiration for you has increased every time I have seen you since."

"Thank you." Emily began to feel uncomfortable.

"Our shared love of astronomy has given me hope, my dear."

"For what?"

He ignored her and instead reached for a door handle as they passed.

"What are you doing, Mr. Jackson?"

"I want to get to know you, Miss Tolly. I thought we could take some time to do that?"

He opened it, then took her hand in his, forcing her to follow him inside. Emily resisted, trying to tug her hand free. Struggling to get away from him.

"Unhand me at once!"

"Come now, I wish only to speak with you, my dear."

"I have no wish to speak with you, however. Release me or I shall scream!"

"There is no need for that, I want only a few moments of your time."

He placed a hand in her spine, and Emily could do little to stop him forcing her forward, as his strength was greater than hers.

He then shut the door behind him.

"I cannot be seen alone with you, sir. I insist you open that door at once!" Emily managed to get her hand free.

"I would like to offer for you, Miss Tolly. I would like nothing more than you to be my wife. Your beauty has bewitched me, and I must have you."

"I have no wish to marry you, Mr. Jackson, and insist you let me return at once to my family."

His face darkened; the expectant look fell away.

"Surely you cannot think I am beneath you?"

"No, of course not. I simply have no wish to wed."

"Oh come now, every woman wishes that. I have accepted your birth, there is no need for you to deny me."

"I-I am denying you."

His smile was no longer pleasant.

"I have put a great deal of time and effort into this, Miss Tolly. You will be my wife, as it is best for both of us if you are."

"P-pardon?" Emily began backing away from him.

"You have powerful brothers, my dear, and I want them in my family. You are my way to achieving that. In turn I will give you respectability by accepting you."

"I am respectable, sir!" Emily felt her anger stir. "How dare you suggest otherwise. My father was a duke, as is my brother!"

"You are a bastard, Miss Tolly. No one thinks your birth respectable." He advanced on her. "Marriage to me will give you that, and I will be doing your brothers a favor."

"How dare you speak to me in such a way!"

"Oh come now, Miss Tolly. There is no need of this pretend outrage. When I realized that you were sister to both the duke and Mr. Huntington, I knew you were the answer to my dilemma, as I was to yours."

"D-dilemma?" Emily moved toward the desk. If she could get to that, she would lure him around it, and run for the door.

"I need the money, and you will be no hardship to bed. We shall make a perfect match."

"How dare you speak to me in such a way. I have no wish to marry, sir. Now let me leave at once!"

"I think not."

He lunged at her, taking Emily by surprise. His fingers bit into her upper arms as he pulled her close to his body.

She tried to escape but he was stronger. "Eden!" She screamed her sister-in-law's name.

"Scream louder, Miss Tolly, because I wish your family to see I have compromised you thoroughly when they arrive."

Wrenching free, Emily ran, but he was on her heels and grabbed her from behind.

"Now there is no need for maidenly fear, my dear."

He forced her backward until her thighs hit something, and then he was lowering her onto it. Emily fought him with everything she had like Max had once told her to if ever she was in such a situation. *"Never stop, Em,"* he'd said, *"until you run out of breath."* She scratched his face causing him to curse. He slapped her hard, and her head spun but she didn't give up.

"I've always fancied a title in my family, and you will help me achieve that. Your brothers will be glad to shower me with money when they realize I am taking you off their hands."

"My brothers will kill you!"

"They won't." He tried to kiss her, but Emily thwarted him, her hands grabbing his hair and pulling hard.

"Bitch!" His face was red and his breath coming in harsh pants now.

She felt her bodice give, and then his mouth was there, on her breasts. He would take her, right here on this desk, if she did not stop him.

"What the hell is going on in here!"

Emily looked to the doorway and saw horror on the faces of Mr. Whitlock, Max's business partner, and his wife, who stood shocked at his side. She struggled upright and tugged her bodice back into place as Mr. Jackson released her.

"Well now, it's obvious what happened, Whitlock. Miss Tolly seduced me. What is a man to do with such inducement but oblige," Mr. Jackson said, straightening his clothes. "Of course I shall marry her, as I am a gentleman and know my duty."

Emily got off the desk, her legs unsteady. She could think of nothing right at that moment, but wiping the satisfied look of Mr. Jackson's face. Curling her fingers into a fist, she then swung it at his face. It landed on his jaw with a satisfying crack, forcing him to stagger backward clutching it.

"C-considering my b-birth, that was expected of me," Emily managed to say. "And I did not seduce him, he dragged me in here, Mr. Whitlock."

"Have the Duke of Raven brought here at once!" Mr. Whitlock demanded, sending the footman who had obviously been lurking scurrying back out the door.

"I will of course wed her, I understand my duty," Mr. Jackson said again, glaring at Emily.

Emily struggled to draw in a breath and gather her shattered thoughts. She then heard the thud of feet; seconds later her brothers appeared.

"Emily!" They ran to her side, ignoring everyone in the room. James grabbed her and pulled her into his arms. She knew only relief to be held by him this way. To feel his strength. "What has happened?"

"M-Mr. J-Jackson…" was all she could manage.

"Eden heard you, but we could not find you," James whispered in her ear.

"Did you accost my sister, Jackson!" Max had summed up the situation with a look.

"She came with me willingly, Huntington. She only cried foul when Whitlock and his wife entered the room. Of course we will wed, as is expected, considering the circumstances. By the morning everyone will know what has transpired in this room."

She couldn't look at him, Mr. Jackson. Couldn't bear to see his smug face.

"Max, no!"

Emily heard Essie's cry, and looked up. Max was advancing on Jackson, fists raised.

"Let him do it!" James snarled, pulling Emily in closer. "And when he's finished I'll kill the bastard."

Max smashed a fist into his face. Jackson stumbled back, and in seconds James had released her and picked him up. Shaking him hard, he roared at him, "You are a liar, you sniveling rodent. My sister would never seduce you. She's kind and sweet, and would never sully herself with scum such as you!"

"Release him, James!" Devon Sinclair arrived with the rest of their family. "Now!"

Emily watched Dev prise Jackson from James's hands, and then thrust him at Mr. Whitlock.

"Remove him now, or he will be lucky to walk again."

"I demand retribution!" James roared.

"And you will have it, darling," Eden said. "But not here."

"I-I've offered to marry the girl," Mr. Jackson stuttered. "Surely you must want that, c-considering her birth."

Max growled softly, advancing on Jackson again. "You made the mistake in thinking we don't care about our sister, Jackson. Believe me when I tell you in that you are sadly mistaken."

Emily was shivering, her body wracked with shudders now as shock set in.

"B-but—"

"Remove him at once!"

Emily heard a scuffle of feet, as it was not often the Duke of Raven roared.

"Come, we will go home at once," James said, his arm around her shoulders now.

"Let me walk," Emily said. "I-I will not humiliate us further by being carried." Stepping away from him, she approached Essie. "Please fix my hair."

The women crowded around her, fussing, soothing, and trying to reassure her, but nothing could penetrate the ice that had taken up residence inside Emily.

"For God's sake, Emily, we care nothing for that," Max said.

"B-but I care."

"No, she is right in this, it is for the best. We must show solidarity," Lilly said, kissing Emily's cheek. Eden hugged her hard.

"She is not part of society—"

"Word travels, Dev, as you very well know."

She knew several looks were being shared, but Emily kept her eyes down and concentrated on not falling apart. She could do that later in her room, when no one was there to see.

"Chin up." James took her hand and placed it on his. "This is my realm, sister, follow my lead."

They walked out into the hall, and Emily did not make eye contact with anyone. Suddenly the hall was lined with several guests; no doubt they had already been informed of her disgrace.

"Duke, you have my sympathies," one woman twittered as they drew near.

"I have no idea what for, Lady Blythe."

"Oh well of course—"

James continued walking slowly, as if he had nothing better to do than stroll. Emily swallowed down the nausea.

"Not long now." James held an arm around her waist as they descended a set of stairs, and then finally they had reached the front of the house. Emily released a long shaky breath, as James's carriage was brought forward.

Emily was bundled inside with her brothers and Eden. Essie, Dev, and Lilly were behind.

"Tell us exactly what happened," James said in a voice that made Emily flinch.

"If you roar at your sister, she will say nothing," Eden said to her husband, who sat opposite Emily, looking like Lucifer.

"Tell us," he said more gently. "Please."

She tried, even opened her mouth, but all that came out was a sob. Dear Lord, it had happened. She had shamed her family, the one thing she had vowed never to do. It had not been her fault, she knew that, but still her shame was now theirs.

"I-I'm so s-sorry," she whispered before giving in to the hot scald of tears she had been holding inside. Max pulled her into his arms, and there she stayed, weeping pathetically until she reached James's house.

CHAPTER 23

*C*am walked slowly toward Max's house. His head hurt from last night's indulgence and as he'd not reached his bed until the ridiculously early hour of 4:00 a.m., fatigue was not helping matters.

He had introduced Wolf to his friends, and met some of his, and they had all gotten on exceedingly well... so well, the night had gone on a great deal longer than he'd planned.

After his argument with Emily, spending time with friends seemed a splendid way to rid his mind of her; however, to do that he'd drunk too much, and was now paying the price.

"I blame her," he muttered. In a roundabout way it was her fault, so he was happy to lay the blame squarely at her feet.

Yawning, he walked up to the front door of Max and Essie's house.

"Why," he wondered aloud, "am I awake at 9:00 a.m.?"

Something had roused him. Restlessness, a burning sensation in his chest, which of course could have been from overimbibing last night, but it had been accompanied by a foul smell. It wasn't fear; this was different. Unease, was all he could put it down to.

Knocking on the door, he hoped his sister was home. He wanted one of Essie's powders to make him feel better. His gentle sister would see him right.

"Mr. Sinclair."

"Good morning, George, is my sister at home?"

"She is, I shall tell her you have called, sir."

"Thank you. I will be horizontal on the nearest piece of furniture. If you could direct her to me, I would be grateful."

The man gave him a polished smile, as butlers were wont to do. "The Duke of Raven and Mr. Huntington are in the conservatory." He walked away at a sedate pace.

Cam wandered into the house yawning. Lord, he needed sleep. Maybe Essie could give him something to help with that also, and perhaps a cool compress for his head. He headed in the direction of the conservatory; he would say hello to his brothers-in-law, then find a corner to crawl into.

As Cam approached he heard raised male voices. Pushing open the door, he found the brothers roaring at each other like two bulls. James stood on one side of a row of plants, and Max on the other.

"What the hell are you two yelling about?"

He'd never seen them like this, not like Cam and Dev, who rarely let a day pass without roaring at each other. Not so Max and James; they discussed matters robustly but never with raised voices.

"Well?" Cam said, louder this time, then winced.

They turned as one, and levelled him with looks that would fell an oak. He'd never thought them the same in appearance, but the look they were sending him was identical.

"I have a sore head, so please keep your voices down," he said, strolling into the room.

"Go away," Max said, swinging back to look at his brother. "We have a problem that needs solving."

"Excellent, I quite excel at problem solving... or at least I will once I have one of Essie's potions to clear my head."

"We have no time for this, Cam. This is serious."

Max's words put Cam instantly on guard. If he said something was serious, then it usually was that and more so.

"What has happened?"

"Emily," James snarled.

"What about her?" The smell in his nostrils strengthened. Something was very wrong, and that it concerned Emily added to the scent.

"You haven't heard?"

Cam shook his head at Max.

"You have not seen your family?"

"I think that's fairly obvious considering I don't know what you are talking about. I rose early and came here to see Essie. As yet I have encountered no one, or eaten," he added, so Max would realize he needed to feed him.

James blew out a loud breath as he ran a hand through his hair in a very un-dukely way. His shoulders slumped.

"Tell me!" Cam demanded as the panic inside him grew.

"Emily was compromised by that soon-to-be-dead Jackson. Mr. Whitlock and his wife saw them together."

"What! How is that possible? What the hell were you two doing? How was she compromised?"

"In the worst possible way. He found her alone, told her he'd take her back to us, but dragged her into a parlor."

"You were meant to be there watching over her!"

"We could not follow her into the ladies' retiring room!" James snapped.

"I should have stayed."

"You could not have done more than us. James and I can care for our sister. According to that piece of scum Jackson, she accompanied him into the parlor willingly, and tried to seduce him."

"I hope you made him pay for that statement!" Rage coursed through Cam's veins.

Max's smile was not pleasant.

"We paid him a visit last night, but he is hiding from us somewhere. His detailed version of what took place came to us in a letter this morning. A letter that outlined his wish to marry her."

"No!"

"Yes, and Max is certain Jackson did this so he could marry into our family. Mine for the title and Max for his business contacts and wealth. He is shocked that we haven't simply conceded and agreed to the marriage, because he believes that to us, Emily is worthless."

Cam swore loudly.

"Yes." Max sighed. "I turned Jackson away when he tried to buy into a venture of mine. He's been trying ever since to insulate himself in my good graces, and sees Emily as his way to do that."

"Did he hurt her?" Cam's words were hoarse. The thought of Emily at the mercy of Jackson made him want to strike at something.

"No, she is unhurt physically, but I know she is hurting. I left the house before she rose, and did not discuss the matter fully last night as she was too upset to do so."

"Bastard!" Cam yelled. "I'll kill him."

"We are her brothers. If there is any maiming or killing it will be us to do so," Max stated grimly.

"The best course would be for her to marry."

"What?" Cam shook his head at James's words. "You would give your acceptance to a match between Emily and Jackson? Her life would be hell with him, especially as he attempted to abuse her just last night."

"No! Christ, Cam, how could you believe I'd consent to that? I have not slept with worry and my head is not sitting on my shoulders right this morning, but I would never allow such a man near my sister."

"In that I am relieved," Cam said.

"But I do believe marriage to the right man will be good for Emily, and make this business with Jackson go away."

Cam walked down a row to cool his spleen; coming back up the other side, he stood beside Max.

"And do you agree?"

"I do," Max said. "I have not lived in society, and so care very little for it or its rules, but it's my belief she will be happier married to someone she cares for. Emily says she has no wish to wed, but I believe she would be happier with her own family.

"No!" The thought of Emily married to someone made him go cold all over.

"You have no say in this, Sinclair."

"She will have a miserable life away from her family. For Christ's sake, James, I cannot believe you would sentence her to such purgatory."

"It will not be purgatory if the man she marries is someone she respects, and one day even loves."

"What man?"

"I don't know!" James glared at Cam. "We will need to give it some thought."

"I'll marry her." Cam cut James off.

He silenced them both with those words, and then wondered how the hell they had even found their way into his head, let alone out of his mouth. *Did I really just say that?*

"I beg your pardon?"

He looked across a large, leafy plant at James.

"I said I will marry her."

"What? Why?"

I don't know why. For some reason he had needed to speak the words. Perhaps he was still drunk?

Max, Cam noted, was staying silent. Glancing over, he wasn't sure he liked the knowing look in his brother-in-law's eyes.

"Because we will rub along all right, and I may as well marry her as anyone." He lifted a hand as the brothers prepared to geld him. "What I meant was, I like Emily, and we will learn to live together. She will have her freedom with me, and access to her family and mine."

"This is not a simple matter, Cam. I will not have Emily hurt, and you and she barely tolerate each other. If you wed, you will be exposed to each other constantly," James said.

Strangely the thought was not an unpleasant one, which surely it should be.

"I have offered. If you do not wish to take up my offer, and instead wish her to live out her days away from you with another, then so be it."

"You are not offering to take her to the park, Cam!" James snapped.

"I understand that, and do not treat me like a fool. I understand fully what I am suggesting, and as I have never wished to marry for love as others in my family have, then I will at least marry someone I can respect, and whose family I like... well, most of them," he added, glaring at the brothers.

"I say yes," Max said, finally entering the conversation.

"What?"

"James, we want her to wed because it will lessen the scandal, that much is clear. Why not have her do so to someone close to us? And of course there is also the matter that he is a Sinclair, so he will make sure she stays safe."

James moaned loudly. "That blasted curse."

"Exactly."

"My investigations have turned up nothing further about that incident with the carriage," James said.

"Mine either," Max added. "Which either means they are waiting for another time to grab her, or she was simply in the wrong place at the wrong time."

This time it was Cam who stayed silent. What the hell was he doing offering to marry Emily? Had he taken a knock to the head and not been aware of it? He had no wish to marry for many years yet.

"It is a very honorable, and selfless act, James, we should not lose sight of that fact. Cam will be giving up much also to wed our sister. There will be no more women in his future but Emily, because one thing I will not tolerate is you having dalliances."

Cam was subjected to a look from both brothers. He withstood it.

Dear Christ. Was he ready for that? With Emily of all people, but something held him silent. Something told him to do this. Perhaps he was losing his sanity.

"He has money of his own now, and a town house, on the same street so we can watch over him—"

"I am not an infant," Cam protested, "and quite capable of caring for my wife should I acquire one."

"We cannot make this decision without first discussing the matter with Emily, and you need to also discuss the matter with your family, Cam. Only then will we agree," James said.

Cam managed a nod, then left the house without a powder for his headache, as right at that moment that was the least of his problems. He'd intended to head for his brother's, but instead he found himself turning the other way.

CHAPTER 24

*C*am walked a while, hoping the cool air would be bracing and clear his head. He had now committed to marrying Emily. Her brothers had heard him say the words, therefore he could not go back now. Did he want to?

The thought of a life with Emily was not an unpleasant one, if he was being totally honest. He liked her, for all they argued constantly. Could they be together until death do them part? Have children and raise them? The thought was a sobering one.

Cam had never believed himself someone who would fall deeply in love, which suggested he could marry Emily, as they did not and were not likely to ever enjoy a great passion... or were they? Something had definitely been growing inside him since that day she was abducted. An awareness of her that had strengthened. He'd also kissed her and enjoyed the experience hugely.

"But how do you feel about taking her to your bed?" he muttered. He found he liked the idea, although he wasn't sure she felt the same way. In fact, he was fairly certain Emily would rebel against all advances.

As he was passing the Raven townhouse, he glanced to the entrance and saw a young boy lurking there.

"Can I help you?"

He leapt at least a foot in the air.

"Apologies," Cam said, to which the now wide-eyed boy nodded. "Can I help you?"

"I'm to deliver a note to the household of the Duke of Raven?"

Small and narrow faced, he looked like any number of young boys running about London streets on any given day.

"To whom in the household?"

Directness, Cam found, was the best way to deal with children. Subtleties and indirect speech rarely worked. Children had not yet become jaded like adults.

The boy's eyes shot left and right. Cam's did the same, but he saw nothing but houses, a tree or two, and a street.

"Who?" he said again, this time louder.

"I have a note."

"How fortuitous. Do you care to tell me who it is for?"

"I'm meant to deliver it into her hands, 'cause it's important."

Cam knew any number of "hers," especially on this particular street.

"I shall see she gets it then."

The boy's fringe stood out from his forehead like a platform, suggesting he'd slept facedown in his bed last night.

"Begging your pardon, but you don't know who it's for."

"You're about to tell me that."

"Am I?"

Cam nodded patiently. When the boy showed no signs of giving him what he wanted, he took two coins from his pocket.

"It's Miss Tolly."

"Excellent, and I shall see Miss Tolly gets the missive you are clutching in your hand."

The boy thrust it at him, took the coins, and ran off down the street with that inexhaustible energy children tended to have. His eyes followed the lad until he disappeared.

Emily has a note. Looking at the crisp white square of paper in his hand, with her name inked in black, he wondered what it said and whom it was from. Turning it over, he found no seal. Could it be from Jackson? She wasn't exactly inundated with friends or acquaintances, he knew this. Nor had he ever seen her leave the house to visit someone unless it was with Samantha or one of the members of their families. Although that wasn't exactly true, as he'd seen her alone twice. At *The Trumpeter* and Mr. Fossett's lecture.

The front door to the Raven townhouse opened, and suddenly there she was, looking... rumpled was the only word he could come up with.

Emily's hair was tied in a bow at the back, and the tail reached her waist. She wore a coat hastily pulled on and he thought the buttons were not done up correctly, but couldn't be sure from this distance. Cam couldn't remember a time when Emily had been rumpled. He found he quite liked the look on her. In her arms was Whiskers, Samantha's little dog.

Cam stepped back a few paces, putting himself behind a pillar, and wasn't entirely sure why.

"Now, you little fiend, I am lowering you to the patch of grass and you will do what you must, then we will return inside to whence we came."

She put action to her words, and the little dog sniffed in circles one way, and then the other.

"Now, Whiskers, as I have no time for your theatrics. Today will be a trying one for everyone, and I have no wish for you to make matters worse. So get about your business."

The dog ignored her and sniffed some more around her feet.

"I have brought you out here to do your business, but next time I am taking you into the rear garden and leaving you there. I'm not entirely sure why this is the only patch you wish to frequent."

The little dog sat and looked up at her, one ear falling forward, the other back.

"Please, Whiskers, I need to go to my room and prepare for my talk with James and Max."

Her voice sounded husky, as if she had been crying a great deal. Cam felt it again, that dull ache in his chest at the thought of her hurting.

"All right. I will do it, but next time you are on your own!"

Cam swallowed his snort of laughter as she started to whistle. To his surprise the dog made for the small circle of grass and squatted, and did as he was supposed to.

"Good boy."

Cam heard the yowl of a cat and watched a bristling feline stalk into view at the exact time Whiskers saw it.

"Whiskers, come here!"

Of course the creature ignored Emily and eyed the cat, creeping slowly forward.

"Come here, Whiskers!"

Disaster struck as the cat ran and the dog followed.

"Whiskers!" Emily shrieked the dog's name and then suddenly she was running. "Stop, you little fiend!"

Cam followed her out the gate, jogging now, as she sprinted across the road before him. The little dog was like a white streak, ears back, body streamlined as he chased the cat, who was now nowhere in sight.

By the time they reached the park, Emily had her skirts in both hands, and Cam was able to glimpse her slender ankles, clad in thick woolen stockings. He lost her briefly as she ducked behind a bush. Reaching her seconds later, he found her on her belly, half under the bush.

"It's freezing, you horrid little beast. Come out here, or I will feed you to a pack of wild dogs," she muttered, wriggling.

Her bottom was nicely rounded, legs long and slender. Cam was now the fiend as he stood watching with Emily unaware that he was doing so.

"Whiskers, come here at once! You are a heathen. I should just leave you out here lost and alone!"

"Such venom, Emily. Poor little Whiskers, surely he does not deserve such a fate?"

Her body stilled, half under the bush.

"May I be of assistance?"

The body did not move.

"I can see you, Emily, so unless you are going in further, you really must come out, as it's brisk, and the ground damp. I suggest you rise at once before you become ill."

"Go away." Her words were muffled.

"I think not."

Cam bent and gripped her trim waist, lifting her out, then placing her back on her feet.

Her hair now held twigs and leaves, and her coat was covered in damp grass. She was stunning, Cam realized, and needed no embellishment to achieve what many sought. Seeing her standing there with the trees at her back gave him a jolt. Completely natural, with no artifice, she was breath-taking. He wondered again how he had not noticed this about her sooner. Her eyes, however, those were weary and red-rimmed, with dark smudges beneath. She looked like a woman who had slept little, and wept a great deal.

Can I marry her?

Running his eyes over her he thought the answer was yes, and not just because she was lovely to look at. No, there was also the matter of her making him feel alive. She challenged him constantly, and also enjoyed astronomy. *The Trumpeter* was something else they shared. Perhaps they could make a marriage work; the only drawback would be in getting her to agree.

CHAPTER 25

*E*mily knew Cam had not been there to witness her disgrace last night, as he'd left the gathering early, but she wondered if the news had reached him this morning.

"Good morning, Emily."

"Good morning, Cambridge."

"Cam will do."

"You do not like your name?"

He shrugged, his wide shoulders rising and falling under the material of his black jacket. His complexion was pale out here in the weak morning light, and although he was still ridiculously handsome, she thought he looked not his usual self.

"I do not know many people with such a name, and I suppose that is a benefit, but it would not have been my choice, were I allowed a say in the matter."

"Do all your siblings feel that way?"

Her life had turned on its head once more, and she was standing here talking to him about his name. She wanted that, wanted to continue to put off what she knew awaited her back inside the Raven townhouse.

No one had spoken of the matter last night, as she had been too distressed, but Emily knew the reprieve was only a short one. She had been ruined irreparably, and while she did not walk in society, her brother most definitely did, and he was a duke. There would be consequences, she was just not sure as yet what they would be.

"Most, but we are quite happy with the abbreviations."

He gave her a gentle smile, and she searched the Sinclair green eyes, but they gave nothing away.

"How did your parents come up with those names, if you don't mind me asking?"

"I can't believe you have not asked anyone before."

"It was rude to do so."

"Lord yes, we would not want you being rude."

"Manners are not something to be ashamed of," Emily snapped. "You should try using yours occasionally."

"I shall give it some thought," he drawled. "The truth is that we were conceived in those places, and named accordingly. Only Eden was born at home, and our mother believed Oaks Knoll to be the Garden of Eden, hence her name."

"Oh... ah, I see. Forgive me for prying."

"I am not embarrassed by it, Emily, and you did ask."

"Are you unwell?" He really did look it, there was almost a green tinge to his skin now. She did not like to think of him suffering.

"No, I simply overindulged last night, and am now paying the price."

"Then your pain is thoroughly deserved." Emily wasn't sure why, but the thought of him enjoying himself while she was being compromised by Mr. Jackson annoyed her immensely.

Had he stayed at the ball, perhaps it would not have happened.

No, there was nothing even Cam could have done about what occurred. Had Mr. Jackson not forced himself upon her then, there would certainly have been another time when he did so.

"That's extremely heartless of you." He looked down. "Your little fiend has returned."

Emily found Whiskers sitting on her feet.

"You horrid little beast!"

"Surely not. Look, he is quite obedient. His business is done, and now he is ready to go home."

"He is a naughty boy."

Emily scooped up the dog and held him close. His little body quivered from the exercise, and he licked her hand. She patted his head. No one could stay angry with Whiskers for long, except maybe James.

"Well I must get back then."

"I know about last night, Emily."

Her heart missed a beat. "I have no wish to discuss this with you." Turning away, she started walking back to the house.

"Jackson will be dealt with."

"I want no retribution. It is done, and there is nothing that can change that."

"I spoke with your brothers."

Emily didn't know how to answer that, so she kept silent.

"They are deciding what the best course of action is, but we shall discuss that further when we return to the house."

"*We* shall not discuss anything. This is not your problem, Cam, it is mine."

"We are all involved, that is how families work. But for now let's leave it until you speak with your brothers. I have a letter for you. I intercepted it just moments before Whiskers make his escape."

"From whom?"

"A young lad who was lurking around the front door, he

was tasked with putting it in your hands, so I offered to do so."

Emily looked at the note he held with dread. She never got letters, or correspondence from anyone. Who would have sent her that? Surely not Mr. Jackson?

"Shall I open it for you?"

"No thank you." She took it, and pushed it into the pocket of her coat. "I am perfectly capable of doing so."

"You do not wish to read it now?"

"No."

"Yes."

"Pardon?" She looked up at him. His hair was messy, eyes squinty, almost as if the dull light hurt them.

"Emily, you do not know many people in London, so chances are that note is from Jackson. I want to know if it is."

"I will tell James or Max if that is the case."

He wasn't happy with that, but said nothing further. Instead, taking Whiskers from her, he then took her arm, and soon they were walking silently back to the house.

James was waiting for her as she entered.

"There appears to be a duke lurking in the front entrance, Emily," Cam said to alleviate the tension that was thick in the air.

"Come to my study please, Emily. You too, Cam."

"But James, why is Cam required?" Emily said as she took off her coat.

"All will be explained shortly."

"Very well. I shall change first."

"It is only family, and while I am curious as to why you have half the park on you, that can wait. Come along now."

Devon, Eden, and Max awaited her inside the room, which surprised her further.

"Hello, darling." Eden came forward and gave her a hug. It

was like all of Eden's hugs, all-encompassing. "Come and sit now, and we shall discuss this horrid business."

She did, sitting beside her sister-in-law and Dev, who gave her a gentle smile.

"I'm sorry, Em. Sorry that bastard hurt you."

"Thank you for your support," she said, swallowing down the tears.

"Before you tell us what happened, Em, I want you to know that in no way are you to blame for Jackson's actions. The blame for last night lay solely with him," Max said.

He sat on the edge of James's desk. Big and intimidating, and yet they all knew now he was anything but with the people he included in his circle. It humbled Emily that she was one of them.

"It's my belief Jackson took the actions he did because he wanted to infiltrate himself into this family, and I'm sorry he used you to do so. What he failed to understand, however, is that we love you, and will protect you no matter what it takes."

"He told me that due to my birth, you would be pleased to be rid of me." She looked from Max to James.

"He was wrong. Now, do you feel able to talk about it, Emily?"

She nodded at James's words, then looked around her.

"Whatever is spoken in here will go no further, Emily. But in order for us to best handle the situation the Sinclairs will need to be involved. They will hear, and as family, I would rather they heard the truth."

"Of course." Emily understood James's words, even if she felt ashamed of what she was to say. "But you know most of it now anyway."

"We do, but I would like you to repeat it once more," Max said.

"Mr. Jackson found me walking along a hallway. He said

he'd accompany me back to where you were. He opened a door and forced me inside, his reason being that he wanted to discuss his interest in me. He then offered for me. I declined. When I said I did not return his interest he began to behave inappropriately, and when I told him to stop, he refused... he was persistent, and then became forceful. He tried... to...." She couldn't say the words, not in front of everyone. "I tried to stop him, but he did not do so until those people arrived. He then accused me of luring him there, and stated he would marry me to save my reputation. You know the rest." Her brothers looked thunderous.

"Bastard!" Cam hissed.

She looked at him standing behind James. His face was clenched in anger, body stiff.

"His words were the truth in part."

"Pardon?" James said.

"I am the bastard daughter of a duke, and nothing will change that. I will always be subjected to such behavior, it is the way of things."

"Have there been many who insulted you?" James demanded.

"A few, but I have not spent a great deal of time socializing and so have not encountered many people."

"Why did you not say something? Have visitors here insulted you?"

"James, please, this is not your fault. It did not happen often, and never when you or one of the family were close, even Max, as he is accepted because of his power."

"I'm sorry, I should have known."

"How? I did not tell you?"

"Still—"

"Still nothing. I am strong enough to cope with a few words, James."

His smile was small. "Yes, you are."

"Jackson is telling all who will listen that even though you seduced him, he is willing to marry you," Max said. "This I know as Edward called just minutes before I left the house, and told me what he had heard. I'm sorry, Emily."

"News travels fast in London," she said.

"James thinks that marriage—"

"I will not marry him!"

"I would never make you do as you do not wish, Emily. I hope you know that. I would also never agree to a match between you and that reptile Jackson. But should you find someone you respect and care for, then—"

"Thank you, James, but my decision is made. I will never marry."

"There is another suitor to consider who you may find favor with," Cam said, entering the conversation.

"Who?" She looked at him.

"Me."

CHAPTER 26

The silence in the room was deafening. No one moved, or it seemed, breathed.

"I—pardon?"

"Marry me." Cam had come around to the idea of marriage to Emily now, and believed it would benefit them both. It was not something he'd planned, and definitely not with a prickly person like her, but at least they knew each other, and he would not be expected to put up with awkward and demanding in-laws, as he already knew them... especially the awkward ones. He would not need to court anyone, or play the pretty with her parents and friends. It was the best course and they would rub along he was sure. There was also the matter of finding himself thinking about her more and more... especially kissing those soft lips.

"Have you gone mad?" Emily looked at him like he had an eye in the middle of his forehead and a set of pointy fangs. "We do not even like each other, why would we marry?"

"My thoughts exactly," Dev said in a terse tone. "And I would have appreciated a little forewarning. I swear my heart just stopped."

"You told us you were going to speak with Dev," Max accused him.

"I got waylaid," Cam kept his eyes on Emily.

"I like the idea," Eden added.

"Me too," Max agreed.

"No!" Emily got to her feet, eyes wide with horror. "Is this some kind of game to you?"

She delivered the words to Cam while backing toward the door. He followed, determined to get her to see reason. Behind him, the others were, for once, staying silent.

"No game. I have to marry at some stage, and it may as well be to you, a bloody Raven. After all, it seems I'm destined to wed one of you, and I'd rather not wait for another one to do something reckless and need saving."

"You're mad, and wh-what's more, I would never accept you... especially not because I'm a bloody Raven!"

Emily was now pressed to the door, eyes wide, hands clenched before her, looking at him as if she'd never seen him before.

"No, I'm perfectly sane, and I'm sorry if my words upset you, but I've always believed we spoke the truth to each other."

Her disbelief was obvious.

"You cannot be serious?"

He grabbed her arms as she tried to turn and reach for the door handle.

"Totally. I have given the matter some thought, and believe it is the best course of action."

"W-well it is not the best course of action for me!"

"Come and sit down, Emily, so we can discuss the matter." He heard Eden's words. "My brother is handling the situation like a bumblehead."

"I-I don't want to sit down, and surely you can all see this is a foolish idea!"

"It is not foolish," Cam said calmly. "Most women would be happy to be wed to me—"

"Shut up you fool," one of his sisters moaned.

"I'm not most women! Dear Lord, have you taken leave of your senses? I'm a baseborn daughter of a duke who has never stepped foot in society. Do you wish to give all that up?"

"You will enter society at my side, just as Max attends functions with Essie, so stop throwing your birth about the place as an excuse for everything."

Her head shook furiously.

"No... absolutely not!" She looked around him to find Max. "Have Essie make him something, I'm sure insanity has taken hold."

"I'm perfectly sane, thank you. And as I have explained, it seems I must marry a Raven, so why not you?" He heard another groan, this time from his brother.

Cam pulled her off the door, and then placed a hand on her stiff spine, nudging her back to the seat.

"How long has this idea been inside your head?" Dev said, but he no longer looked shocked. In fact he appeared relieved, which Cam thought odd.

"I thought of it this morning when I encountered Max and James discussing what happened last night."

"No!" Emily did a neat little spin and then ran for the door. "You are all foolish to believe we could ever be married."

She wrenched the door open and ran from the room.

"That went well," Dev said.

"Cam, you are a fool," Eden said. "You handled that entire situation badly."

"I was truthful!"

"No woman wants to hear a man is marrying her in such a way, even if it is truthful."

Dev held up a hand as Cam prepared to launch a verbal attack on his sister.

"While I am not displeased by the idea, given what has been occurring between you lately, there is the small matter that you and Emily cannot be in the same room together without fighting. My fear is that we would wake one morning to news in *The Trumpeter* that you had disposed of each other in a bloody battle over the dinner table."

"I have no wish to marry for love." Cam scowled at Eden. "Indeed I have made that quite clear. So why not marry Emily? It would save her reputation, and as I have just explained it's likely I will end up with a Raven if history is any indication, so better one I already know, and I have already saved."

"God's blood, Sinclair, we are discussing the future of my sister!"

"Do you think I take this matter lightly, James?" Cam looked at his brother-in-law. "That I do not see the gravity of the situation? Indeed, when I first offered this morning, it was an impulse, but I have since given it serious thought, and believe marrying Emily is the best course of action. I will give her my name and protection."

James put his head in his hands and Max began to pace the room. Eden rose and approached Cam.

"What now?" he snapped at her.

"You are a very noble man, brother. I love you."

He grunted something, not entirely comfortable with her words, as no man would be, and hugged her back.

"But you still could have handled this better."

"She will need to agree," Max said. "We will not force her to marry you."

"Of course."

"You are sacrificing any chance of a love like we, your family have, Cam. Are you happy to do that?"

"I think they will love," Eden said softly. "Just as we do, James."

"You can stop those fanciful notions right now, sister. I have no wish to love as you do. And if I may remind you again, I have no wish for the messy emotions accompanying that state. I will add to that, marrying someone I know will be a great deal easier than someone I do not. Plus, Emily knows about us, even if she has never outright said anything. She has observed and is an intelligent woman."

"You will be loyal to her."

Cam held Max's eyes.

"I believe in the sanctity of marriage. I will not stray, as she will not."

"I can't believe we are actually contemplating this," Dev said, impaling Cam with a fierce green look. "You know it is my belief we wed for love... and that our colors must match anyone we choose to live our lives with?"

"What color is she?" Cam made himself ask. His brother's smile was small, but a smile nonetheless.

"A very pretty shade of orange."

"Is Cam the same?" Max asked.

"He is."

James and Max looked relieved, as both held a great deal of stock in Dev's belief that no one should marry unless their mate was a color match.

"She would be safe with him," Max mused. "There is that thing they all have."

"It is not a thing," Eden said calmly. "It is a sense, and may I remind you, it saved your life, Max."

He looked rueful. "How could I forget."

"There are many positive factors to this situation," James said. "And if he misbehaves we can thrash him."

"You could try," Cam said, glaring at the duke.

"Christ," Max hissed. "It is almost more than I can take in. Cam married, but more importantly, to Emily."

"She must agree," James added. "It will not happen if she does not."

"Jackson needs to pay for what he has done to this family," Dev growled. "And pay dearly."

"He will. I discussed the matter with Edward, he is going to find every secret and dealing the man has with anyone. I want to crucify him. But it will not be enough to do so physically. I want him to suffer in every way, and the first part of that plan is take away what he loves: money. If we can break him, I will force him to state he dragged my sister into that room with the intention of ruining her."

"We have to find him first," James added.

"And then?" Cam said.

"Then what is left of him will be put on a boat somewhere. We are just not sure as yet where."

Cam nodded. Jackson would pay, her brothers would make sure of it. But so would he, because Cam would track the bastard down, and make it so.

CHAPTER 27

"We are to go out, Emily, and would like you to come with us. We are visiting Lord and Lady Cindery, and you like them."

"I will stay home, but thank you, James."

Her brother frowned.

"You cannot stay inside this house indefinitely, Emily. The Cinderys will not mention the incident with Jackson, and are lovely people."

"I know they are, but I wish to stay home, thank you."

"You won't talk to anyone, and constantly hide in your room. Samantha is the only one you spend time with. Surely you do not wish to live your life in such a way?"

"Let me go to Raven Castle, and then you will no longer have to worry about me, and everything will return to the way it was."

"I will always worry about you," he said quietly, his voice deadly serious. "And I have no wish to send you away from us."

"But surely it is the best for everyone." Emily tried to make him see reason. "I like Raven Castle."

"The same castle you told Eden was chilly even on a warm day? The castle you said echoed with the ghosts of my ancestors?"

She had said that. However, it had been on a particularly cold day, and the castle had seemed a dreary place.

"Oh, but if I am there constantly I will—"

"I am not discussing this now." James raised a hand. "Eden is awaiting me with Samantha and Isabella downstairs. I would ask that you do not leave the house until I return."

"I will not leave, I promise, but please just think about me going to Raven Castle, James."

"You will be isolated there, and alone. Is that what you really wish?"

The thought made her heart weep. To not see those she now loved would be devastating.

"I will see you all when you return."

"And then we will leave again. We are a family, and have no wish for you to be away from us."

"Oh." Emily sniffed. "Thank you."

"Emily." James sighed. "I had thought things between us were improving, but since Cam's proposal they have regressed. When will you understand that I love you no matter how you feel about me—"

"Oh... really?"

"Really, why is that so hard to believe?"

She had to tell him the truth, she owed him that much. She could not fix everything but perhaps in this she could do what was right and stop hiding behind her fears. "I do care for you, James, very much."

Her words surprised him, and that shamed her. She had withdrawn into herself since the incident with Mr. Jackson. Shame had forced her back into hiding, and that was wrong. She'd vowed to be stronger, vowed to be part of this family, and she'd failed once again. It had to stop; at least in this she had to try harder.

"I'm sorry if you believed otherwise, James. It was never my intention to hurt you. In fact, I love you as you do me," Emily added softly. Because she did love him, and it was wrong not to say so. This man had done so much for her and she had repaid him by hiding her true self.

"Really?"

"Really, and it was wrong of me not to show you that after what you have done for me."

"I had thought your actions were because of our father," he said. "That I am a duke, and therefore—"

"No!" Oh how wrong she had been to not speak out sooner. He had carried this belief with him, and it could not be further from the truth.

"My shame kept me distant from you, James. My brother's actions, and my birth. It was never you."

He folded her gently into his arms.

"No, never could I think that way. You are one of my miracles, Emily. The sibling I always hoped for, but never believed I would have. You, Samantha, and Max complete me. I would never blame you for your brother, or your birth, as I realize now you would not blame me for my father."

"I'm sorry, James, I should have spoken sooner. It was just so hard to adjust to this life, so hard to try and fit in when I had lived so differently. I did not want to make a misstep."

He held her arms, placing a soft kiss on her forehead.

"I constantly make missteps, but having my family at my back makes me stronger, and able to cope. Use our strength, Emily, because we are at your back too."

She managed a nod, but could find no words around the lump in her throat.

"And now I must go, as my daughter is likely wailing

loudly, and my wife will not be pleased if we are late. But always remember that I love you very much, and you are a part of me, Emily."

"Thank you," Emily whispered.

"The rest we will talk about later, but for now know you always have a home here with us, no matter what future choices you make."

He kissed her cheek, and hugged her close briefly. Emily found herself holding him tight, and then he was gone, leaving her alone, as she would be if she went to Raven Castle.

Her heart felt lighter, and yet there was still the shadow hanging over her of what to do. Emily decided on a walk in the gardens to clear her head. Surely that was permitted? Pulling on her coat, she patted the pockets searching for gloves, and heard a rustle.

Pulling out the note Cambridge had given her, she realized it had been in there since the day he offered to marry her. She quickly read the words. Excitement raced through her, chasing away all other thoughts… well perhaps not all. Cam was constantly inside her head. She read it again.

Miss Tolly,

I was extremely interested in your paper. It was well written and researched. Of course I knew all it contained, as I have studied the subject of astronomy for many years. However, I am having a private viewing of my Reflective Telescope on the third Tuesday of the month, and would like to extend you an invitation to come along. I shall expect you at midday.

It was signed Mr. Fossett, and the third Tuesday of the month was today.

"Oh, I must see it!" Emily clutched the letter to her chest. To look through a reflective telescope was something she had never thought she would do.

"But how can I?" she whispered as the memory of James's words quelled her excitement. If she left the house, her family would be furious. "Think, Emily."

Dressing in her bonnet and gloves, she wrapped a scarf around her neck and went to find the butler.

"Buttles, is there a carriage available?" She found him reading in his small office.

"You should have rung for me, Miss Tolly," he said, hurrying to his feet.

"My legs work perfectly well, Buttles. Now, is there a carriage that I could use?"

"No, Miss Tolly."

"I have a need to go somewhere at once, indeed it is quite urgent."

The man gave her a steady look; like all servants, he was fully abreast of what was what in the household, and in his case more so.

"I'm sorry, Miss Tolly, but the weather is deteriorating, and I'm sure you would be better advised staying inside."

Had James told him she was not to leave? Thoughts churned furiously inside her head as she tried to come up with a plan.

"I wish to have a footman and my maid accompany me, Buttles. I will leave the house shortly."

"Can I advise his grace of your destination should he return before you, Miss Tolly?"

"I am to walk to Mr. Huntington's." Emily had to stand firm, or the man would convince her to stay. But if Max was home, he would take her where she wanted to go, and James would surely be happy with that?

"Of course, please excuse me."

Hurrying to the front entrance, Emily waited. Tapping her foot, she realized there were only two hours left to get to

Cribridge House, which she believed was at least an hour's drive from London. It would likely take longer in these conditions, so she must make a move soon.

With John the footman and Belinda, she hurried out the door that Buttles held open minutes later.

"Good day, Buttles. I shall be all right." She patted his hand, as a line of worry had formed on his forehead. "If my brother should return before me, tell him I am with... my other brother."

Now she had cleared the air with James, she felt freer somehow, even though this business with Jackson and Cam's proposal still hung over her. It was one less burden to shoulder.

Knocking on Max's front door yielded her nothing, as she was notified by his butler that the entire household was out. She then walked to Lord Sinclair's next. Perhaps Lilly would accompany her? No one was home there either.

"Why is everyone out on such a day?" Emily looked skyward. It was gray and cold, with the promise of snow. Surely the best place to be was home?

Should she just get into a hackney? Would her brothers ever let her leave the house again if she did so?

Without realizing it Emily's feet had begun walking once more, and soon she was standing before the Earl and Countess of Wynburg's house. Lady Wynburg was aunt to the Sinclair family and had often enjoyed discussing astronomy with Emily. Perhaps she would like to accompany her? James and Max would not be angry then, surely?

Five minutes later she was back out on the street. They were not home either.

I am doomed. She looked skyward; had a snowflake just settled on her nose? The weather was deteriorating. With a sigh, Emily thought about just turning around and walking home. It was only a telescope; surely one day she would be presented with another opportunity to see through one?

"But I want to see it."

"What?"

Dear Lord, why did it have to be him of all people?

CHAPTER 28

*E*mily faced Cambridge Sinclair. He was only a few feet away, but she had not heard him approach. He, however, had heard her words.

He looked large and intimidating dressed in a black hat, heavy black greatcoat into which was tucked a tan woolen scarf, and black hessians. His hands were encased in tan gloves, and she realized that when he was not surrounded by Devon, Max, and James, he was actually a large, intimidating man. The man who wished to marry her.

She'd avoided him for days, and now suddenly here he was. Her tongue felt as if it was stuck to the roof of her mouth as she looked at him. He had such a presence about him, such a charisma that it almost took her breath away.

"Hello."

"Hello," Emily said, digging her toes into the soles of her leather boots. She felt awkward seeing him. When last they met, he had asked her to marry him. Actually, what he had said was he needed to marry at some stage in his life, and as history suggested it would be to a Raven, it may as well be her.

"What has you out in this weather, alone?" His tone was polite.

"I have a maid and a footman with me," Emily said quickly, shooting a look over her shoulder at the servants who were standing several feet behind her trying to appear inconspicuous. "I would never leave the house alone."

"My mind is at ease."

It didn't look at ease, Emily thought. In fact, he looked angry.

"It was reckless of you to leave the house at all, Emily."

Emily bit back the words she wanted to say. Right at that moment retreat was her best option. It seemed likely that she would not be looking through Mr. Fossett's reflective telescope today.

"Good day to you. I shall return to my house."

"But why have you left it?"

He stepped closer, and suddenly something dangerous hung in the air between them, more dangerous than that little charge of excitement she'd previously felt.

"Perhaps you have come to accept my offer?"

"No, I have not, and you very well know it is not the right thing for either of us. I want to go to Raven Castle, but at the moment, James is not allowing that to happen." Emily blurted the words.

"You would rather live in that ancient, freezing pile of stones and walk the halls filled with your ancestors' ghosts than stay here with your family and marry me?"

"I—yes" was all she could come up with. "But James will not let me," she said again. Excellent, now she was rambling.

"As he should not."

"Why... no, I have no wish to discuss that now. I will return to the house."

"Emily, I believe I have told you before that I am no fool. Something has you outside in these frigid conditions without a family member at your side. Something important enough to have you defying your brothers. I would like to know what that something is."

Would he help her? She shot him a look. He did enjoy Astronomy also, so perhaps for this brief moment they could put everything else aside and call a truce. Did she dare ask him?

"I am waiting, Emily."

Emily swallowed her response to those arrogant words.

"It's cold and your nose is turning red, which is not flattering on anyone."

She refused to cup the appendage.

"I need to ask a favor of you." The words tumbled out before she could stop them.

His smile was slow, but it eventually reached his eyes, making them come alive.

"Oh, now this I cannot wait to hear."

"If there was another option I would take it."

"Of that I have no doubt."

"It is just that I don't... have another option, that is."

"And this is important to you, whatever it is?"

"Yes, very important."

"Well then, you better tell me what it is before we both turn into ice sculptures."

It was cold, Emily realized, now she'd stopped moving.

"I received a note—"

"The one I handed you?"

"Yes, and I only read it today—"

"Why did you leave it so long?"

"Because I forgot it was in my coat pocket due to this other business."

"You being ruined, and me proposing?"

She nodded. It was so like Cam to speak bluntly.

"Well then, what did the note say?"

"Here." She pulled it from her pocket and thrust it at him. "It is simply better that you read it for yourself."

He held her eyes briefly before taking the paper. Emily stood in tense silence while he read the words.

"How exciting for you."

"I thought so."

"You do realize this is today?"

"Of course I realize that, hence I am now out here with a maid and footman standing before you!" Emily took a deep breath to calm down.

"Ah, I begin to see now what has transpired," Cam said. "James and his family are out, as are the Huntingtons and I suspect every member of my family also?"

"Yes."

"You were that desperate you even approached my aunt and uncle?"

"Your aunt likes astronomy," Emily said in her defense. She absolutely would not shuffle her feet.

"She does, and it shows your desperation that you left the house for this, when over the last few days you have not spoken to anyone... even your family, and absolutely not me."

"I have so spoken to people."

"No, you have not."

She reached for the note, intending to snatch it back and return to her house. She would find some other way to get there. He lifted it high, out of her reach.

"But what of your poor head? Surely it is not faring well out in this cold? And your chill; should you not be in bed resting? And lastly, let us not forget your unsettled stomach."

He was mocking her now.

"Would you rather I'd just said I had no wish to see you?"

"I always prefer the truth to lies, Emily."

Emily wasn't sure how to answer that so she huffed out a breath.

"Do you wish for me to take you to see Fossett's reflective telescope?"

"I...." Emily swallowed down the resentment.

"Say the words, Emily."

"I do, because if I took a hackney, my family would be most displeased."

"At least in this you displayed a modicum of sense."

"Give me my note!" Emily jumped in the air and tried to grab it; he simply lifted his arm higher.

"Ask nicely and I will take you to see your charming Mr. Fossett."

His green eyes were now filled with wicked humor. Emily swallowed several times and forced a sickly smile onto her lips. She could do this to see through that telescope. A few hours, perhaps less, was all the time she would need to spend in his company.

"Please take me to see Mr. Fossett's telescope."

"That smile would scare children."

"Cam!"

He laughed. "All right. Send your servants away, and accompany me inside my house, and I shall have my carriage brought around."

"Oh, but I should take my maid."

"For propriety's sake?"

He had a point, damn him. She was already ruined, it would not matter if she accompanied him.

"We are not to discuss that other matter," she said, unmoving. That must be cleared up before they entered his carriage.

"I'm doing you a favor, so you don't get to tell me what we can speak of, Emily."

Drat.

CHAPTER 29

*C*am bundled Emily into his carriage and took the seat opposite. Her eyes, of course, were focused out the window. To say he was surprised to see her on his uncle's doorstep was an understatement, but it had been a pleasant one, as had the jolt of awareness.

"Are you cold?"

"No, I am fine, thank you."

He doubted she would be a demanding wife, but he also wasn't entirely sure any of them knew who the real Emily Tolly was. Cam doubted she'd ever really shown her true self.

He let the carriage travel out of their street and through London before he spoke again.

"One thing James will never tell you, Emily, is that your disgrace will touch Samantha and Isabella."

"Pardon?"

Her eyes were locked on his now; suddenly he had all her attention.

"Your actions will affect your family."

"I am an illegitimate daughter of a duke, I'm sure that

alone brings shame with it, and surely by the time Samantha and Isabella enter society they will have forgotten me."

"Perhaps."

"But perhaps not?"

He could see his words had her worried.

"Would you have them subjected to the whispers and snide comments I now suspect you have suffered?"

"I have not been in society to suffer these supposed comments."

Those lovely lips were pursed in a tight circle now. She wore a deep sable gray coat today that came to her ankles and buttoned to her neck. Inside was tucked a cream scarf and on her head a matching gray bonnet with black trim. She looked like any lady he would see on any given day... and yet she was so much more to Cam.

"You have been to several of those occasions with James or Max. Social events with industrialists and a few peers."

She nodded, wary now.

"Have people insulted you at these functions, Emily?"

"I don't want to marry."

Not precisely an answer, but telling nonetheless.

"I don't either, but at least if we marry each other, then we can live our lives as we choose."

"What do you mean?"

Cam had given the matter of how to get her to agree to marry him a great deal of thought. His life need not change overly, other than he would be sharing a house with this woman, and perhaps she would have more freedom carrying his name.

"You will be able to share the paper with me, Emily. As part owner you will have a say in its running."

"I— You would make me a part owner?"

"Of course, you will be my wife."

"But...." Her words fell away.

"Did you think I would be a controlling husband?"

She didn't answer, but her silence was confirmation enough.

"I will not, and if you marry me it will go easier on them, your family. James will not say this, but your disgrace will always be there, even though you are completely innocent of any wrongdoing and your brother is a duke." Cam wasn't sure this was true, strictly speaking, but he was using it to strengthen his case anyway.

"Plus, if you become my wife, you will have your own household to run, and will not be reliant on anyone for your care into your old age."

"Yes I will: you. I am not a fool, Cambridge, I know that a man often thinks of his wife as chattel. I know men can be cruel and get away with it, just as I know women are rarely able to fight back."

Who hurt her? He wanted to ask the question, but knew she would not give him an answer. One day she would. One day he hoped she would trust him enough to share some of herself.

"Do you believe I would hurt you in any way?" That she could angered him. When had he led her to believe he would be a tyrant?

"I don't really know you."

At least she was being honest now.

"You know enough about me to know I would never mistreat or starve you. I would never stop you from seeing your family, nor from pursuing this love you have of astronomy. With me you would not be forced to move away from your family. I would see you as my equal, Emily."

She thought about that for a few seconds. Her eyes running over his face, and he felt suddenly exposed. As if she could read his every thought and feeling.

"I could never be your equal, my birth—"

"I don't care about your birth!"

"Don't yell at me."

"Forgive me," Cam said, reining in his temper.

"I don't understand why you want to do this when we have rarely been comfortable in each other's presence."

"I have explained why. I also have no wish to marry a woman who makes demands of me and wants me to be nice to her horrid mother."

Her smile was small. "Surely they are not all horrid."

"Most."

"But what happened will linger over me for the remainder of my life, surely?"

"Perhaps we can do something about that, and our marriage will be a start."

"But what about him... Mr. J-Jackson?"

"Leave him to us to deal with."

"What does that mean? I have no wish for you... any of you, to exact revenge on that man."

Cam remained silent. Emily huffed out a breath.

"But, Cam, marrying me means you cannot wed another. What if you meet the woman of your heart?"

"Em, Em, Em," he sighed. "When will you realize that I do not have the ability to love that deeply? Shallow is what I am."

"No you're not," she defended him. "You love your family, and I have seen the great capacity for caring that you have."

"I do believe that was a compliment."

"Don't let it go to your head."

He looked at her for long drawn out seconds, and she looked back.

"One question?"

She had never instigated it before, so Cam nodded to indicate she go first.

"Do.... Have you ever raised your hand to a woman?"

He held her eyes, willing her to believe him when he said, "No. I never have, nor will I. I would never hurt a woman by using my strength against her."

Her look was intent, trying to see if he spoke the truth. He exhaled when she nodded. *Who had raised his hand to her? Who had caused her pain?*

"Who is your favorite Sinclair?" He'd said it to make her smile, anything to chase the darkness from her eyes. The questions he wanted to ask could wait. Those he would get to when she was his wife.

"Warwick, of course... oh no, perhaps the twins, but then there are Eden and Essie, plus Dev. The decision is not an easy one."

"You left out a name," he teased her.

"Did I?" She smiled, but it soon fell away. "I'm scared, Cam, as you should be."

He reached across the carriage and took both her gloved hands in his.

"I'm terrified, actually. For so long I've barely been able to look after myself, but now there may be another I need to consider. It is not easy for one as self-centered as I."

"I-I shall think about it."

"That is all I ask of you, Emily." Cam then moved to the edge of the seat and hauled her closer.

"What are you doing?"

"Kissing you, because I quite enjoyed it last time."

"What? You can't."

He took her mouth beneath his and tasted her. Kept it soft and light until her resistance eased; only then did he pull her closer and take her deeper. Kiss her as a man did a woman. His hand cupped her head and angled it perfectly, and then he lost himself in the wonder of Emily's lips.

Cam lost all thought but this woman as one kiss fell into another. His body grew hard, and his hands went to the buttons on her coat. Opening it, he slid a hand inside and stroked her back through the material of her dress.

"Cam—"

"I would never hurt you," he breathed against her lips.

The hand moved, touching her ribs and then higher. He could imagine the beautiful weight of one of her naked breasts cupped in his hand. Needed the reality with a desperation that shocked him.

"Emily." He said her name into the silken skin of her neck, and then his hand was there, touching the gentle curve restrained beneath her clothes. She tensed but did not pull away. "It would be like this between us." He moved his hand in a circle and the breath hitched in her throat.

Finally, when he felt his head start to lose reason and the only thought he could form was how it would feel to unwrap her so he could ravish her lush body right here in the carriage, he reluctantly pulled away.

"Oh."

"Oh indeed," he rasped, shocked at what had just occurred. He wanted her, Cam realized. Desperately, and that rocked him to his toes.

"I-I cannot believe you did that."

"Did I hurt or force you?" Cam gritted out.

She shook her head. At least in that she was being truthful.

"But if we married, it would be convenience only." She scuttled back on the seat, out of his reach. "Not a marriage in every sense. I don't want that."

He didn't smile because at that moment he didn't have one readily available.

"We will have a marriage in every sense of the word, Emily. I will not marry you and seek my pleasures in another. I will stay true to the woman I wed, and what we just shared proved we are at least compatible in that way."

He could tell she was shocked that he spoke so plainly.

"I-I don't want that."

"How very forward thinking of you to allow me permission to seek my pleasures elsewhere, however I must disagree. I will not be like so many others. We will stay true to our vows, Emily."

She huffed out a breath. "I have not agreed to a union with you, Mr. Sinclair. Pray do not forget that."

He felt more rational as they bickered. This, after all, was their usual way of communicating. Not with their mouths fused, and he holding the lush weight of her breast in his palm.

"You will, because I am hard to resist."

She actually spluttered. It turned into a cough that forced the conversation to suspend briefly.

"I can resist you with ease, sir."

"And yet right at this moment you are at my mercy, so perhaps you should try to be nicer, so I will not turn the carriage around and you will not see your sainted Mr. Fossett, nor his reflective telescope."

Cam swallowed his smile as her top teeth sank into her bottom lip, and silence fell in the carriage. A surprisingly comfortable one for all that it was Emily who sat across from him, and he'd just kissed her soft, sweet lips.

CHAPTER 30

*E*mily did not look at Cam again; how could she? That kiss had shocked her, as had the burst of need she'd felt when he'd touched her breast. She'd believed herself a cold woman. A woman who did not want a man's touch. Yet when he touched her, she'd felt so much. His mouth had been gentle to start, his hands holding her like she was made of spun glass, and with each brush of his lips, each stroke of his hand, she had lost the ability to think of anything but the feelings that were building inside her.

It would not happen again, she vowed silently. Fear had made her demand that. Stating she had no wish for intimacy.

You are not marrying him, Emily reminded herself.

"What are you thinking?"

"Pardon?"

Cam raised a brow, the Sinclair green eyes focused on her.

"Your lips formed a straight line, and one can only assume that was because your thoughts were not pleasing."

"As they are my thoughts you will never know."

He chuckled low in his throat, and Emily decided it was best to ignore him and looked out the window.

He'd touched her breast.

Was Cam right, would Samantha and Isabella be tarnished because of her disgrace?

"You're frowning now."

"Can you not be quiet for even a minute?" Emily glared at him.

The man made her feel so many emotions she found it hard to name them all.

"Oh now I object. I have been quiet for at least fifteen minutes while you sit in the corner and seethe."

His smile told her he knew exactly what he did to her, and enjoyed doing it immensely.

"We can never marry, as one morning the servants would find you dead in your bed, for I will have had enough, and killed you!"

"My brother thought that was a possibility."

"A sensible man then," Emily said. "Then there is your legion of admirers who will be devastated that you are wed. Although what they see in you I fail to."

"Ouch."

"You, sir," Emily waved a finger in front of him, "are the devil himself!"

"And you, madam, are no saint. In fact, you beg me to tease you, and always have with your uppity behavior."

"I do not!"

"Please," he scoffed. "You've disapproved of me since our first meeting, and there is nothing I can do that you like. I simply walk into a room and bid everyone good day and your hackles raise."

She was not ready to concede to this, so she looked out the window once more. The carriage was passing through gates and rolling down a long driveway.

"One wonders why you feel the need to censure me constantly, but then perhaps after that kiss I have more of an understanding."

She made herself look at him, let her eyes rest on his face, hoping to unsettle him a little as he did her, but he simply smiled back at her.

"I have no idea what that means, and no wish to," Emily said in her most haughty tone. "I am not one of those... those ladies that fall about themselves to get your attention."

"How do you know about those ladies when you have not entered society?"

"I have ears, and hear what people say, plus I have attended a few social functions and see how women behave when you are near. It is nauseating. However, right now, I wish for you to keep a civil tongue in your head, as we have arrived."

"I am always civil to everyone but you," he said, having the last word.

He opened the door and stepped down, holding out a hand for her. He then retained it and placed it on his arm.

"Come, I can hardly wait to bask in Fossett's magnificence," he whispered in her ear.

"Stop that."

"I shall leave his house a better man for just being in the presence of greatness."

Emily refused to smile.

"I shall leave brimming with knowledge, and the better for it."

"S-stop it."

He peered down at her.

"Is that a smile, Emily? God's blood, I do believe it is."

"You, Cambridge Sinclair, are a wicked man, and I'll add to that by saying jealousy is unattractive in a man."

"You think I'm jealous of Fossett?" He hooted with laughter.

"Of course, and threatened, but don't be, because your family love you and that is what counts."

Emily refused to acknowledge how alive she felt verbally sparring with Cam.

"You, Emily Tolly, are a witch, and I have seen through your insipid disguise since day one. This is your true nature, shrewish and caustic. You would cut a poor humble man to shreds with your tongue."

Ignoring him, Emily looked at the large house. Made of dark stone, it had several turret windows and three floors.

"It's very grand," she found herself saying.

"Our prince has rewarded Fossett by offering him this house for as long as he wishes, due to his magnificence—and finding that comet of course, which I'm still dubious of."

"Only because you did not find it," Emily said as they stepped up to the front door.

Lifting a hand, she wrapped her knuckles on the polished wood.

"One hopes it is answered before we are chilled to the marrow."

Emily ignored this, and waited patiently, hoping her teeth didn't begin to chatter, it was indeed dastardly cold.

"Hello," she said when finally it opened. "I am Miss Tolly, and have an invitation to visit with Mr. Fossett and view his reflective telescope."

The butler looked at Emily as if she was something nasty he'd stepped in, which didn't bother her overly as many people had looked at her in just that way in her lifetime.

"Mr. Fossett did not mention your name to me as a guest for the viewing, Miss Tolly."

As Emily had the invitation in her hand, she began to extend it, but a large hand stopped her.

"I am Mr. Sinclair, and this is Miss Tolly," Cam said in a tone she'd rarely heard him use before. Looking at his face she noted the muscles bunching in his jaw. "We have an invitation, so please tell Mr. Fossett immediately we have arrived. However, you will first show us to a room to wait."

The butler paled.

"Now," Cam added softly.

"Please follow me."

They were shown into a small room that held a narrow side table, a painting, and one chair.

"Please wait here."

"And where are we to sit?" Cam said.

"I'll stand," Emily said quickly. She had lived constantly with conflict before coming to live with James, and tried to avoid it now where possible.

"I will stand," Cam snapped, glaring at the butler.

The man left, leaving the door ajar.

"There is no need to be angry with the butler."

"He was rude to you, Emily, and you do not take that from anyone, especially when you have done nothing to provoke it."

"There is obviously some kind of mistake. I'm sure he will return and collect us directly."

Emily was walking the room; turning, she bumped into Cam. His hands steadied her, and held her before him.

"You are inferior to no one, no matter what your birth is. I need you to understand this, Emily."

"I-I know what I am."

"And what is that?" He shook her gently forcing her eyes back up to his.

"Stop this, Cam." She tried to get away from him.

His hands lifted her to her toes, so their eyes were level.

"Why can you not see the woman others can, and stop allowing people to make you feel small?"

"My f-family do not make me feel small," Emily managed to get out. Her eyes were fixed on his, and the green depths were filled with so much emotion. No longer was he the humorous Cam she saw most often. "I am making strides to be stronger," she found herself saying. "In fact, just today I told James I cared for him and we talked. And why I am telling you this I have no idea."

"Husbands and wives should not keep things from each other."

"We are not married!"

"We will be. But this business between you and James is a good start. Did you also share with him why you behaved as you had?"

She nodded.

"Excellent. I have great hopes that now you have started, the changes will continue."

"I'm not sure why my behavior concerns you so much?"

"Because I will not have my wife believing she is beneath anyone."

Emily's heartbeat kicked at his words. She did not want to marry this man; he was too much of everything for her. Too vibrant, too strong, too funny, and yes, too well respected among those that ignored her.

"I... I am not your wife, and will never be so."

He hauled her closer and kissed her hard. Releasing her, he stalked to the door.

"I shall return soon, do not go anywhere."

Emily slumped into a chair. As if she could move when her limbs had turned to liquid.

CHAPTER 31

*C*am took the stairs two at a time. With distance from Emily his body temperature had lowered once more. Christ, the woman had lips to tempt a saint. Every time he was near her now he wanted to kiss her. Which was surely a good thing if she was going to be his wife.

He wasn't sure why he was so committed to the idea of marriage to Emily, but he was, very committed. Now, however, was not the moment to think through why; he had a hunch why Fossett had not given the butler Emily's name. He hoped he was wrong, but as he climbed the last set of stairs and a raised voice greeted him, he knew he was not.

"You allowed her inside my house!"

"Problem?" Cam approached Fossett from behind. The man spun to face him and the butler took the opportunity to scurry away.

"Who are you?"

Fossett's face was flushed with color, lips drawn tight in rage. There was no sign of the handsome countenance women worshipped.

"Mr. Sinclair."

"You brought that woman to my house!"

Cam wasn't a man who angered easily, for all his volatile ways. It usually took a great deal and a direct threat to someone he cared about for him to reach the state.

"That woman," he said, leaning into Fossett, deliberately intimidating him, "is worth ten of you!"

"I-I know of her reputation. I was informed what she did with that man, Mr. Jackson!" Fossett thundered, his face turning puce with rage. "I was willing to overlook the unfortunate circumstances of her birth, but I want no contact with a woman who would behave as she did!"

Cam grabbed Fossett's collar and lifted him to his toes, shaking him as he did so.

"She is a duke's daughter, and under the care of her brother the Duke of Raven, who will be most interested in this conversation and your behavior. The brother who is a close confidant of our prince. Her other brother, Mr. Huntington, is one of the wealthiest men in the United Kingdom. I'll throw my family into the mix also, as they are noble, unlike you. In fact, you were born the son of a blacksmith."

"I-I...." Fossett's eyes were bulging now.

"Did you hope to keep that a secret? Believe me, word spreads to all corners of London very quickly. However, due to your work, most people overlook your birth. Now, back to Miss Tolly. What happened with that scum Jackson was not of her making, in fact he frightened her, and—"

"Let him go, Cam."

Cam closed his eyes briefly before releasing Fossett. He didn't want to, but the fingers on his arm had him looking down into Emily's pale face.

"He is not worthy of your anger," she said.

Fossett staggered back clutching his necktie, which was now a mess, and gasping like a landed fish.

"H-how dare you?"

"How dare I, you sniveling little rodent? How dare you!"

Emily stepped in front of Cam as he advanced on Fossett again.

"That will do, Cambridge."

Instead she advanced on the man, and he took a backward step which made Cam feel better.

"I wish for you to hand me back my papers please, Mr. Fossett. I'm sorry you believe me unworthy of seeing through your reflective telescope, however, I will not beg you to let me view it."

"I-I do not know where your papers are."

He knew, Cam realized. The bastard just wanted to keep them for himself.

"Yes, you do." Cam stepped to Emily's side. "Now fetch them or I will go through every room in this house until I find them."

With a last furious, terrified glare, Fossett turned from them and hurried away.

"I'm so sorry, Emily." Cam put a hand on her shoulder. It was rigid with tension. "Really sorry."

"I-I had thought him a better man than that." The whispered words were loaded with pain.

"He should be considering he is the son of a blacksmith and should know better than most what it is like to struggle in such a world."

"Thank you for defending me, Cam."

"I hate snobbery, especially when the snob is ignorant."

Emily sighed. "It is the way of this world you inhabit. I'm just glad I never truly entered society."

He made an understanding grunt.

"Have you looked around these walls? They are covered in the most amazing pictures," Cam said, hoping to distract her. She followed as he moved closer to the paintings.

"Dear Lord, is that... oh it is."

"A naked man and woman," Cam said, smiling. "Several different versions of them actually."

"I shouldn't be looking at them," Emily said, not moving an inch. "They are quite depraved."

"Look all you want, darling, they are quite educational."

"No." She made herself turn, and Cam saw color had filled her face, replacing the pallor of before.

"Oh come now, surely you are curious. After all, these things are what take place between a man and a woman."

"Th-they do not!"

"They do with couples who enjoy each other in bed sport. See this one—"

"Cam!"

He chuckled.

"Don't be a prude, Em. Your reputation allows you to look at these, so why not."

"My reputation is unjust!"

She turned on him, eyes flashing now. He liked Emily when she was angry, because she forgot to be the timid mouse the rest of her family saw. Her beautiful eyes flashed, and her cheeks flushed. Shoulders back, she was glaring at him.

"Yes it is, and I'm glad you realize that fact."

"You did that on purpose."

"What?"

His eyes roamed her features. She really was a beautiful woman, Cam thought. He wondered what she would be like in the throes of passion. The hell of it was, he wanted to find out... desperately.

"Don't let him weaken you, Emily. Show him only your strength now."

"Here, now leave my house." Fossett arrived and thrust the papers at him. Emily stepped forward and took them, making the man look at her. *Good girl.* She had a backbone, it was just hidden under years of submissiveness.

"You are a fraud, Mr. Fossett. A blacksmith's son who has no right to judge me for something that I had no hand in instigating, and no wish to participate in. Good day."

Cam watched Emily turn and walk away, then leaned closer to Fossett. The man scurried back a few feet.

"Pray that I never encounter you alone when there is no *lady* present, Fossett." Cam emphasized the word lady. "For it will not go well for you if I should."

Cam turned and followed Emily from the room. He left the house on her heels.

Placing his hand on her waist, he lifted Emily into the carriage, and then joined her.

"I have tried my entire life to be a good person, Cam."

She spoke the words to the window after the carriage had been moving for several minutes.

"Put him from your mind. Fossett is an idiot."

"Yes, because it is that easy to do so."

"There is no need for sarcasm."

She sighed again and turned to face him.

"I'm sorry, and thank you again for defending me."

"You're welcome."

She'd lost all that wonderful fire now they had left the house.

"I wish I could have stopped that from happening, and yet I had no way of knowing that fool would react in such a way. Had he been a peer, I would understand, as most of them can't form a sensible thought."

"I had hoped my disgrace was not common knowledge, it seems I'm wrong."

Cam snorted. "Society thrives on gossip, even if it is not one of the nobles disgraced. Your brother is a duke. People love to glean any tidbit of gossip attached to such a man, as do most Londoners. I should imagine even the mice have heard about it by now."

Her eyes held his for long seconds and he knew what was coming. The breath locked inside his chest, and suddenly the palms of his hands inside his gloves grew sweaty. The air was full of a spicy scent, as he watched her mouth open to say the words.

"I will marry you."

CHAPTER 32

*T*hey chose a small church, just outside of London. James had wanted them to go back to Raven Castle and marry there in the little church on the hill, but Emily had not wanted that. Not wanted to wed Cam in the same place their three siblings had married for love. She was to marry Cam to save her reputation, such as it was, and to protect her family from her disgrace.

"He is a good man, Emily."

"I know that, James."

"But it is not too late to stop this, if that is what you wish."

"It is not."

"For heaven's sake, James, stop it, you will scare her."

James, Eden, and Essie were accompanying Emily to the church. He would walk her down the aisle and the sisters would stand at her side.

Samantha and the twins had been disappointed not to be included, but she'd had no wish to turn it into a celebration when what it actually was, was a disaster.

A disaster for Cam more than her, because this selfless act would change his life forever. He'd said he would be faithful to her, but would he? Was it possible that the man who had loved the company of many women could actually do such a thing?

"You are frowning, Emily."

"Sorry, Essie."

Her sisters-in-law looked stunning, as they always did.

"No, if you are to frown," Eden said, "then today is probably the day to do so, but let me tell you something about my brother."

"Oh Lord, are you going to list his virtues again?" James groaned.

"Shut up," Eden snapped, kicking her husband in the shins.

Emily giggled, and the noise surprised all of them.

"Begging your pardon."

"Don't apologize for giggling, Emily," James said. "It is a wonderful sound, and one we do not hear nearly enough."

Emily had thought she was done with tears, but felt them choke up inside her as James cupped her cheek.

"Come now, there is no need for tears. You know I love you, as you love me, just as we love the others, and that is all that matters, Em. The love we all share in this family. It completes us."

"Oh," Eden wailed, sniffing loudly. "That was lovely."

"I want only for you to be happy, so if at any time you are not, then you need only contact me and I will come, Em."

"My brother will not make her unhappy." Eden sniffed.

"Eden, Essie, will you give me a minute alone with Emily please," James said as the carriage stopped outside the church. "I know you'll listen, but at least it gives the appearance of time alone with my sister."

"Of course we will." Eden kissed his check, then Emily's, and left, taking Essie with her and closing the door behind them. James took her hands in his.

"Let me tell you something about Cam, Emily, which may help you understand him better."

She nodded.

"When I first met him he was angry and confused. His father had betrayed the Sinclair siblings, and Cam took it the hardest."

"I did not realize. Cam has always seemed so confident and assured. I envied him that." She had, and perhaps that was another part of the reason she always bristled when he was near; he was everything she could not bring herself to be.

"Yes, I also. You and I were not raised to inspire confidence in ourselves."

"I'm sorry you suffered at our father's hands, James. Samantha told me that she was mistreated, which led me to believe you must have been also."

"It is the unfortunate truth that our father was not a good man."

An understatement, Emily was sure.

"But back to Cam." He squeezed her fingers. "I understood quickly that his loyalty would never be questioned by those he loved or respected. He owed me money; I will not get into how that came about, should he wish it he will tell you. He had no means to repay it, so he worked for me, and worked harder than three men."

She was curious as to how this had come about but did not question him further, understanding that this was a matter that lay between James and Cam.

"There was something else I came to realize about Cam. He could not be forced into doing what he did not wish. The man is as malleable as wood."

Emily thought about this as James placed her hand on his arm and started walking to where the sisters waited for them.

"In a roundabout way I am trying to tell you that he would not be marrying you, Em, if he did not want to. The choice was his to make, and he made it because it was his wish to do so. Perhaps you can think about that if you have doubts."

She did think about it as Eden straightened her black velvet cloak, opening the front so her rose silk dress could be seen. *Did Cam really wish to marry her?* Essie then fussed with the band of matching pink flowers on her head, to which was attached a veil.

"It is too cold to take off the cloak, Emily, but you can see the skirts of that lovely dress at least."

Emily had wanted to wear one of the many dresses she already owned, but no one had allowed that. Eden had gathered the other women in the family together and they'd come up with this dress, and several other new items of clothing and nightwear, all of which she had secretly left behind in another case, and brought her own.

"Right, you're ready. Now smile, and remember, my brother is a good man, and it's my belief you will be very happy together."

"As do I," James said solemnly. "But also remember if you need me I am here. To hell with the fact he is a Sinclair. I will not tolerate him upsetting you."

"I am a Sinclair, thank you very much, husband, and I object to you thinking my brother would hurt Emily. Cam is a good, kind man, and what's more, you should know that by now."

"You are a Raven," James said firmly. "And I do know that, but I need Emily to know I am here should she need me."

"I know it, brother."

He nodded, and she saw that he was emotional, just like Eden and Essie, who were also sniffing back the tears.

James was to accompany her down the aisle. Max had

told her he thought it right and was happy to stand beside Cam. She rose to her toes and kissed his cheek.

"Thank you for rescuing me, James. My life has been wonderful since I came to live in your house."

"As has mine."

"I promise you there is no need to worry. I feel better now we have spoken. As Eden has said, Cam is a good man, and I'm sure we will rub along together."

"I don't want you to rub along together!"

"Pardon?" He looked fierce as he impaled her with his gray eyes.

"I want you to fall in love with him, Emily. I want you to experience what Eden and I have."

"Oh darling." Eden reached for the duke's hand.

Emily thought it unlikely she would ever have that, but she forced a smile on her lips and lied. "I shall try."

"That is all I can ask of you then."

As they'd arrived at the church, conversation stopped, and Emily wasn't sure she could talk anyway, as the nerves that had been fluttering inside her stomach intensified.

"You look lovely."

"Thank you, James."

The church, she knew, held only a few Sinclairs and Ravens, all who wished her well, but the steps up to it were some of the hardest she had ever taken, and there had been plenty of hard ones in her lifetime.

"A nice deep breath in now, Em. That's it, good girl," Eden said, fussing about with her dress again as if she was about to marry the man of her dreams.

Emily walked into the cool, dim interior seconds later and looked to the end of the aisle, and there he stood. Tall, elegant in deep brown, flanked by her brother and his. Somehow she made it down the aisle, but did not remember the journey. To her surprise there were a handful of nonfamily in attendance, all smiling at her. She recognized Cam's aunt and uncle, and others she had become acquainted with over the years. Family friends, and it was a shock to see that many of them were indeed her friends now too.

Emily did not look at Cam as she arrived at his side. Instead she concentrated on the vicar who was to marry them. James squeezed her hand, and then stepped away.

"I think Emily looks lonely with only Eden and Essie at her side."

Samantha's voice was loud enough to carry through the church, as was the shushing noise Lilly made.

"I agree, and Dorrie and I have the flowers Dev gave us, so maybe we should stand beside her... just to keep her company."

Beside her Emily felt Cam's arm shake. Casting him a quick glance she saw he was trying not to laugh, as was Max. Dev however was attempting to intimidate his siblings by scowling. Emily had absolutely nothing to laugh about. She was to marry a man who until recently she'd wanted to throttle at every occasion they'd met, *although there was the kissing*, but suddenly she did. Turning to where the little girls all sat in the front pew, she watched their little legs swinging back and forth.

"I think Cam looks lonely also, Lilly," Warwick Sinclair said. "I should stand at his side, especially if those three are with Emily."

"Come along then." James sighed, signaling for them to come forth. "Sorry, Em."

"It is all right," she said, and meant every word. She should not have stopped the children from enjoying the moment, even if she was not.

"Yes it is." Cam touched her hand briefly, just a brush of his fingers over hers. She met his eyes, and found him smiling.

"Thank you," Emily said. "For everything."

"Well, I cannot in all conscience take the credit for how you look today, but can I say you are quite magnificent and that beautiful seems inadequate, because you are so much more than that."

"Thank you, and you also look handsome."

"Do I?" He looked down his body. "I believe that is the first compliment I have received from you."

The sound of running feet interrupted them as the children rushed to join them. The guests laughed, but she could not tear her eyes from Cam's.

"It will be all right, sweetheart, trust me... trust us," he added.

She nodded. "I trust you, Cam... it is just—"

He leaned in and placed his finger on her lips.

"That you trust me is enough for now."

The children jockeyed for position, and then there they were, bright-eyed and alert, wedging themselves between Eden and Essie. Warwick was pressed between Dev and Max.

"If you are ready," the vicar said with heavy sarcasm.

"Oh indeed, pray please continue," Samantha said, now smiling.

There was laughter from the guests and the wedding party, which now totaled nine.

Looking at her little sister, who smiled up at her, Emily felt the urge to weep... loudly. Tomorrow she would not wake up and see Samantha and Isabella. Not share story time with them. She would wake next to this large, handsome, and disturbing man at her side. The thought was an unnerving one.

"Dearly beloved, we are gathered here today...."

She got through the vows, and even managed to speak

her part in a clear voice. Cam appeared calm and sounded steady.

"You may now kiss the bride."

"I hate this part," Emily heard Warwick say. "It seems to take a great deal of time to complete, when surely it is only a matter of touching each other's mouths—which by the way is revolting, and I will never do."

"One day you won't mind," Dev assured him.

Emily turned to offer Cam a smile, as if to say she knew he would not do that, not here with so many watching, but there he was, lowering his head.

"Wh-what are you...." Her words fell away at the first touch of his lips, brief and soft. She felt his hand slide to the middle of her spine and move her closer so her body now touched his.

It was over in a matter of seconds, but it left Emily's head reeling, as it had when they'd last kissed.

"Hello, Mrs. Sinclair."

"H-hello," Emily managed to stutter out. Her cheeks felt hot, and the imprint of his mouth was on hers.

Dear Lord, she was now Mrs. Sinclair.

CHAPTER 33

"$\mathscr{I}$'m not sure why we need to go away for a few nights, Cam. It is not a wedding in the conventional sense of the word."

"And yet we are, and what would you know of a wedding in the conventional sense of the word, when you have only witnessed those of our families. Believe me when I say they are unconventional."

She was fussing about with her gloves, the small bag on her wrist, in fact anything that kept her eyes from him. Emily was nervous, and Cam could not fault her for that, as he felt the same. This woman was now his to protect, his to care for until he drew his last breath; the thought was a daunting one. It was also what he'd wanted, and he would do whatever it took to make her happy.

When she'd entered the church on James's arm and looked down at him, he'd felt something deep inside his chest. Relief? A rightness? He hadn't known what, but he'd been extremely happy she'd arrived. There had been a niggling doubt she would not appear, and simply flee London.

"Go to sleep, your eyes are half-closed, Em."

To his surprise she did, resting her head on the back of the seat.

Cam had decided the best course of action was to leave London and their families for a few days immediately after the wedding. James and Max hadn't wanted this, but he'd stood firm. He and Emily needed time alone together without constant interference from them.

His eyes followed the curve of one cheek. It was soft and lightly tinged with color, and he wanted to touch it. He knew her dress was rose silk, but as she'd yet to take off her cloak he was unsure what the top looked like. His mouth watered at the prospect of seeing it... seeing her.

He'd struggled to breathe watching her walk down the aisle toward him. She'd looked like an angel with those flowers around her head and the small veil down her back. Her face was flushed, bottom lip clamped between her teeth. He'd had the ridiculous urge to meet her halfway, gather her up in his arms, and tell her everything would be all right.

The truth was he had no idea if it would. Their beginning had not been auspicious after all. But she'd said she trusted him, and for now that was a start.

The service had been a blur to Cam. He'd read the concern on the faces of their families and tried to make light of the situation as he usually did. Only now while she slept did he draw a deep, steadying breath. She was his. The thought was a sobering one, when for most of his life he had been the irresponsible Sinclair.

Moving to her side when he was sure she slept deeply, he pulled the satin bow of the bonnet she wore, and eased it from her head. The circlet of flowers still sat beneath. Small white buds decorated it, and rose satin ribbons. Finding the pins that held it in place, he removed each, then tucked them into his pocket. Lifting the circlet off her head, he placed it on the opposite seat.

Emily slept on, her slumber deep, breathing even. Samantha told him her sister had not slept well last night, which was hardly surprising. He had, but then it took a great deal to keep him awake. The little girl then told him to look after her, as Emily was vulnerable, and sometimes woke at night upset. To which he'd replied solemnly that he would, and that she was welcome to come and stay with them whenever she wanted. She'd seemed happy with that.

Pulling the blanket from beneath the seat, he tucked it around Emily as he eyed the mass of curls someone had pinned on her head. Surely her head ached having so many things poked into it?

She murmured and wriggled, looking for a comfortable position. Cam eased her into his arms, and leaned back on the seat, turning his body slightly so she was half on his lap.

"Cam?"

"Sssh, sleep now, sweet."

Her eyes closed as he ran a finger between her eyebrows and down her nose, as he used to with his younger siblings when they failed to sleep. It worked, and soon she was breathing deeply.

She was sweet, he thought. He had no idea what the future held for them, only that she was part of his, as he was hers.

Closing his eyes, he let himself sleep for the first time, holding his wife in his arms.

He woke with a start as the carriage rolled into the yard of the inn where they would change horses.

Emily had wriggled until one side of her face was pressed

into his chest, and an arm was flung over his waist. She still slept even as the carriage stopped.

"Emily, wake up, love." Cam leaned in to kiss a soft cheek. It was smooth under his lips.

Her eyes fluttered open, and she turned slightly to look up at him.

"Dear Lord!" She sat so fast the top of her head connected with his nose.

"Ouch!"

"Oh dear, forgive me."

"You use me as a pillow, and then punish me for it," Cam groused, rubbing the offended appendage.

"I'm not sure how I got into that position." She squinted at him, struggling to focus.

Delightfully rumpled, she wore the imprint of his lapel on one cheek, and her face was sleepy. One hand went to her head.

"Where is my bonnet and the circlet of flowers?"

"There." He pointed to the opposite seat. "I thought you would be more comfortable without them."

She wasn't sure what to make of that, and as her mind was still a bit foggy, Cam took the opportunity to open the carriage and step down.

"Come, wife, let us eat and find some warmth inside while the horses are changed."

She threw him a look as she pulled on her bonnet, but didn't comment further.

The conditions had deteriorated since their journey had begun, now, howling wind and biting rain accompanied them as they hurried into the small building, Cam requested a room to sit in while they waited, and a meal.

"Where are we going, Cam?" Emily said as she warmed her bottom by the fire

"A friend's country house. It is not huge, but comfortable and will afford us some breathing room for a few days."

"I could breathe in London."

She wasn't looking at him, but his right ear. He doubted she'd spent much time alone with men, other than family, and though she knew him, much had changed. Now they were married.

"Are you tired, Emily?"

"A little."

"We could stay here for the night, and press on in the morning."

"No! I mean, no, we should press on now, and reach our destination."

What she actually meant was no, she was terrified about what would happen when she reached her bed tonight. Cam wondered what knowledge she had about what happened between a man and a woman, and if any, who had taught her.

"Emily, I will never hurt you."

Her eyes widened.

"What will happen between us will be enjoyable for you, I promise. Perhaps a little discomfort to start but—"

"I have no wish for that," she interrupted him. "No wish to discuss the matter or to partake in it."

"And yet you will."

Their food arrived, and he did not pursue the matter further.

"Roads are set to get bad this evening, Mr. Sinclair," the innkeeper said.

"Are they?" Cam kept his eyes on Emily as she avoided his.

"Rain, and sleet. It'll be icy out there."

"Do you have a room available for the night, sir?"

"Cam." Emily started toward him. "I don't want to stay here."

"I do. I shall get it ready for you at once," the man said, ignoring Emily.

"Before you start in on me, may I remind you that you are not the only life at stake here. I have drivers and horses that need my care. Would you have them travel in such conditions just to ease your maidenly fears?"

It had been just the right thing to say as Emily was a soft-hearted person, and putting anyone in danger would go against everything she believed.

"Of course, forgive me. I thought only of myself."

"And the monster your husband obviously is."

"I did not say you were a monster, only that...." Her words trailed off.

"Did anyone talk to you about what happens between a man and woman?"

"Eden tried, but I told her I knew everything." Emily didn't look happy about the confession. "Perhaps I was too hasty there."

He couldn't help it, he laughed.

"I'm glad my fears amuse you, sir."

"They don't," Cam said, sobering. "Now eat up, Emily, and stop worrying, I will do nothing you do not wish for."

Her smile was blinding, and he knew why. She believed he would ask nothing of her now. Cam, however, had other ideas.

"Take off your cloak and come and eat. I'm sure you are as hungry as I."

Cam watched as she removed the velvet cloak. He nearly swallowed his tongue when he saw the dress it revealed.

The neckline swept low, exposing soft cream skin and a hint of cleavage. The material caressed her breasts and then fell in silken folds to her ankles.

"That is a lovely dress," he managed to get out.

"I had planned to wear one of mine, but your sisters and Lilly refused to allow it."

"They can be quite forceful" was all he could manage as his eyes ran over her lovely body. He was suddenly on fire with need to hold her, make love to her. The thought made him smile, as she was his wife after all.

CHAPTER 34

*C*am escorted Emily up the stairs to the room they would share—after she had insisted he ask the proprietor if there was another room available. There wasn't, he had informed her solemnly.

"I shall return once I have checked the drivers are settled for the night. A bath will arrive soon."

Relief flooded Emily as he left; his heavy feet made a sturdy sound as they descended the stairs once more.

Looking around the small space, she saw a bed, floor rug, chest of drawers, and washing water. A small fire spluttered in the grate.

A knock on the door heralded two footmen who carried in a small bath. They placed it before the fire, and when it was filled, steam wafted upward, urging Emily to climb in.

"Do you have a screen that I could use?"

"Yes, Mrs. Sinclair, I shall get it at once," one of the footmen said.

The embarrassment of having Cam return to find her naked was more than Emily could stand.

Once the screen was in place, Emily opened her valise to find her nightwear. Shock held her still as she looked at the clothes inside. She recognized nothing. Lifting a wisp of peach satin, Emily watched dismayed as it unfurled to the floor. Delicate straps held up the fitted sheath but offered little by way of protection from anyone who saw her wearing it.

"I cannot sleep in this!" Frantically she dug through the case, but not one of the items was hers. Holding up a matching sheer over-jacket, she clutched it to her chest.

"How could they?" Outraged that her sisters-in-law could have done this to her, she sat on the bed. What was she to do? She could not sleep in these. Surely Cam would be horrified. He would think Emily had purchased them, think that she was luring him to bed her.

She had no choice but to sleep in her clothing, or wear her cloak over the nightwear, as it was cold. Deciding upon that course, as her clothes would not be comfortable, she took the garments from the valise and the bar of sweet-smelling soap someone had tucked in there, and went behind the screen to quickly undress. Releasing her hair, Emily groaned with relief as if fell over her shoulders. Her head ached from the pins poked into it many hours earlier. Stepping into the water, she enjoyed the heat as she submerged from the waist down. She washed quickly, and was done when a knock sounded on the door.

"Can I come in?"

Cam was back.

"I—ah, yes, I am bathing."

"Excellent, and I shall bathe after you."

Emily quickly stepped out. Rubbing herself dry, she pulled on the offensive nightwear and her cloak over the top. Only then did she come out from behind the screen.

"Are you to sleep in that then?"

Cam was lounging in a chair; the man could look comfortable anywhere. She saw none of the tension in him that she felt.

"Yes, it's cold."

"Surely not that cold."

"Yes, it is."

"No, it's not."

He climbed to his feet.

"I can sleep in whatever I like." Emily backed up a bit as he approached.

"I am having a bath, and when I get out, you will have removed that and climbed into bed."

He looked determined, but she was equally so. No way did she want him to see her nightwear. *Drat his meddling sisters.*

Another knock on the door stopped her from answering him. It was a maid bearing a tray.

"Brandy," Cam said when she closed it. "I thought it would warm and help relax you."

Emily glared at the screen after the maid had left, which was of course totally wasted as he was behind it.

"I do not need relaxing."

"You're strung tighter than a piano."

Emily ignored him and opened the stopper, then poured a small measure into a glass and took a gulp. It caught in the back of her throat, making her cough.

"Brandy is to be savored, not gulped."

"Shut up," Emily snapped. "I have no need of your comments."

Nerves had her taking another mouthful, this time a smaller one, and she enjoyed the fiery heat as it traveled through her body and down to her belly.

She walked around the small room, lifting the curtain to look out into the black night. Rain was falling steadily now, and although she loathed to admit it, Cam had been right to make them stay the night.

Sipping the brandy, she listened as Cam washed, imagining what he looked like. Not that she wanted to know, of course. In fact if she could, she'd leave the room and find another, but there was no other to be had.

"You are still wearing your cloak."

He walked out from behind the screen wearing a heavy sable dressing gown that came to his calves. It shouldn't make him look dangerous, it was a simple garment many men wore, but it did. It was as if he was prowling across the floor toward her. His hair was damp and stood off his head, and she refused to look lower, to where the robe had opened in a V, exposing his skin and the hair on his chest.

"I have no wish to remove it." She clutched the velvet folds in one hand, and her glass in the other. "You cannot make me."

"I have told you I will not hurt you, Emily, will you not trust me?"

"You said we would not do that."

"Actually what I said was, I will do nothing you do not wish for."

"It is one and the same thing."

"No, it is not. Please take off your cloak, sweetheart."

"I cannot," Emily squeaked. She felt a silly flutter inside when he called her sweetheart, just as she had when he'd used the endearment in the church.

"Why?" He was before her now, close enough that Emily could smell the soap on him.

"H-how do you stand it?" Emily leaped on the opportunity to distract him.

His brow wrinkled. "What?"

"Being able to smell everything as well as you do?"

"How much do you know about us?"

"I have been witness to things that cannot be explained. Things that the average person could not do. I know you are all special."

"That is a lovely way of describing our peculiarities, thank you."

When he smiled like that she found small lines at the corners of his eyes. They only added to a face that did not need more appeal.

"I will not say a word."

"Thank you again." He nodded, the damp locks falling forward over his forehead. "Do you wish to know more?"

She nodded, sipping her brandy, enjoying the feel of it sliding down her dry throat.

"If you will bear with me, I have to go back into history to explain where it all started."

Emily watched him, relieved that for now her cloak could stay in place and she had distracted him.

"In 1335 a Sinclair saved the Duke of Raven, who was a powerful man. The king was so grateful, as the duke was an ally to him, that he gave our ancestor his title and the land at the base of Raven mountain so they could watch over the Ravens, hence we are their protectors. From that day forth our senses have grown in strength."

"It almost seems too far-fetched to believe, and yet I know what you are."

"Try living with it," he drawled. "Dev can see in colors. Every person has one, and he can tell when a person is ill or gripped by a strong emotion."

"I've seen his eyes change, the green so vibrant, and his pupils so large."

"Bright colors can hurt his eyes sometimes."

"Do people have the same colors, or are they all variations of each?"

"Some are the same, with a slight variation." He hesitated before continuing. "Dev believes that people should not marry those that are not their color match."

Emily cupped the glass in her hands. She had to ask, and yet.... "What I—"

"We are a match," he said in a steady voice, his eyes holding hers. "Eden can hear anything from a great distance, which is why she wears earplugs."

They were a match, why did this make her happy?

"Essie can taste, and has a special talent for healing, and I can smell things, sometimes before they happen."

"Like a warning?"

"We can sense danger or trouble, sense when the other is hurt or needing us. That has simply grown since our family and the Ravens have become intertwined through marriage and the birth of children."

"And Lilly?"

"She is both a Sinclair and a Raven. Centuries back a Sinclair was badly behaved with a Raven, and that is the link. She can heal with touch."

"And that is why she wears gloves?"

He nodded.

"It hurts her sometimes, but bringing Dev back to life when he was shot nearly destroyed her."

"I did not realize he had died. That must have been terrible for you all."

She could not begin to grasp how someone brought another back from death, but she did not doubt Cam's words, as he had done just that for her.

"I have felt that fear several times now, and never wish to do so again."

Emily knew that Devonshire Sinclair's death would have torn his family apart, just as the loss of any of them would.

"I'm am so glad that she was able to do that, Cam. But what of Warwick, Essie, and Somer? Do they have the sense also?"

"They do, each is different. Now, shall I take your glass, Emily, so you can remove your cloak?"

"I have to tell you something, Cam."

"All right."

He eased the glass from her fingers and placed it on the table, then reached for the fastenings at her throat.

"Wait!"

"Emily, you're being foolish now."

"Y-your sisters have done something foolish."

"Is that meant to surprise me? Because I've known them for many years, and to be honest they rarely do anything that isn't."

"That's a harsh way to speak about someone you love," Emily said, playing for time and wishing she could sip more of that lovely warm brandy.

"I may love them, but I am as aware of their faults as they are of mine, my sweet. You don't spend your life retrieving them from trouble and not know this about them."

His hands went to her throat, where he stroked a finger down the front; his touch was so light Emily barely felt it.

"Now tell me what they've done?"

"They exchanged my clothing for new pieces they acquired. M-my nightwear is terrible, and my dresses are different also. It is most distressing."

She could see he was attempting to swallow a smile, but failed.

"This is not a laughing matter! I have no wish to parade about like a trollop."

"You, Mrs. Sinclair, could never be considered a trollop; you're far too much a prude."

"I am not a prude."

"Show me what you are wearing beneath that cloak then."

His fingers still played with her skin, but this time they'd moved lower, his hand easing hers aside to open the cloak.

"I will remember to thank them," he rasped as his eyes ran over her exposed body.

CHAPTER 35

She was exquisite, every inch of her. Waves of golden hair hung to her waist, and just the smell of her was arousing him painfully.

"I never knew you had so much of it." He picked up a lock, running it slowly through his fingers. "It's beautiful."

"I had to take it down, as my head was hurting." She said the words in a rush, as if she'd done something wrong.

"I was not criticizing you, Emily. I should imagine the pins needed to keep this all on top of your head must number many. Your scalp must be quite sore by now."

She nodded, watching him warily. Raising a hand, Cam ran his fingers over her head, sifting through her hair to touch her scalp. The moan escaped before she'd realized it.

"Good?"

"Yes, th-thank you. I would like to go to bed now."

She wanted to back away from him, but had nowhere to go. Only the window was behind her.

"I will never hurt you, Emily."

"I know that."

"No you don't, but you will."

Cam eased her forward into his arms and held her gently. "Relax now."

She was stiff with tension, so he placed his palm on her back and rubbed softly while his other hand continued to stroke her head.

Cam fought for control. No good would come from forcing his attentions on her, but the hell of it was he was harder and more aroused than he could ever remember being.

When he'd seen what she wore under that cloak he'd nearly swallowed his tongue. The silken material was gossamer thin and the palest peach. One satin ribbon held the robe together, and he'd wanted to open it and slide his hand beneath to caress her warm flesh, but not yet. Emily would run for the hills if he scared her.

Her skin was tinged pink from the bath, and the soap she'd used was blended with lavender. That mixed with Emily's natural scent was like a bloody aphrodisiac.

Easing back, he kissed her softly.

"Cam?"

"The lace here is pretty." He touched a thin band of peach lace that ran in a line above her breasts. Pleased when her breath hitched, he did it again.

"We're not doing that, Cam."

"What?" He traced his finger down the opening.

"Cam." She sounded unsteady.

He leaned in and took her mouth again, just a soft brush and then another. When he felt her yield, he took it deeper.

God, she was sweet.

Cam had not dallied with innocents in his lifetime; the women he'd taken to bed were experienced... until tonight. How was it possible that Emily inflamed his passions more than any?

"Open your mouth for me, sweetheart."

She did, her lips trembling beneath his as he continued kissing her. He found the ribbon for the robe and tugged it undone, then slid his hand inside, acquainting himself with her slender body.

"Just feel, Emily."

"I'm scared."

Cam removed his hands and cupped her face, tilting it so her eyes met his.

"Can you not trust me?"

He could see the fear mixed with passion. Saw the battle that was being waged inside her.

"I do not trust easily."

"I know that."

"Lessons learned early in my life are still with me, Cam. I cannot change that."

"What lessons?" He did not like to think of her living in fear.

She lowered her lashes.

"It matters not."

"It matters to me, but we will get back to that. For now I want to make you a promise."

"What?"

"If at any time you tell me to stop, then I will do so."

She looked uncertain.

"But surely you won't.... I mean what if you're...." Her words trailed off as a blush colored her cheeks.

"I am not an animal, Emily, and can control myself. Should you wish to stop at any time, then I have promised you I will do so."

"Truly?"

He nodded. Someone had hurt this woman deeply, he'd just never known how deeply until now. Her trust, Cam realized, was something he wanted... needed, if they were to make this marriage work.

"Raise your hand and make a fist."

She did as he asked. Cam then opened the first two fingers. Doing the same to his, he then curved them around hers.

"This was the highest form of Sinclair promise when we were children. To break this was a treacherous thing indeed. A two-fingered promise is a vow."

Her smile was slow to come but worth the wait.

"You Sinclairs and your traditions. It must have been wonderful to grow up surrounded by so many people you love."

"It was, but then there were moments when you wished for just a minute of solitude. Those days, I barricaded myself into the room I shared with Dev, and I would stuff Eden's earplugs in tight and lie on my bed reading."

"I suppose that did not last long?"

"I usually got an hour." Cam smiled down at her. Their fingers were still linked, but now he held them on his chest. "What about you? Did you have any childhood rituals?"

She shook her head as the smile fell away, and Cam cursed himself.

"We shall make some then."

With his free hand he cupped the back of her head, tilted her chin with his thumb.

"Remember the promise, my sweet."

He kissed her, taking his time to coax her lips open again, savoring the sweet taste of her. She was an intoxicating combination of innocence and sin. Her scent wrapped around him like an alluring cloak.

They stood there like that for some time; the kisses grew more heated as she began to respond, their fingers still twined. He let his free hand wander softly over her, touching her shoulders and running down her spine. She shivered, but did not pull away. He slid the sheer robe from her shoulders.

"You are beautiful."

"No." She whispered the word against his mouth.

"Allow me to know best here, Emily. I have spent many years researching the female form."

The sweet-smelling skin of her neck drew him. Placing his mouth there, he kissed her.

"Oh."

Her response had him licking her; this time she shuddered.

Releasing their fingers, he took her hand and placed it inside his robe. The feel of her fingers on his chest was exquisite. Touching her neck, he ran a finger around the low neckline of the nightdress, dipping lower with every pass until he eased them inside the material. He could feel the swell of her breast, and blood pounded through his body at the thought of cupping it in his palm. Raising the nipple to his mouth to lick.

"I want you very much, Emily."

"Really?"

"Really," Cam rasped.

Gripping a handful of the silk, he raised the hem and slid his hand beneath to cup her thigh. He bit back a moan at the feel of her warm skin. Moving upward, he took the material with him.

"Raise your hands."

"I...."

"Trust me."

She did as he asked, and he slid the nightdress off her body.

"Christ, you're exquisite," Cam breathed, looking at what he'd uncovered. Long slender limbs, pale, satin skin. Breasts the perfect size for his hands, and nipples his mouth wanted to caress.

She tried to move away, tried to cover herself, but he

wrapped a hand around her waist and pulled her back into his body. Taking her mouth, he kissed her once more. Deeper, more urgent, he let Emily feel his need for her; she did not believe his words, but perhaps she'd believe the evidence she felt in his body.

Lifting her into his arms, he carried her to the bed, pulled back the covers, and lowered her.

"I'm going to take off my robe now."

CHAPTER 36

*E*mily could not make herself move. Her limbs were no longer her own, and her body was infused with a need she'd never experienced before. Cam's touch had ignited her, his kisses driven her to seek more. It was as though a fever chorused through her veins.

She could not draw her eyes away from what he revealed. The hard-muscled plains of his chest appeared first, and then the shoulders ridged with more muscles. Her eyes ran over the first man she had ever seen naked, and Emily fought the sudden urge to flee. With so much power and strength, he could harm her with little effort.

"I will not hurt you. Remember our promise."

She found his green eyes, steady on hers. How had he known her thoughts?

"I remember."

She did not look lower than his chest, not wanting to see his arousal. She wished now she had let Eden tell her what happened between a man and a woman, because the only stories she knew were those her brother had told her. His mind had become twisted and warped, and he'd told her horrible things about what a man did to a woman, and yet here now, with Cam, she did not believe him capable of such terrible deeds.

He held her eyes as he moved to where she lay. Placing a knee on the bed beside her, he leaned in and took her mouth again, and Emily could do nothing to stop from reaching for him. Even through her fear she wanted his kisses again. Wanted him to take away her thoughts and replace them with that wonderful burst of heat.

"Don't hurt me, Cam." Emily had no wish to be weak or pathetic, but right at that moment she needed his reassurance again. Needed it more than her next breath.

"Never," he whispered against her lips. "Remember our promise, love."

She nodded. Cam used endearments as others used names, it was his way, Emily knew that, but even so it warmed her to hear them spoken to her now.

"One question?" he asked the words into her neck.

"Wh-what?"

"Do you like my touch, Emily?"

She could not lie.

"Yes. And you, Cam. You are the one with experience, can you find pleasure with me... an innocent?"

His lips trailed over her face, kissing her nose and chin then down the column of her neck, leaving heat wherever they roamed. The breath escaped her lips on a sigh as his hand smoothed the skin of her ribs.

"I have never felt as I do now with another woman."

She cupped his face, needing to see his eyes for the truth. He held still and let her look.

"You really meant that."

"Of course. I would never lie to you about something like this."

He eased out of her hands and placed a kiss on her lips before moving lower.

"Beautiful." His words brushed the damp skin of her neck that his kisses had left behind, making her shiver. "I want to worship every inch of you."

No man had spoken to her in such a way. No man had wanted her like this. It was a heady thought. Lifting a hand, she touched his hair, running her fingers through the black locks. Soft and springy. She dug deeper and found his scalp. He moaned as she stroked.

"I like your touch."

His words were hoarse, and Emily heard the passion. Her body felt different suddenly, her breasts fuller, and heat pooled between her thighs.

Emily gasped as he cupped her breast, his thumb stroking a nipple, making her arch as a spike of desire shot through her.

"Just feel, sweet."

She was. His masterful hands were creating a torrent of sensation inside her, and she wanted more, wanted his mouth. Dare she seek it out? Dare she touch more of him?

Tentative at first, she stroked the skin of his shoulder, feeling the heat and strength.

"Yessss."

Encouraged by his response she trailed her fingers down his side, enjoying the warm slopes and planes of muscle. Her fingers clenched as his mouth reached her breast, the sensation beyond description as he licked around her nipple.

"You have delicious breasts, Emily. The perfect size for my hands and mouth, and your nipple... ah now, there are no words to describe the beauty of it."

"I-I'm sure you've seen m-more." She arched off the bed as the last word left her lips. His mouth had closed over her nipple, tugging on the peak, sending fire through her body.

"Dear Lord!"

She hardly dared to believe what was happening, that she and Cam were doing this, but she could scramble no other thought but one. *More.* Her body craved more.

His lips moved then, traveling downward.

"Wh-what are you doing?"

Emily struggled to roll away but he placed a hand gently on her stomach, holding her there.

"Trust me."

The look he sent up her body made her stop struggling. Such smoldering heat in the green depths. He was as consumed by passion as she.

"Remember our promise," he whispered, moving lower.

"B-but...."

The word fell away as he reached the curls between her thighs. *Dear Lord.*

His tongue found the damp folds and burrowed through to the hard peak. Emily forgot to argue at the first sweep of his tongue. She writhed as pressure climbed inside her, begging for more... begging for something but she knew not what. His mouth stirred her to a frenzy, and soon she was clutching the bedcovers and making noises she'd never uttered before.

"Cam, oh please," she cried, as he slipped a finger inside her. Emily was hit with a storm of sensation that made her arch off the bed. When she regained her senses, she found him braced above her.

"I don't think I'll ever tire of seeing that particular look on your face."

"I... what...." Before she could finish he'd settled between her thighs.

"This will hurt, love, but briefly and only the first time."

The muscles of his jaw were bunched as she felt him

probing her entrance. His face, like that of a warrior going into battle, was tense and focused.

"You won't hurt me."

He stopped moving, his eyes seeking hers.

"You believe that?"

Emily nodded. She knew this now. No man could have treated her as he just had, and then hurt her. He'd shown her ecstasy, shown her gentleness, and so much more.

"I do."

His eyes closed briefly, and then he leaned in and kissed her as his body took possession of hers. She wondered how he would fit as he breached her barriers, but soon he was there, sheathed deep inside her. It hurt, burned, and yet she did not dislike the feel of him inside her as she'd once believed she would.

"Em?"

"I'm all right, Cam."

He braced himself on his arms above her, reading the truth in her eyes.

"I don't want to hurt you," he gritted out.

"Would you stop if I asked you to?" She had to know, had to ask if his words had been the truth.

"Yes," he rasped.

"I don't want you to stop."

"Thank God," he moaned, easing out of her and slowly back in. There was a lingering tightness and pain, but it was not unbearable. Reaching for him, Emily grabbed his shoulders and pulled him down so their lips met. He came willingly. She felt it again, the sweet tension climbing higher inside her erasing the pain.

"Again, my sweet," he whispered. "I need you to find your release for me again."

His hand cupped her breast, stroking her nipple, and she felt herself reach the pinnacle once more, this time gripping a handful of Cam's hair as she traversed it. He followed with a hoarse cry, collapsing on the bed beside her.

Both struggled to breathe.

Turning her head, she found him facing her. Eyes closed, hair tousled. He looked like a fallen angel. *Her fallen angel.* The long line of his body was lax and replete, unworried of his naked state. One large hand rested on her stomach.

Emily reached for the covers but he beat her, pulling them higher. He then eased her onto her side. Wrapping a hand around her waist, he pulled her back into his front.

"Sleep now," he said, his words followed by a yawn.

Emily didn't think she could sleep with a man... her husband. Looking down at the large hand holding her, she finally let the feelings inside her flame to life. Feelings that had sat dormant for so long. Since her first glimpse of Cambridge Sinclair she had felt something for him, only now could she put a name to what that was.

CHAPTER 37

*C*am was on his back when he woke. Sniffing the air as he always did, he smelled her, his wife. He found her pressed to his side, still sleeping. Her head was burrowed under his arm, and she lay on her front. He saw a cloud of blonde hair, the ends curling right and left, but little else as the covers were pulled to her shoulders.

Last night had been a revelation; he could find no other word to describe what had happened between them. Once she'd lost her inhibitions, Emily had been right there with him each step of their first sensual journey together. Smiling, he thought about the years they had ahead of them exploring the passionate side of her nature.

Who'd have thought that prim Miss Tolly, now Mrs. Sinclair, could be such a passionate woman in bed?

She stirred slowly, rolling out from under his arm and onto her side. The blankets slipped and he saw the swell of her breast and one rosy nipple. Cam's body reacted in a typical manner but he quelled it. She would be sore this morning, and did not need him pouncing on her. Her face looked peaceful in sleep, as if the life that sat hard on her shoulders when she was awake did not hurt her in slumber.

Her eyes were still shut and he wanted to lean in and kiss her lips. They were soft, the bottom slightly fuller than top. She moved again, this time away from him, much to his regret. The covers slipped lower and his eyes traveled down the delicate line of her spine.

His wife.

There was a great deal of emotion inside Cam at that moment. All of which he knew was leading to something, but he was not ready to form it into a word yet. With one finger, he eased the covers lower, and it was then he saw it.

His body jerked as he studied the scar. Leaning closer, he followed the wicked line that ran from the middle of her back outward for several inches. A foot long a least, it was half an inch wide. His first thought was a knife had done that. It was old, the skin flattened and faded. He'd not seen it last night, because she'd been lying on her back, but he saw it now, and the rage inside him was swift.

I may never have met her!

"I'm going to kill someone," he growled before he could stop himself.

She turned onto her back, eyes opening to look up at him. The gray depths were soft and sleepy.

"G-good morning."

"Who hurt you?" Cam should have waited, should have let her wake with a kiss, but the fury inside demanded answers.

"Pardon?" She blinked several times, attempting to clear her head, then pulled the covers higher.

"Who inflicted that wound on your back."

"I-I don't know what you speak of."

She quickly sat upright against the headboard, arms wrapping around the legs she'd drawn up to her chest.

He saw the gesture as protection; it was instinctive and he hated it. Hated that she felt the need to do so around him.

"Emily love, tell me who hurt you... please," Cam said, moving closer, trying to cool the anger inside him.

She tried to turn away from him, but he held her chin in a hand.

"I fell on glass."

"You're lying. That mark was inflicted by a knife."

"H-how could you know that?"

"I've seen knife wounds."

"They are no different from being cut by glass. You cannot possibly tell between the two."

"I can, and that was done by a knife. Who hurt you?"

"I don't want to talk about it, and you should not have looked."

"You were lying on your side, I could hardly fail to do so. Plus, your skin is like silk, and you're beautiful. A saint would have struggled not to look at you lying there like that."

She was silent, her eyes big as she studied him. There was a distance between them again, and he had put it there with his words.

"Forgive me, I had no right to wake you in such a way." He hauled in a deep steadying breath. "I saw that scar and felt your pain."

"It's all right."

She still had her hands wrapped around her knees, and Cam was not having her withdraw further from him after what they had shared. Reaching for her, he lifted her into his arms.

"What are you doing? Unhand me!"

"No. Now sit still and let your husband wake you properly."

"I am already awake, thanks to you."

"And there is my acid-tongued wife."

"I'm not—"

He kissed her softly until she responded, as he'd known she would. Emily, Cam realized, would always respond to his kisses... his; no other man would have her.

"Good morning, wife." He tucked a lock of hair behind her ear.

"G-good morning."

He would not push her about the scar now, which was hard for him as he was not a patient man.

"Are you hungry?"

She nodded.

"It was all the exercise we did last night," he said with wicked smile. She colored up delightfully. "I had no idea you could scream my name that loud."

"I did not!"

"You did actually. 'Oh, Cam, more, Cam,' you cried."

"I did not." She scowled.

"Perhaps not, but I enjoyed the lovely little sounds you made, and shall make it my life's work to ensure I hear plenty more."

She grabbed a handful of his hair and pulled it hard until he released her in a howl of pain.

"Eden told me that this would bring you to heel. It seemed she was right."

"As long as I can bring you to heel as well, and I know just the way to do so."

He kissed her breast, circling her nipple slowly. Her answer was to gasp.

"Alas, we cannot continue, as you are sore."

"Oh."

He didn't laugh at her disappointment, but silently rejoiced in it.

"Tomorrow," he whispered in her ear.

"I-I am not used to speaking of things openly," she said,

scrambling off the bed. "You Sinclairs like to discuss everything in such a manner. You will understand that I am not used to that."

"Surely not everything," Cam drawled as he watched her. He saw the scar again, and then she wrapped a blanket around herself, covering up all that delectable flesh.

Who had hurt her?

She attempted to glare at him, but looked like a rumpled angel. The blanket was around her Grecian style, and her hair fell in a tangled mess to her hips. She looked luscious, and he had to drag his eyes from her, or get off the bed and carry her back onto it.

They washed and dressed, and Cam teased Emily as she attempted to put her hair back on top of her head, until she laughed.

"You, sir, are a scoundrel."

"Surely not?"

"Yes, and far too used to having your own way."

"You are not serious surely? With as many siblings as I have I'm not sure how I can have achieved that."

She was dressed in one of his sister's selections. Long-sleeved, the velvet was the color of blackberries that grew wild all over England. The style was simple, and the bodice a great deal more revealing than Emily usually wore. Cam liked it very much. Her usual clothing covered every inch of her. He must remember to thank his sisters for their meddling.

"These dresses are horrid," she said, attempting to tug it higher. "There is no lace to tuck into it. I feel half dressed."

"And yet you look beautiful."

Her hands stopped fiddling with her hair.

"Only because you can see more of me."

"I have always known you were beautiful, my sweet, even

when you wore those hideous sacks made of equally hideous fabrics, in horrid colors."

"They were not hideous, and extremely comfortable."

"They were designed to disguise the female form, Emily, and as yours is lovely, I am glad that is no longer the case."

"They will be waiting for me upon my return," she muttered.

"I would not bank on that. My sisters can be ruthless when required."

She gave up on her hair, instead putting it in a simple braid and twisting it into a circle on the back of her head.

Excellent, he would be able to release that later with very little effort on his part.

Cam watched as she picked up a small bottle of scent. Removing the stopper, she lifted it for a sniff at the same time a knock sounded on the door. The scent bottle slipped, spilling the contents on Emily.

"Oh dear, now I shall have to change."

"Yes, and I will deal with whoever is at the door, and leave, as the strength of that scent is making my head hurt. I shall then go and see to the carriage and our morning meal."

"Oh, Cam, I'm sorry—"

"It's all right." He brushed a kiss over her cheek and answered the door. It was his driver, so he left with him to settle their bill and ready everything for their departure.

He found himself smiling as he met with the innkeeper, and felt ridiculously happy, which of course was all down to Emily.

CHAPTER 38

hey ate, then Cam bundled Emily back into the carriage. A servant placed a ceramic bottle at her feet and then closed the door. Seconds later the carriage was rolling out of the inn's courtyard.

"What is that?" Emily was looking down at the bottle.

"Place your feet on it."

She did, and the wonder on her face made him laugh.

"Oooh, that is blissful."

"I will get it refilled when we stop for a meal at midday."

"Thank you, it is the most wonderful gift I have ever received, kind sir."

Her smile was playful. In just one night, so much had changed between them. Cam was sure there would be plenty of arguments and heated debates in their future, but he looked forward to that. In fact, he looked forward to life with Emily.

"One question?"

She looked suddenly nervous.

"All right."

"Who hurt you?" It had been riding him since he'd seen it.

The need to know the identity of the person who had inflicted pain on her so he could extract retribution.

"I would rather not speak of that time."

At least she acknowledged that it was not an accident now.

"That time? Do you mean before you came to live with James?"

She nodded.

"Surely it was not all bad?"

Cam had told himself not to push her, but he was not a patient man. If he wanted to know something he went after it. Emily was a mystery even her own family had not uncovered. He was her husband, and he wanted no secrets between them.

"Shall I tell you a secret of mine in exchange for one of yours?"

She didn't nod, or shake her head, simply continued to look at him.

"I was a gambler for many years, hating the world my father had left us in. He was a wastrel who left Dev to run the family and find the finances to feed us. I used whatever money I could to lose myself in women and spirits, and the rest I gambled. My family suffered because of it... because of my selfishness."

He was not proud of the man he had been, but it was a part of him, and she deserved to know this.

"Why?"

"I was resentful of the fact my father had died leaving us penniless. I hated Dev for the sanctimonious bastard he was, and my family for the burden we carried by being different. I loathed that. Loathed walking into a room and smelling every foul smell ten times sharper than anyone else."

"It must have been a hard time for you."

Her eyes held pity.

"I didn't tell you so you would feel sorry for me, Emily. I told you because I wanted you to know the man I had once been. I want no secrets between us."

"But are no longer," she said softly. "James told me you were one of the most honorable men he knew."

"Did he? That is very kind of him, considering he saw me at my worst."

"Don't make light of it, Cam. You are a good man, and a strong one for changing who you were."

Cam had fought many demons and battles to become the man he was today. "I have no wish to go back to that self-pitying, indulgent fool."

"But I think some of us learn through life lessons to become the people we can be proud of. That you were strong enough to change is something you should take pride in."

He was proud of the man he had become. His business interests were prospering, and he was now respected among his peers and associates. More importantly, his family was proud of him.

"And you, what will you tell me about yourself, Emily?"

He kept his eyes on her as she studied her gloved hands.

"I have not always been proud of my actions, or things I have done, but some were through necessity."

"What were you forced to do?"

She shook her head, which Cam guessed meant she was not about to elaborate. He was wrong.

"My brother, Edward, protected me as best he could for the early years of my life, but when he was forced to watch my mother die a slow and very painful death, his mind started to go."

"Where you not there also?"

"Of course." She flicked her wrist, dismissing his words. "But it affected him more than me."

Cam fought back the anger at the mention of the man who had nearly taken his sister from him.

"Where did you live?"

She was silent again, thinking through what she wanted to tell him. He knew it would be abbreviated, but for now he would take that. One day she would tell him the whole story.

"We moved a lot. We had a horse, and mother rode that, and then when she couldn't, Edward rode holding her, as he was strongest."

"And you walked?"

She nodded.

"We relied on the generosity of others, sleeping in their barns or wherever we could find shelter. When mother's illness became apparent, people did not want us close. Edward approached the duke, but was sent away."

"All the late duke's children suffered at his hand. It is my fondest wish he is residing in the fiery pits of hell for his crimes."

She nodded.

"That was when Edward came to resent the Ravens with a ferocity that robbed his sanity. Revenge became the only thing he cared about."

"I'm sorry for what you suffered, Emily."

"'Tis in the past now."

But it still haunted her, Cam knew this. Knew in order for her to heal whatever pain lay in her past, that like him, she needed to speak of it. However, he didn't think that would be an easy thing to get her to do.

"Tell me who hurt you?"

"Cam—"

He moved closer, onto the edge of the seat, and drew her to the edge of hers, forcing her to face him.

"To know a beast inflicted pain on someone as sweet and

innocent as you makes me want to go after him and pay him back in kind, Emily."

"I am not sweet and innocent, Cam."

"To me you are."

She shook her head.

"I have seen things that no innocent should see—"

"And you think I care about that? You may have seen things, but you are still an innocent, Emily."

"My brother would take me gambling with him. I went into the most disreputable places and distracted men so he could steal from them. He cheated, and I helped him!"

"That sin is his not yours, as I suspect you did not go willingly, and my only sorrow is that I was not there to protect you."

She tried to pull away from him, but Cam held her still.

"Who hurt you?"

"He did," she whispered. "He tried to kill me because I refused to do it anymore."

Cam pulled her onto his lap and held her while she cried.

"I hated him, and it w-was not his fault. He was sick, and twisted in the head and I could do nothing to stop him."

"Sssh, I have you now."

"He made me come to London with him, and I knew he was here to seek revenge. Knew, but could do nothing to stop it from happening."

He gave her his strength as the words poured out. Wrapped her in his arms and held on. Her fingers fisted on his coat as she held him back.

"Wh-when he left, the last time I saw him, I begged him to stop, but he simply told me I was a traitor to our mother, and that she deserved revenge for her suffering. The n-next p-people I saw were Devon and James."

She was sobbing now, and Cam wanted to stop her,

wanted to ease her pain, but knew the words needed to be spoken.

"When Eden and James returned to tell me Edward was d-dead, I was glad my brother was gone."

He let her weep until the cries eased to sniffles, and then a small catch in her breathing. Only then did he speak.

"You could not have stopped him, Emily, you know that don't you? Know that the poison inside his head could not be cleansed. What drove your brother to do what he did was nothing to do with you, love. You must remember the brother you once had, not the latter one with the twisted mind. Forgive him, Em, and move forward... with me."

Cam would never forgive the bastard for hurting her, but Emily did not need to know that. All that mattered now was she had trusted him enough to share her past, and that humbled him.

"It's all right, now, love." He kissed her brow. She lay against him, warm in his arms, and he realized something as he looked down at her... his wife.

"I love you," Cam whispered, but she didn't hear as she'd drifted off into an exhausted slumber.

CHAPTER 39

"*I* smell danger!"

Emily woke to these words, and the next second the carriage veered wildly, jostling them.

"Christ!"

Cam's curse as he held her was loud in the small confines of the carriage.

"I have you."

"Was that a gunshot?" Emily asked.

"Yes." He lowered her to the seat beside him and moved to the window. Emily did the same from the other side. The carriage was moving at speed now.

"Pull your head back inside at once, you silly woman! We are being pursued!"

Cam grabbed her again, hauling her to his side.

"Wh-why would someone be following us?"

His face was grim, eyes dark and intense. This, she realized, was the other side to Cambridge Sinclair. Gone was the devil-may-care man who teased and played the fool with his family, and also the gentle man who had held her while she stumbled out the story of her life.

"That I don't know, but there are three riders following this carriage, and it is clear they want to stop it, and in likelihood will."

"Oh dear." Emily felt sick at the thought. "What is to be done?"

Cam reached behind him.

"Stab anyone who gets close to you."

He held a knife in his hand.

"All right."

"Except me of course." His smile held no humor.

Emily took the knife and lifted her skirts. She tucked it in her garter, retying the ribbon tight. "I hope it holds."

When Cam didn't reply she looked at him, but his eyes were fixed on her thigh.

"Cam!"

He blinked.

"Sorry, but I think that is the sexiest sight I have ever seen."

"We're being pursued by God knows who, and you think about that? Cam?"

"What?" He was looking out the window again.

"Thank you."

"It would be my honor to hold your secrets, Emily, if you will do the same with mine."

"I-I..." He looked at her as she stuttered. "I think I love you," Emily said.

"You think?"

"Well, it is a new feeling, but yes," she said, testing the word in her head as the carriage continued to pick up speed. "I don't know what is about to happen, but I know I want you to hear those words from me before it does."

He reached for her and hauled her close to kiss her hard.

"I love you, Mrs. Sinclair, and unlike you, I don't need to think about it."

"Oh... really?" Emily felt the ridiculous urge to smile. "B-but how do you—"

"Really," he cut her off. "Now shut up, I need to concentrate."

The carriage was flying now.

"We'll discuss this further later... hopefully in a big bed."

Reaching under the seat, he pulled out a shotgun and went to the window, but as he did the carriage wobbled. They heard a crack, and then it was listing.

"The wheel, Cam!"

"It has broken, the carriage is stopping," he said calmly... way more calmly than the situation warranted to Emily's mind. She was panicking. Her breath was coming in pants, and her body was trembling.

"I want to have children!" she cried.

"I'm hoping I'm included in the conception."

"I don't want anything to happen to us!" Emily was battling the panic. Happiness was in her grasp. Real happiness, and a life that she would live to the fullest with the man across from her.

"It won't. Trust me. Now say nothing, stay at my back, and do exactly as I say, do you understand me, Emily?"

"Yes."

An arm banded around her waist and pulled her close. He kissed her hard again.

"We will get out of this, I promise. But I need you to be strong, sweetheart."

"I can do that... be strong for you."

"I know you can. Just as I know you can be strong for yourself."

His absolute faith in Emily made her shoulders straighten. He believed in her, so it was time she did too.

They didn't speak again, as a loud voice was demanding

they step from the carriage. Cam pulled up the hood of her cloak, then touched her cheek.

"It will be all right."

Emily prayed he was right as she followed him from the carriage.

"Are you well, Bids? You also, Clivers?" Cam spoke to his drivers. Both acknowledged they were unharmed. "Nothing silly now, boys," he added.

Emily looked at the three men on horseback before them. The lower halves of their faces were covered, hats pulled down so their eyes were shielded.

"What is it you want from us?" Cam's words were steady, eyes locked on the men now.

"I want your drivers to step down beside you."

Cam nodded to indicate they do as the man said. A coil of rope was thrown down.

"The woman can tie them up to that tree." He pointed to the left.

"I can do it," Cam said, reaching for the rope.

"I said the woman!"

"It's all right, Cam." Emily took it from him and went to do as the man bid. Cam's drivers gave her a reassuring nod as they sat on either side of the trunk, which she had no idea how to interpret.

"Wrap it around their waists," the man pointing his gun at her directed.

"I won't make it too tight," she whispered.

"Do what you must, Mrs. Sinclair." Emily knew Bids, as he was usually Devon's driver, but had offered to travel with Cam and her for this trip.

"Stop talking!"

"I don't like this, Mrs. Sinclair. Something smells off," Bids whispered. "Be on your guard."

She nodded, wondering what he meant. Surely the fact

that they were being held at gunpoint was treacherous enough.

"You, bring me your money."

The man was pointing at Cam.

"Don't go," Emily whispered as she returned to his side.

"They will shoot us if I do not, love," he whispered. "Let me do this and they will leave. Remember our love, Em. Hold on to that now."

"Cam—"

She could not stop him from walking away from her, but something inside her wanted to run after him, and drag him back to her side.

Her eyes followed the long line of his back and broad shoulders as he walked. When he stopped beside the man who had spoken, he lifted a pouch of money. The man took it and threw it to the rider beside him. He then pointed his gun at Cam.

"No!" Emily screamed, and ran forward but it was too late, he had lifted the butt of his gun and brought it down hard on Cam's head. His knees buckled and he dropped to the ground.

"Cam!" She threw herself down on top of his still body.

"Grab her!"

"Cam?" Emily dug her fingers into his neck. There was a pulse, the relief made her light-headed.

Hands grabbed her but she struck out with her foot. She would not leave him, as he would never leave her.

"Grab her!"

Remembering the knife, Emily burrowed under her skirts and grabbed it. Leaping to her feet, she lunged at the nearest man. He howled in pain.

"Get away from us!" Emily swung the blade from side to side as the three men began to circle her. "I will never leave him."

She was outnumbered but fought with everything she had left in her body. Slashing with the knife, and kicking, she kept them at bay as long as she could, but there were too many of them and soon they had her. Forcing the knife from her hands, Emily's arms were wrenched behind her back.

"Give her to me."

She was dragged to the man who still remained on his horse, and lifted up before him.

"Ride!"

She looked up into the face of the man who held her. He had removed his mask.

"You!"

"Hello, Miss Tolly."

His smile flashed, and Emily felt icy fear slither through her.

"No!" She fought again, but he was too strong. Seconds later Cam had gone from her sight, and Emily felt the agony of realizing that she would never see him again. The happiness she had glimpsed had been ripped from her, and now there was only the terror of darkness inside her.

CHAPTER 40

"Mr. Sinclair. Mr. Sinclair!"

Cam roused to the sound of his name being roared repeatedly. Moaning as his eyes opened, he touched the side of his head. His hand came away covered in blood.

Emily!

Sitting upright, he battled the nausea and looked for her.

"Emily!"

"They took her, Mr. Sinclair."

He found his drivers still tied to the tree. Climbing to his feet, Cam staggered several times as he tried to clear his head.

Christ, someone had taken Emily.

The breath came from his throat in painful gasps as he tried to focus, tried to see past the terror. His love, Emily, the woman who had been part of his life for so long, but only recently had he loved with a desperation that made his chest burn.

"They knew her, Mr. Sinclair."

"What?" Cam blinked several times, he was struggling to

think clearly. His body was shaking, and his veins were filled with icy fear. Someone had taken Emily away from him.

"The man who put her up before him on his horse called her Miss Tolly," Bids said, looking worried. "Heard it clear from here."

"Christ!" *Think, Cam.* Panic was clawing at his insides, scrambling his thoughts. He had to find her.

"Unhitch the horses. We'll ride for the next village or inn and secure faster ones."

"I'll bind your head first," Bids said when he was standing.

"We have no time."

"We don't have time for you to bleed to death either," his driver said. "Necktie please, sir."

Cam ripped it from his neck and handed it to him.

Minutes later he was riding as if his life depended on it. His head had settled into a dull throb, but it was nothing compared to the pain in his heart.

He'd taken Emily away from London and her security, and this had happened. Was it connected to the abduction in London... surely it had to be. How was she suffering? Were they hurting her, where had they taken her? Thoughts tumbled with relentless consistency over and over inside his head. *Does she think me dead?*

She loved him. That thought alone pushed him harder. They had a life to live together, and he would do everything he could to ensure that, no matter how long it took or the cost to him.

His family would know what was happening; he could sense their distress, feel their urgency. They would come, he never doubted that, but were still hours away.

The acrid stench in his nostrils refused to abate, telling him that his connection to Emily was now even stronger. The union of their bodies had bonded them, but the union of their hearts had made them one, and now he would smell her fear, and yes, pain, although he could not stand to think of her hurting.

"A village up ahead, Mr. Sinclair!"

Bids's words had Cam urging his horse faster, until they were galloping into the small town. Dismounting with haste, Cam made for the stables.

"How may I help?" A man came to meet him.

"I need three of your fastest horses at once!"

"You're bleeding, sir. If you'll allow it, I'll have my wife tend you."

"I have no time, I—"

"Fetch her," Bids said. "He needs tending. Send something to fetch the carriage please, it has a broken wheel, some thirty minutes back."

"I'm not waiting, Bids. Once the horses arrive I am leaving."

"You'll be no help to her if you faint, and I'd be remiss in my duties to your family if I don't have you tended afore we leave."

"Damn it, Bids, Emily—"

"Has a head start, but with fresh, fast horses, and your head feeling better, we'll catch them with hard riding. A matter of minutes, Mr. Sinclair, and nothing more."

"I'll see to it at once, and have my wife here in a trice, sir."

Cam nodded, then watched the man throw out orders with the skill of a drill sergeant.

"Have you seen three riders? I doubt their faces were still covered, but they were in the company of a lady?" Cam asked as the man returned with his wife.

"Four riders did come through here a while ago. Three stopped at the end of the village, while one came in and collected supplies from the inn. I was watching from the doorway, as I like to see who comes and goes."

Cam bit back a curse as the man's wife dabbed something on his head.

"It needs cleaning and stitching. You shouldn't ride on it, sir."

"No time," Cam said. "Just pour something over it, then bandage it and we'll be leaving."

"They could have disguised her, but they only had three horses," Bids said, looking worried, which was his usual expression, but in this case it was warranted.

"They hid one," Cam said, he then cursed loudly as the woman poured alcohol over his wound.

"It had to have been planned. In fact, they were possibly following us since we left London," Bids said as Cam tried to regain his breath. "I'm not sure why they waited until now to stop you if that was the case."

"That I don't know," Cam gritted out. "But likely they waited for the weather to ease."

He chaffed at the seconds it took to have his head bandaged.

"She fought you know."

"What?" He looked at Bids.

"At first Mrs. Sinclair threw herself down on top of you, and then when they came at her she pulled out a knife from her skirts, and fought. Three men there were, and she held them off, standing over you, keeping you safe."

Cam swallowed down the emotion inside of him.

"Takes a powerful love to behave in such a way, and a powerful lady is my belief."

Cam could imagine how fierce she looked, and prayed she stayed strong until he found her.

I'm coming, Emily.

. . .

Emily could hardly breathe through the smelly cloth that covered the lower half of her face. She rode on her own horse, hands tied before her, and was consumed with worry for Cam.

Is he all right? Has someone come to his aid?

She knew he would be all right, knew it inside her, but the fear still consumed her.

I love you. He'd said those words to her, and her heart had felt fuller. Even though the situation had been dire, the feeling had gripped her. Now all she could think was that he was lying somewhere hurt without her, and she could do nothing to help him. With every mile she traveled, her despair increased... but so did her anger.

"I will remove the gag if you promise not to scream, my dear."

The man she knew as Mr. Jackson rode beside her. Keeping her eyes forward, she refused to acknowledge him.

How had he found them? Had he followed them from London, been planning this all along when his attempts to wed her had failed?

For now she would do as he asked, but when and if the chance arose to escape she would be taking it. She was stronger now, stronger because of Cam's love. She would cower to no one again. Emily Sinclair would no longer live in the shadows, but at the side of her husband, and she would not let this man take her away from the life she wanted.

He would come for her if he could.

Cam had given her strength, and self-belief. He had annoyed, irritated, and teased it into her, and then last night he'd given her heaven in the guise of his body. Today he had given her his heart. She wanted that in her life and more. Emily was now greedy to go after all of it... everything that she had once believed herself unworthy of having.

Disguising the anger that raged inside her, she looked at

Mr. Jackson and nodded to indicate she would behave... for now. But when the chance presented itself for her to scream for help, she would be doing so at the top of her voice.

"Why are you doing this?"

His lips thinned as an angry snarl formed on his face.

"Had my original abduction succeeded, then I would not have been forced to take such drastic measures."

"It was you that day who took me off the street?"

"It was, and then your family would not let you out of their sight, so I could not make another attempt. So I tried to court you, show them I was a candidate for your hand, but no, they would not have it. Your brothers have a misguided belief that you are important to them, Miss Tolly. However, we both know that cannot be true."

"My name is Mrs. Sinclair," Emily said, controlling her temper.

"Ah yes, they married you to one of their own to stop the gossipmongers tattling about you. It matters not, I simply want you as a ransoming tool, then I will release you."

"I don't understand." Emily grappled with what he said.

"I need money, Miss Tolly. When I abducted you that day, I would simply have held you until your brothers paid the ransom, as they would have, and everything would have returned to normal when I released you to them, but that idiot husband you now have saved you. Then one of those fools I paid to take you, chose to cut the carriage free rather than hurl you from it, leaving me without transportation."

"He is no idiot," Emily said as calmly as she could. "He is my husband, and the man I love."

She did love him very much, Emily realized as a flush of heat suffused her chest. She loved Cam, and oh the feeling was wonderful... or it would be if he was not lying injured somewhere. Dear Lord, let him be all right; she could not believe anything else, would not let herself imagine him anything but the large, vital man she had always known.

"He saved you, and thwarted my plans! The carriage was destroyed forcing me to hire one, and thus I am more out of pocket because of you!"

She remained silent.

"So I was forced to do this. I will ransom you, and then return you."

"But surely there was another way?"

"I can borrow no more money, and after the time and expense you have cost me, it became something of a challenge for me to get your brothers' money, especially as Mr. Huntington refused me twice when I applied to join one of his consortiums."

"So this is revenge, and a need for money?"

"Exactly that, and your brothers have enough of it."

"You are quite mad," Emily said as calmly as she could. She'd lived with a madman and knew the signs.

"No, I am desperate and you have thwarted me at every turn. This time I ensured that would not happen, and in capturing you I will get my revenge on your family."

Emily now knew his identity and what he had done, and that he was in debt. He would never release her, especially if he was to return to the life he had led before in London. It was not logical, nor feasible. The thought was a chilling one, as that meant he would dispose of her in some way.

"We shall ride to a location, I will send word to your brothers, then when I receive the money, I will let you go."

She had to escape, or she would never see Cam or her family again.

I love you, she vowed silently, praying that Cam was safe.

291

CHAPTER 41

*E*ach village Cam rode through told him they had not seen Emily, but a group of four riders.

"It has to be her, Bids."

"'Tis my belief you are right, Mr. Sinclair." The driver's expression had not changed since they had started. Like Cam, his fears for Emily had grown with every mile they traveled.

"How is your head?"

Cam grunted a response. It hurt like the devil, but anger was keeping it under control. Emily, his wife, the woman he loved, was now vital to his existence. She was his, and someone had taken her from him, and that someone would pay, and pay dearly.

He felt it then, the small fission of awareness.

"My family is coming, Bids."

The driver had been with their family for many years; he had seen much, and did not question Cam's words.

Bids's core role in the Sinclair family was as a driver, but also a worrier. He worried if one of the twins or Warwick hurt themselves. He worried if anyone in the family left the house without him driving them; in fact he was worse than an over-protective parent, but they tolerated him as it was well meant. But Bids also knew that they were different, and his loyalty to them was unflinching, thus he never shared this knowledge with anyone. Cam could think of no man, other than those in his family, that he would have at his side at this moment.

"I don't mind telling you that's a relief, Mr. Sinclair."

"We will change horses here, and continue," Cam said, riding into the inn's small courtyard.

They had been riding for hours now, and were he had soon realized, heading back toward London. Anger had held him upright, and his need to get to Emily. The bandages on his head were soaked with blood, and he was dizzy, but he would not stop, not until he had her safe.

"You need to eat here, and have that wound cleaned and rebandaged, Mr. Sinclair."

"I'm well, Bids, don't fuss."

"Just the same, I'd like you to do it."

"There is no time."

"They can't keep up the punishing pace, just as we can't."

He looked at the stubborn set of both his drivers' faces.

"My wife has been abducted, and I need to get to her," Cam said slowly. "I must get to her, just as you would, were our positions reversed."

"I'd not stop at anything, God's truth, and yet I'm afeared for you."

"I am well, and my family will be there to help soon. A while longer, Bids, is all I ask of you."

Grim-faced, the driver nodded.

They changed horses, collected food, then ate it on horse-back. By the time day eased into dusk, Cam's body ached and his head swum with pain and blood loss. He would not be able to stay upright for much longer, no matter how much he willed it.

"Food is what you need," Bids said as they rode into yet another village, this one bordered by a stream. Cam had long since stopped feeling the cold that sliced through his body and buffeted him. He was numb to all but Emily... his love.

"They are here," he said suddenly, dismounting as a charge of awareness ran through him. He staggered a few steps. Righting himself, he looked up the road he had just traveled. Cam watched seven horses thunder into town.

"Thank God."

He stepped into the street, and seconds later they were all there. Each talking over the other as they dismounted and ran to him. Touching him, hugging him, letting them know they were close, as they always did. He had never been more grateful for his family than at that moment. Wolf, too, had come.

"Are you well, brother?"

"He took a blow to the head." Bids stepped up and answered Dev's question.

"Emily," Cam said, leaning into the arm his brother had wrapped around his shoulders. "They have taken Emily, Dev. We have to get her back." He heard the raw emotion, just as they did. The need and desperation to have her back with him was etched in each word.

"Let's get him inside."

"No," Cam said in answer to James. "I must go after her."

"We will." Essie stepped up and cupped his cheek. "I promise we will find her. But first let us care for you. Ten minutes, and then we can be back on the road."

He could not fight them all, so found himself being propelled into an inn. A private parlor was procured in minutes by James, who was not opposed to throwing around his title when required. Cam was then forced down onto a chair. Bids started relaying the story as Essie leaned over him.

"Let me see now, Cam."

"'Tis nothing."

Ignoring his attempts to push her away, she began to unwrap the bloodied bandage while James and Max asked questions. He watched her face, but she kept that lovely smile on it like she always did when she treated him or anyone who needed her attentions. The gentle sister who could be fierce as a lioness when required.

"You'll live." She leaned in and kissed his cheek. She then stepped aside and Lilly moved closer.

"Let me help you now, Cam."

He felt the heat of her hand on his head, and then the burning sensation followed by relief.

"Only a little." He gripped her wrist. Lilly could heal with a touch, but it hurt her to do so.

"It will not cause me too much pain, brother, rest easy. Plus, your siblings are helping, which gives me strength."

He found Dev's eyes; they were bright with his power. He had his hand on Lilly's neck; Eden held his hand and Essie hers. He felt the humiliating sting of tears behind his eyes and tried to blink, tried to will them away.

"All done," Lilly said.

"Sit now, Lilly, and drink the tea I prepared for you, my love," Dev instructed as he dropped down to his haunches before Cam. "Food also, Essie. Ensure she eats."

Cam heard the hum of voices behind him as his brother looked at him, the green eyes so bright they glowed like gems.

"We will find her, Cam."

"I-I feel as if my heart has b-been ripped from my chest."

His brother held up a hand and Cam gripped it as if they

would arm wrestle, as they had often as children. He gripped it tight.

"Help me find her, brother."

"We have everything on our side to do that, Cam. My sight, Eden's hearing, and you and Essie only add to that, as does Lilly. Her brothers will do whatever it takes also. Put your faith in us now, as we have ours in you many times."

"God's blood, I never wanted this," he hissed. "Wanted this vicious emotion and pain. Vowed to leave that to you lot."

"And yet now you feel it because you love her, as I suspect she loves you."

Cam nodded. "It is all-consuming, Dev. My heart feels bigger, and my need for her is obsessive. Tell me it will pass. Tell me this insanity will ease, for I fear I cannot live like this forever."

"The love will never go, but the madness of it will ease given time, Cam, and then you and Emily will have your life together. This is my vow to you."

"I'll take it, and hold you to it."

They held tight for a few more seconds, then Dev released him and rose, as did Cam. He was stronger now his family were here. Lilly had healed him, and he was ready to do what he must to find Emily.

"You did what you could, brother, never doubt that." James stepped forward.

"I did not do enough."

"Your wound tells a different story," Max said, his eyes banked with rage. "But now we ride."

The door opened, and a man told them fresh horses were ready.

"Yesterday, Edward came to see me," Max said. "He had some interesting news."

Cam was instantly alert. Edward was Max's right hand man.

"A man called Mr. Carmichael allegedly tried to abduct a merchant's daughter in Scotland two years ago to ransom her for a large sum of money. He failed, and then disappeared."

"And this is important because?" Cam demanded.

"He reappeared in London and changed his name to Mr. Jackson."

"That bastard!" Cam roared. "I'm gutting him!"

"He has been after our money from the start. It was he who abducted Em before. When we tightened the protection around her he tried to woo her, and when that failed he compromised her thinking we would simply hand her over."

"That failed, so he simply took her," Cam finished for him.

"Yes." Max sounded grave. "But unlike last time he tried, she can now identify him."

"He'll kill her." Fear choked Cam.

"We won't let that happen," Dev said.

"They felt you, your siblings," Max added as they left the room. "Essie was with me, and simply doubled over wrapping her arms around her waist, calling your name. Her fear was something I will never forget. They all came then, together within minutes. Wolf sprinted in my front door wearing only a shirt and trousers. His feet were bare and his hair stood off his head."

"I have yet to recover from the fear that filled my veins suddenly, cousin," Wolf said, gripping his shoulder. "We will get her back safe."

"It's my belief, for sanity's sake, that you must never live more than a mile from each other, and all travel destinations are shared from this day forth. Never do I want to see the woman I love in that kind of pain again," Max added.

"Agreed," James said.

They reached the horses and began to mount.

"Jackson is going to London, I'm certain of that. It is his jungle, and a place he knows well. He has contacts who have warehouses there. It's my belief he will hope to hide Emily there, and then make contact with us," Max continued.

"Then let us ride hard, family, for I have a man to kill," Cam said with the scent of revenge thick in his nostrils.

CHAPTER 42

hey arrived long after dark had fallen. Her eyes had adjusted to the night and the fatigue Emily kept at bay with anger. She'd been gagged once more as they entered London for fear she would scream, which she would have done given the opportunity.

Cold had long since turned her toes and fingers numb, and her body was one large ache as they pulled up before a large house in a neighborhood she was not familiar with.

Cam was alive, she was sure of it. The knock to his head had been hard but she felt him, and if he was dead, she would not do so. His family would have reached him by now, Emily was sure of this also. The bond they had was strong, and they would have felt his pain.

"Swing your leg over, Miss Tolly."

Glaring down at Mr. Jackson, she did as he instructed, her legs buckling after so long on horseback. She leaned away from the hand he held out to steady her and into the horse.

"Come." He grabbed her arm and started up a step and through the gate, the hinge squeaking as he opened it.

Reaching the front door, he knocked on it twice, and then turned the handle and entered. Emily followed him into the long, dimly lit hallway that had a doorway at the end and a set of stairs leading to the next floor.

"I shall remove your gag now."

"He will find you," Emily spat as soon as the foul cloth was removed. "And then you will be made to pay for the harm you have caused."

"Your husband has no idea it is I who has taken you, Miss Tolly, nor do your brothers. He may track you to London, but he will not find you here. I have left no trail, and this house is rented. Only the men accompanying me and the woman who will care for you are aware of who I am, and I am ensured of their silence as they will be paid handsomely when your brothers hand over the money for your return."

"Let me go. No good can come of this."

A door at the end of the hall opened then, and a woman appeared.

"This man has kidnapped me!" Emily started forward. "I shall reward—"

"Don't bother, she will pay you no mind, will you, Mrs. Dobbs?"

"No. I know what needs doing, then I'll have me money."

Mrs. Dobbs raised the candle she carried, and Emily saw her mouth was a grim line. She wore black, and a lace cap that had once been white, but now was a grubby grey.

"I've readied the room," the woman said as she started up the stairs.

They followed, she and Mr. Jackson. It was cold in here, cold and damp, Emily thought, shivering. She wanted Cam. Was it just last night she'd been in his arms? It felt like much longer. She wanted to see him laugh again, wanted that desperately.

They walked into what appeared to be a small parlor.

Four chairs stood around a table. Emily watched Mrs. Dobbs moved to a set of shelves on one wall that held books. Bending, she did something, and suddenly the shelf moved and an opening appeared.

"In you go."

"No!" Emily fought with everything she had. If they got her in that room, no one would find her ever, and she would have no means of escape. Lashing out with her foot, she kicked Mr. Jackson in the leg, forcing him backward, thereby releasing her. Freed, she sprinted for the door. She reached the stairs and hurried down, trying to keep her footing. Unable to use her hands as they were still bound, she stumbled, but managed to right herself by jumping down the last three. Emily ran to the front door and wrenched it open. She hurried outside.

"Stop her!"

The roar came from behind her. Mr. Jackson was in pursuit. Emily made it down the path and through the gate. She leaped off the step and started screaming loudly.

"Got you!"

Hands grabbed her, and she realized it was one of the men who had accompanied them to London. Stomping on his foot, she tried to escape, and did briefly before hands gripped her coat.

"Grab her!"

She bit the hand that tried to muffle her screams, but he did not relinquish the punishing grip he had on her.

Emily was soon carried inside and back up the stairs. Once in the parlor, the man walked through the opening in the wall and dropped her onto her feet.

"Try that again and I'll shoot you!" Mr. Jackson roared from behind him.

"You're going to kill me anyway!" Emily cried. "I know you won't hand me back!"

She saw it then, the guilt in his eyes, and felt a savage twist of desperation.

"Please let me go home." She didn't want to beg, but could do nothing else.

"I won't kill you, and once I have fled London and your family cannot find me, then you will be released." He untied her hands. "Mrs. Dobbs will bring you food and water to wash with soon." He left, shutting the door behind him. She heard the scrape of the bookshelf and then she was alone.

The candle showed her the chair. Falling into it she wept then, for Cam, for herself, and for the future she'd never thought she'd have, but for a brief shining moment had believed in. She wanted desperately to see her family again. Hold little Isabella and play with Samantha. Her relationship with James was still so new, and now she had told him how she felt to be part of his family, she would never see him again.

Crying did little for Emily but give her swollen eyelids and scratchy eyes. It definitely did nothing to get her out of her current situation. With a loud sniff, she wiped her nose on her sleeve, then rose to investigate the small room.

She'd been in dire situations before, and this was just another. The difference this time was how desperate she felt to survive. Before she'd wanted to live, because... well, who wanted to die, but now, now she had Cam, and so much more.

"I will see him again," she vowed.

The candle was about ten inches, which would give her a while before she was in darkness. The room held a narrow cot and the small chair. She could see no windows until she tilted her head back and there, right at the top, she found a small rectangle of glass.

"All right, so there is no means of escape here," Emily muttered, making herself walk as she was freezing. Slapping her arms and stomping her feet, she felt a little better. When the door opened, she'd managed to build her anger back up to a furnace.

"Mrs. Dobbs, how charming to see you. Are we to dine together?" Emily said for no other reason that she wanted to annoy the woman and not let her see the fear that warred with the anger inside her.

"I brought food, and washing water, but don't try anything funny, as there is a man outside who will stop you."

"You are too kind." Emily's words dripped with sarcasm. "I hope they're paying you well, because when my husband and brothers find you, the rest of your years will be spent in a small, cold cell." Emily look around. "Not dissimilar to this one actually."

"I need the money."

"I'll double it."

Mrs. Dobbs grunted something she could not understand, then left the room. Emily ate, because she needed the strength, although what it was she ate she had no idea. She washed her face and hands. Once that was done, she took the cutlery, and tucked them into the inside pocket of her cloak. Pulling the blanket over herself, she lay down.

"I love you, Cam," Emily whispered. "Find me."

She slept then fitfully, and when she woke she remembered: Eden could hear great distances. Climbing to her feet she started yelling for help as loudly as she could. When her voice was hoarse she stopped for a while, and then continued until she could not. They would find her if she kept yelling... they had to.

CHAPTER 43

*T*hey had lost the trail of the four riders several hours from London, but Cam knew this was where Emily was. Felt it inside him, that she was close now. He was numb with worry and fatigue, but he would not stop until she was in his arms again.

"The warehouses and location of Jackson's acquaintances are close to the docks," Max said as they rode through the streets. "We shall head there."

"I don't think she's there," Cam said. "I don't think he'd take her somewhere obvious. Think about it, Max, why go where you know he has business? It makes no sense. No, it's my belief he's got her somewhere else."

"He doesn't know that I know... any of us know, it's him."

"Max has a point there."

"I believe he has her somewhere else," Cam said, looking at his family. "Call it instinct, or whatever you want, but Emily is close, I can feel her. We need to ride around and listen. Eden will hear her."

"We can't walk all the streets of London, Cam!" James growled.

Cam's skin prickled as he sniffed the air. "She's close."

"And I repeat, we cannot simply walk the streets."

"I know that, James." Cam kept his horse moving, eyes going from left to right, looking at buildings, searching for someone who may have seen something. "But we did this to rescue Lilly, and Max. I see no reason why it won't work with Emily, as we are all together."

He found two men standing outside a small tobacco store.

"Have you seen four people on horseback? They are cloaked and would have come through here in the last few hours." He flipped a coin, and one caught it.

"Two hours ago. They went that way."

"Dressed in dark clothing, hats pulled low?"

The man nodded.

They continued on their way, and their next clue came when a young boy dashed across the street before them.

"You there!" The lad stopped, startled, and looked at Cam. "I'm looking for four riders, all dressed in dark clothing."

Children were often seen and not heard, and could be an excellent source of information.

"Four horses headed up Boxley Street a while ago."

"Are you sure?"

The boy nodded. "I was up that way and saw them."

Cam flipped him a coin.

"There are many people who ride about London in fours, Cam," James said.

"I know that, but she is close, I can feel her."

Boxley Street was a ten-minute ride. Tension had replaced the tiredness and everyone was alert as they entered the street.

"Bids, you hold the horses," Cam said, dismounting. "We'll walk from here."

"Whistle if you need me," the driver said. Nodding, Cam started walking with his family.

"Listen carefully now, my love," James said softly to Eden.

The road was a long one, with many houses, and many voices for Eden to work through. It was late, but still people were awake.

"Everyone in," Dev whispered. "We're tired. We need to use each other to build our strength and find Emily. Hold hands now," he added.

They formed a circle right there in the street. The surge of power revitalized Cam as he focused on her. His wife, his love. Wolf's strength added to their power, and the look on his face could only be described as wonder.

"She's near," Essie and Eden said together.

"Yes." Dev nodded, his eyes glowing green in the dark.

Cam sniffed the air for anything that would direct him to Emily. He caught it then, a faint scent.

"I smell her scent. She spilled a bottle of it over herself this morning. She's passed by here recently."

Cam found Dev's eyes on him.

"Your sense is strengthening, brother, as mine did when I fell in love."

Cam said nothing and continued walking.

"I hear her!" Eden started running. "She's yelling for help."

Blood surged through Cam as he ran after his sister.

"Oh, she's stopped." Eden slowed her pace. "But I believe she is in one of these two houses."

"The left," Dev said. "I see her color."

Cam tried the handle but it was locked, so he banged hard on the wood. He then put his shoulder into it, but all that achieved was pain.

"Someone is coming."

Dev, Max, and James pulled out their pistols, as did Essie.

The door opened slowly, and someone peeked out. Cam leaned on it and forced his way inside.

"You have my wife here. I want her now!"

The woman backed up several steps as his family followed.

"I don't know who you mean?"

"She's here, we heard her scream. Take me to her at once."

"There is no one here but me and my son," the woman said.

"She's here," Dev said, looking upward. "Let's go."

They ran up the stairs and searched each room. "This one," Dev said, running into a parlor.

"But where is she?" Essie asked, turning in a circle.

"I see her color, she's behind that wall." Dev walked toward a bookshelf. Cam joined him, urgency riding him as together they started removing the books.

"There must be a lever, anything," Cam said, desperate now that Emily was close.

"Here." Max had dropped to his haunches. "A lever." He pulled it, and the wall started moving.

"Emily!"

She ran through as soon as the gap was wide enough, and threw herself at him.

"Thank God." Cam's arms banded around her. He pushed his face into her hair and breathed her in. "I have you, my love."

"I watched you fall, Cam."

"I'm here." He kissed her cheek. "Lilly healed me so I am well."

"I did not know how you would find me."

The words were muffled against his chest, but he heard her anguish.

Cupping her face, he urged her to look at him. "I will always find you, Emily, you are part of me now."

Her face was dirty, hair a mess, and she was exhausted like he, but to him she was the most beautiful woman in the world.

"Jackson," Eden whispered. "I hear him outside."

Cam thrust Emily at Lilly and sprinted for the door; the great wave of fatigue he'd felt when he realized Emily was safe had left him. Now he had blood in his eyes. With Dev, James, and Max on his heels he headed outside.

They sounded like a stampede of cattle running down the stairs and out the door. There they found horses, and Jackson about to mount one.

"You bastard!" Cam ran, hurdling the gate, and landing a foot from the man. Jackson was attempting to get his foot in the stirrup, but in his haste was failing. Cam was on him in seconds. "I'm going to rip you apart!"

He managed to get three punches in before he was dragged off.

"Let me have him!"

"No, his death will not be by your hand," James said.

"He will be dealt with," Max added, stepping in front of Cam. "He will be dealt with by the law, and by me."

"And me," James added.

"I may have a hand in that also," Dev said in a deadly calm voice.

"Cam?"

He turned, shaking off the hands that held him, and saw her appear in the doorway. She hurried down the path to him, grabbing his hand and squeezing it hard.

"You will not kill Mr. Jackson."

"He deserves to die for the torment he put your through." He cupped her face.

"But he did not win, Cam, we did. You, me, and our family, as we always will."

"The thought of not seeing you again nearly killed me," Cam whispered. "To know you were somewhere, scared and alone, and I could not reach you—"

"But you did reach me." The smile on her lips was gentle, and so sweet it made him swallow. "As I knew you would."

"Fear made me doubt," Cam conceded.

"As it did me, but I felt you, Cam. Felt that you were all right."

"Did you really?"

She nodded, and he pulled her into his embrace.

"God, I love you, Mrs. Sinclair."

"And I you, Mr. Sinclair."

Behind them decisions were made, and then Jackson was removed by Max as he pleaded with them for clemency, which of course was ignored.

Cam cared little as to where the man went, only that he never came near Emily again. He lifted her onto his horse and rode home with their siblings flanking them.

He refused his family's offer to house them for the evening, and instead rode to his home. Wolf, Dev had told him, had relocated into his house, a fact that pleased Warwick, Dorrie, and Somer immensely, as supposedly he was a great deal like Cam.

His staff were surprised by the arrival of the recently wed Mr. and Mrs. Sinclair, but rallied, and soon food and a bath were readied in Cam's rooms.

Exhausted, they made their way upstairs leaning on each other. Cam just had the strength to carry her over the threshold and into his room; he then stumbled to the bed and threw Emily on it. Even her giggle sounded weary.

"Now strip, woman, and bathe, then you can get into bed and eat."

"I have no strength to move. I just want to sleep."

Cam watched as she curled on her side like a kitten, and his heart expanded. She was here safe, and Lord, he loved her.

"Em, you smell," he said, gently rolling her onto her back.

"Do I?" She opened her eyes and sniffed. "Oh, I do. That must be awful for you."

"Nothing about you could be awful," Cam said. "But I prefer your natural perfume."

"That is a big bath."

"Yes, I've always believed it was big enough for two, and now I can test that theory."

Emily's hands stopped as she turned to stare at him. "P-pardon?"

"Care to share my bath, wife?"

She was shocked, which made him laugh. He was going to enjoy stripping away her inhibitions.

"Come on, don't dawdle, the water will cool." Naked now, Cam stepped closer and stripped her out of her clothing. She did not put up much protest. When her boots were hurled across the room, he picked her up and lowered them both into the water.

"Bliss." Cam sighed, leaning back with her. "Relax," he said as she tried to struggle upright. "One thing you should know about me, Emily, is I am not a man for conventions or prudish behavior."

She made a choking sound in her throat. "I already know that about you."

"There you go then; life will go easy now."

"Oh, that I doubt very much."

He felt her relax under his hands as he ran them slowly down her arms.

"I had never thought the day would come when I would bathe with a man, but I have to admit that you make an ideal pillow."

He tweaked a curl.

"One question?"

"Anything," she said.

"Did he hurt you?" The question had been burning inside

Cam since he'd found her in that room. He needed to know if that bastard had harmed her.

"No, he did not hurt me. The ride to London was long and tiring, but the only pain I felt was from leaving you. I was so scared for you, Cam, knowing you had been hurt."

"And I for you."

"How has this madness happened between us, when for so long we loathed each other?"

"Perhaps it was not loathing, but something else that we fought, my love."

"Perhaps you are right. I remember thinking about you a great deal more than I should."

"And I you, and my thoughts were not always pure."

She turned and lay along his body, looking up at him. Cam could lose himself in those eyes. "How is it that every time I look at you I see more beauty?"

Their kiss was long, and left them both gasping for more. They washed, and then stumbled to the bed. She wanted a nightdress, he said she wouldn't need it, and seconds later she was wrapped in his arms slumbering.

Cam pressed his face into her hair and inhaled. He had it all now, family and Emily. The small space inside him that had once been empty was now full. He was complete.

EPILOGUE

"*B*ut it does not read right, Cam."

Emily was bent over Cam's shoulder reading the newspaper.

"I'm sure it does," he said, attempting to stay calm.

She jabbed a finger at the column.

"No, it doesn't. That piece needs to be at the top of the page."

"Remove your finger, madam."

Emily jabbed it again just to annoy him.

"God's blood, you would tempt the patience of a saint!" he roared. Pushing back his chair, he tumbled her into his arms. "It is lucky for us both that I am not one, however."

Emily wrapped her arms around his neck and kissed him. Very soon the only sounds in his office were sighs and moans.

"You did that deliberately," Cam said, nibbling her ear.

"Of course not. I do think those changes would make that article for *The Trumpeter* better. But I defer to your superior judgment, of course."

He snorted. "No you don't, you've just learned to manipulate me."

"I would never manipulate a person... and most especially not my husband." Emily went for an outraged look, which had him snorting again.

Life with Cam six months after they had married was, to her mind, bliss. They still argued, but for the most it was a vigorous debate, and both had learned to concede when they realized they were wrong... for the most part anyway.

Emily loved him so much it terrified her, but he said that was a good thing, as it would keep her doting on him.

She loved his laugh, his exuberance, the love he had for those in his circle, but most of all she loved the woman he had made her become.

"Thank you."

"For what?"

"Loving me. Believing in me, and for making me be a better person."

He stopped nibbling her ear and looked at her, those Sinclair green eyes intent as he tried to read her thoughts.

"You were always a good person, sweetheart, I just helped you to understand that. As for loving you, well that was the easy part. You are a very loveable person."

"As are you."

"Christ!"

"What?" Emily was suddenly on her feet, and Cam was straightening her clothing.

"They are here."

"Who?"

"All of them... the whole bloody lot!"

A knock sounded on the door, and their butler appeared looking harried.

"What is it, Bodkins?" Emily asked.

"The Duke and Duchess of Raven, Lord and Lady Sinclair—"

"Yes, yes, there is no need to recite the entire list of names, Bodkins, we know who they are," Cam growled. "Seat them somewhere, and bring plenty of food, especially if that reprobate cousin of mine is here also."

"Captain Sinclair is present, sir."

"And is there any indication as to why I have been descended upon?"

"I believe Lord Sinclair said that you have eaten at their table plenty of times, therefore, they are reciprocating."

Emily laughed as Bodkins left.

"What has you so happy?"

"You... family, the feeling of being part of all this."

He caught her as she launched herself at him.

"I'll let you in on a little secret," he whispered into her ear. "It makes me happy too, but don't tell them that."

It would be several long minutes before the once again immaculately attired Mr. and Mrs. Sinclair went to greet their families.

THE END

VISION OF DANGER

Thank you for reading SCENT OF DANGER. I hope you enjoyed Cam and Emily's story. Book 5 in the Sinclair and Raven series VISION OF DANGER is available now!

War had left him a changed man. Could she be the one to heal him?

Wounded war hero Captain Wolf Sinclair has recovered physically from the hell he endured fighting for his country, but in his head, he still exists in the dark. Living among a big, boisterous family allows him somewhere to hide, until the day Rose Abernethy storms into his life. She challenges him, makes him feel again. Soon he's addicted to her touch, and her kisses have him wanting more. But danger stalks her, and Wolf realizes he must keep her safe because in Rose he's found someone to bring him into the light.

Rose is a runaway. The life she'd always known changed with the death of her aunt, and she was forced to flee Scotland. She chose the big city of London to hide in. But hiding isn't an option when your life is in danger, and the big, handsome Captain Sinclair becomes your guardian angel. She battles her growing need for the man who is from a different world. A world where money and status are everything. The closer she gets to him, the more she realizes he's fighting demons, and Rose knows that helping him heal is important to her, especially as she's given him her heart.

SEDUCED BY A DEVIL

Deville Brothers Series

From USA Today bestselling author Wendy Vella comes a sizzling new series full of passion, scandals and intrigue. Tasked with protecting the King, the Deville brothers are part of a secret alliance forged centuries ago, but when it comes to affairs of the heart they are yet to be tamed.
Seduced By A Devil

Desperate for his help

Gabriel Deville, Earl of Raine, has never met a woman like Dimity Brown. Mysterious, alluring and utterly infuriating, she has no respect for him. In fact, the piano teacher treats him like he is the underling, not her. His beloved sister, however, calls her friend, and when Dimity disappears, he cannot refuse his sibling's urgent plea to find her.

Gabe's first shock is finding Dimity in a seedy tavern, dancing on the bar. The second is seeing the feisty young woman vulnerable and scared. He soon realizes that what he feels for her is a great deal deeper than anger and he will stop at nothing to keep her safe. Earning her trust and uncovering her secrets will be a challenge, but securing a place in her heart will be the biggest challenge of his lifetime.

Powerless to resist

Dimity had believed her life would never be anything more or less than it currently was, but then her father dies, and everything changes. She is thrown out of the only home she has ever known, and finds a letter in her father's things that turns her life completely on its head. Penniless, confused and desperate, she has nowhere to turn until Gabriel Deville steps back into her life.

Lord Raine is arrogant, ridiculously wealthy, and far too dangerously handsome. Despite the sparks that had always flown between them, their interactions had been coldly civil. When he insists she accept his help, Dimity takes it, certain she can resist him, and what is growing between them long enough to unravel the secrets of her past.

Can they overcome their differences and society dictates to forge a life together?

Seduced By A Devil
Rescued By A Devil
Protected By A Devil
Surrender To A Devil
Unmasked By A Devil

ABOUT THE AUTHOR

Wendy Vella is a bestselling author of historical and
contemporary romances
such as the Langley Sisters and Sinclair and Raven series,
with over a million copies of her books sold worldwide.

Born and raised in a rural area in the North Island of New
Zealand, she shares her life with one adorable husband, two
delightful adult children and their partners, four delicious
grandchildren, and too many cantankerous farm animals.

Wendy also writes contemporary romance under the name
Lani Blake.

Sign up for Wendy's newsletter
www.wendyvella.com/newsletter